JUST DATE AND SEE

PORTIA MACINTOSH

D1324922

9580006

First published in Great Britain in 2022 by Boldwood Books Ltd.

Copyright © Portia MacIntosh, 2022

Cover Design by Debbie Clement Design

Cover Photography: Shutterstock

The moral right of Portia MacIntosh to be identified as the author of this work has been asserted in accordance with the Copyright, Designs and Patents Act 1988.

Every effort has been made to obtain the necessary permissions with reference to copyright material, both illustrative and quoted. We apologise for any omissions in this respect and will be pleased to make the appropriate acknowledgements in any future edition.

A CIP catalogue record for this book is available from the British Library.

Paperback ISBN 978-1-80048-789-5

Large Print ISBN 978-1-80048-788-8

Hardback ISBN 978-1-80483-816-7

Ebook ISBN 978-1-80048-790-1

Kindle ISBN 978-1-80048-791-8

Audio CD ISBN 978-1-80048-783-3

MP3 CD ISBN 978-1-80048-784-0

Digital audio download ISBN 978-1-80048-786-4

Boldwood Books Ltd
23 Bowerdean Street
London SW6 3TN
www.boldwoodbooks.com

For my family – who I love to spend Christmas with

1

The house I grew up in is full of ghosts.

Well, not ghost-ghosts. I've seen plenty of scary things in my thirty-two years on this planet, but none of them supernatural, I don't think. You know what I'm talking about, right? The lingering things that trigger memories; things that, to the untrained eye, don't seem like things at all.

In the kitchen pantry, on the inside edge of the doorframe, there are the markings Mum used to make to document mine and my sister's heights as we were growing up. To a stranger, these markings must seem pretty straightforward, but when I look at them, I remember how competitive Jess, my younger sister, and I used to be. Bizarrely, we always strove to be the shorter sibling so, when the time came for Mum to check our heights, we would always try to find ways to make ourselves appear smaller. It doesn't make much sense to me now, although, funnily enough, Jess does still love to shrink away from things.

Take today, for example. Emptying Mum's house – a large detached in the heart of picture-perfect suburbia – is a huge job.

You would think my only sibling would be here to help but she's MIA. I could give Jess the benefit of the doubt, perhaps she's not here because it's a difficult thing to do, taking all of Mum's things out of the house that she lived in before either of us were born, loading them into the van that's going to take them away. Perhaps that's why she isn't here. Of course, it's equally likely Jess hasn't turned up because she's had a better offer. Either way, she should be here. It's not fair to leave this all for me to do.

I'm currently emptying the fridge and the freezer out into black bags. Bloody hell, there's a jar of Branston pickle in the back of the fridge that looks like it's been there since I sat my A Levels. I'd imagine she got it for Dad, back when he was still around. It's been a long time since he lived in this house, and even he is managing to find a way to linger.

With everything bagged up, apart from the single white chocolate Magnum I found, I drag the bags out into the back garden and place them in the wheelie bin. I unwrap my ice-cream and take an enthusiastic bite. It's December, and chilly outside today – it's cold inside too, given that there's no heating on and all the doors are open. Either way, it's a bit cold for ice-cream, but I'm starting to feel hungry from all the hard work, plus I can't quite bring myself to throw chocolate in the bin.

There are a few things I'm keeping – not just chocolate. I'm taking some sentimental things from my old room home with me, as well as an impressive collection of boardgames amassed over the years, and an old Nintendo Wii that would otherwise end up on a scrapheap somewhere. It's amazing how it hasn't worn as well as the edition of Monopoly that Mum and Dad had before I was even born, but I'll see if I can get it working one day when I'm bored, perhaps.

'Hello, Billie,' I hear an unfortunately familiar voice call out.

Now, there's something I'm glad to be leaving behind.

I'm so close to the back door. I could probably ignore him, save myself from one last encounter with everyone's least favourite neighbour, if I just pick up the pace.

'Oi, Billie,' he says, his voice much louder this time.

I may as well get it over with. After today, I'm never going to see him again.

'Hello, Mr Baxter,' I say, trying to mask a sigh.

Elliot Baxter has been a pain in the arse for pretty much as long as I can remember. He's our seventy-something neighbour from up the street, except, because the road curves around, it means that his back garden backs on to ours. I thought sharing a garden with him was stressful. I can't even imagine what it must be like to be next door to him.

Elliot just loves to complain, it's his all-time favourite thing. Whether it's because his neighbours' dog does its business too close to the boundary fence or the kid with the 'especially noisy bike chain' who rides past his house, Elliot always has a problem and when Elliot has a problem, the whole street knows about it.

'What's up?' I ask him, hoping he makes this quick. I'm really not in the mood.

'Finally sold the house,' he says. I can't tell if he's making a statement or asking a question, but I know it's probably the former. There's no way he doesn't know. He makes it his business to know other people's business and, let me tell you, it's a full-time job that he works hard at.

'Yep,' I reply. The less I say, the less he has to work with.

'New people moving in?' he asks.

'I would imagine so,' I say – although, you know, that is typically the idea when someone buys a house.

'The, er, the new people,' he starts.

I raise my eyebrows expectantly, bracing myself for whatever Elliot is about to say next. He always has the same look on his face, he looks as though he's just been slapped but he doesn't understand why.

'What are the new people like?' he eventually asks.

'Oh, I don't know them,' I reply.

'But what are—'

'I'm really sorry, I need to go help the removal men,' I insist. 'All the best, Mr Baxter.'

Honestly, if that's the last time I ever have to speak to him, then it's not all bad news today.

I don't give Elliot a chance to reply. I hurry indoors and up the stairs where I find one of the removal men in my old room.

It's strange, seeing it being emptied, my memories slowly being stripped away, resetting the room for the next person who will occupy it. With every item that is removed, it's like I hardly recognise it. It isn't only my things that are being removed, it's me.

'You all right, love?' he asks as he stacks boxes.

Inside those cardboard boxes are all the memories from my childhood, attached to various items. The good memories, the bad – speaking of which, the removal man has just revealed an ugly one, by rolling up the rug that used to be next to my bed.

I stare down at the ding in the wooden floor. Another ghost. It catches the removal man's eye.

'Oh, God, I remember that happening like it was yesterday,' I tell him. 'There's only a year or so between me and my sister. Anything I got before her – or anything I had that she didn't want until she saw me with it – made her so jealous.'

On this occasion in particular, it was my rainbow-coloured Beanie Baby rabbit that she decided she had to have, after previously mocking me for having such a childish toy. I don't remember how old I was – but we were still quite young.

'It all happened so quickly. I was lying on my bed when she came in and decided she was taking a toy from me,' I explain, grabbing a small box, heading downstairs with the removal man. He does genuinely seem interested in what happened, unless he's just being polite. 'She tried to grab it from me – something she often did when she wanted something, and sometimes I let her – but there was no way I was going to give it up that day, so I kept tight hold of it. I don't remember how long we struggled with it, probably not that long, although it felt like an epic battle at the time. Eventually, when she couldn't hold on any longer, she let go, sending me back with a force that knocked the lamp off my bedside table. My sister scarpered as soon as she realised something might be broken. I averted my eyes, too terrified to look, terrified that the bedside lamp I've had for as long as I could remember – one that was my mum's when she was a young girl – was broken and I could have cried with relief when, unbelievably, I finally looked down and it was absolutely fine. The floor, however, was not.'

'That's siblings for you,' the man says through a smile. 'You'd never think she was the type, talking to her now.'

'My sister, what, is she here?' I ask, surprised.

'Yeah, she's down at the van with Tommy,' he replies. 'Although they're flirting up a storm. That's why muggins here is doing all the work.'

'Well, that does sound like her,' I say with a laugh.

My smile quickly falls as we reach the front door.

'That rug has been hiding that mark on the floor for maybe twenty years,' I muse. 'The day I dragged it across the floor, supposedly as a temporary fix, while I figured out what I was going to do about it, marked the start of this fear that Mum would find out. Eventually I would forget it was there, being reminded of it less often, no longer feeling that guilty burn in my feet when

I would get in and out of bed each night. I hadn't thought about it in years and years, until you uncovered it today, and it's just hit me.

'Mum is never going to know. She's never going to discover it. It weighed so heavy on my mind, for so long. Mum loved her wooden floors, that's why I was so scared of her discovering what had happened, and why I had to make out like I wanted the responsibility of cleaning my own room from a young age – which was not fun at all – but she'll never know, she'll never walk on her prized wooden flooring again.'

The removal man places the rug down in the garden and gives me a gentle pat on the shoulder, very much at arm's length, but I've got a lot of time for men who are never quite sure if it's okay to touch women – even if they mean well – so it's appreciated.

'I'm sorry, love,' he tells me, his genuine sympathy apparent in his tone. 'I can't even imagine what you must be going through, losing your mum, it must be so difficult. I'd be a mess if my mum died.'

'Died?' I repeat back to him. 'My mum isn't dead.'

'I'm so sorry, I just assumed, with you being so upset...'

Oh, no, now he looks like he feels even worse. I need to iron this out, as quickly as possible.

'I'm not upset because she's dead, I'm upset because she's moving in with me.'

The man quickly withdraws his hand of support, his face shifting from confusion to something somewhere between feeling embarrassed and judging me with his eyes.

I don't suppose that came out exactly as I intended it to, although I'd be lying if I said I was happy about the situation.

The main reason I'm so upset to be emptying my mum's house is because it's the house I grew up in, the one I lived until I left for uni, built on a plot that she and my dad picked out when it was nothing more than a patch of dirt. My mum has sold our childhood home to buy somewhere smaller now that it's just her, which makes sense... it's just so difficult to see the place go.

As if that's not bad enough, originally, when plans were being made, I told her that she could stay with me for a night, before collecting her keys to the new place the next day. Unfortunately, due to a whole mess of circumstances with the chain on her buyer's side, and the newbuild Mum is buying not being ready due to delays, her one-night stay in December has turned into her moving in for the foreseeable, until the new year, at least.

For someone so used to living on her own, who has gone to great efforts to arrange herself a nice, quiet Christmas period alone in her finally finished house project, the thought of having to live with my mum again isn't something I'm jazzed about.

'That's her over there,' I tell him, pointing my mum out, over by the removal van.

'That's your mum?' he replies in disbelief. 'I thought that was your sister!'

I sigh. I hear that all the time these days.

'Billie, my darling, how's it going?' she asks as we approach the van.

I might be feeling like crap about this entire situation, but Mum is positively glowing. She looks cold, with her coat belted up tightly, and her pink cheeks – oddly it suits her, though, it's like the kind of healthy look I try to achieve with blusher, only to end up looking like a clown. I doubt the weather is suiting me so well. I've only been back outside for a few minutes and I can feel my nose trying to run, so I sniff hard. So attractive!

'Yeah, all good,' I reply. 'I emptied the fridge and the freezer of the last bits – Elliot had one last stab at being the world's nosiest neighbour, but otherwise I think the place is pretty much emptied, apart from a couple of boxes.'

'I'll go get them,' the man I've been chatting to says. I think he'd do anything to get away from me now.

'No worries, pal,' the other man – I'm assuming this is Tommy – replies.

He briefly takes his eyes off my mum and turns to me. As we make eye contact, there's a shared look of recognition between us. We know each other. He's...

'Tom Paulson?' I say, my voice shooting up at the end, because I can't be certain.

'Yeah,' he replies, his smile growing as he realises where he knows me from. 'Billie May, right? I remember you.'

My mum looks at me expectantly, her curiosity clearly getting the better of her as she waits for an introduction.

'Mum, do you remember Tom from my class at primary school?' I ask her.

I went to secondary school with him too, but I was too old and too cool to have my mum taking me to school then, obviously. Still, I remember him. He somehow looks so different, but also not really that different at all. He looks like I remember his dad looking – he was a policeman, who dropped by the school when we were in Year 2 or 3 to give us a talk on stranger danger. I don't waste time wondering whether or not I look as much like my mum, I know that I don't.

'Your *mum*?' Tom says in disbelief as his jaw heads for the floor. 'This is never your mum. I can't believe it.'

'Believe it,' I practically beg.

This happens all the time now and, while I'm happy for my mum, I still don't find it easy.

'I would have noticed a MILF like you at the school gates,' Tom tells her with a wiggle of his eyebrows.

My mum, visibly delighted to be referred to as a MILF, laughs and bats her hand.

'Oh, yeah, I remember you being such a charismatic nine-year-old,' I reply sarcastically. 'Didn't you pee your pants during sports day?'

Tom frowns. He turns back to my mum.

'So, is Mr May still on the scene?' he asks curiously. Gross.

'Sadly not,' my mum replies, with a tone and a look that implies she is anything but sad about it.

My dad left my mum (and me and Jess in the process) years ago, when I was barely a teenager. He 'fell in love' and styled out leaving us as this bold, romantic thing, as though that's going to mean anything to a couple of kids staring down the barrel of occasional evenings and every other weekend (which we only did for as long as we absolutely had to). He thought he was heroic, following his heart, leaving his marriage for true love. Of course, in a not-so-shocking turn of events, it turns out the woman who he was seeing behind his wife's back wasn't his true love.

Anyway, things may not have turned out so well for my dad, but my mum never let herself become a casualty of divorce. Divorce, it turns out, looks great on her. Or divorce settlements do, at least. My mum didn't just wash that man out of her hair, and she didn't waste any time scratching his face out of photos of the two of them, my mum had a series of cosmetic surgeries that made her look so different it effectively scrubbed the old her from the photos instead. I'll never know the full extent of the work she had done – she didn't even tell me and Jess, on the day when she had the bulk of the heavy lifting done, until she was back home again – but she's in great shape, her skin looks like there's an Instagram filter over it, I cringe to even admit it, but her boob age is way younger than mine now. The new Kate May looks incredible, she's happy, she really is living her best life. Don't get me wrong, I am happy for her, it's just massively uncomfortable for me when things like this happen.

I never would have guessed Mum would be the type to have work done – she certainly never used to be – but my dad left a massive hole in her life when he broke her heart. I think their relationship had become such a big part of her identity, all she wanted to do was reinvent herself. She's certainly achieved it – and good for her.

Tom begrudgingly turns his attention back to me. I can't help but sigh – not that he notices – because somehow my mum looking so good makes me feel like I look crap in comparison. I know, we're apples and oranges, and more than anything I think it's the fact that my mum defies her age that fascinates people, but it's hard not to feel unremarkable in her shadow – not that it's her fault, and not that I begrudge her it, after wasting all those years with my dad.

'Actually, it's weird, I was talking about you the other day, someone at football said you'd moved in with Declan Clancy? Mad that anyone could still be with their Year 11 boyfriend or girl-friend, innit?'

Tom looks to my mum. There's a car driving past so she takes this opportunity to look away for a moment, leaving me alone in my awkward moment.

'Well, we weren't together the whole time,' I explain. 'And, erm, we're not together now, actually.'

I probably should have opened with that, but I still find it so uncomfortable to talk about. I don't even like to admit it to myself because it sets me going down a path where I question everything, until I start being overly critical of myself, and that's no way to live. *Declan* was Declan's problem, not me.

Tom's cheeks flush.

'Sorry, Billie, love, I was sure one of the lads said you'd bought a house together recently,' he says sincerely.

'Oh, no, we did,' I reply. I pull a sort of playfully irritated face, as though I'm talking about some minor inconvenience. 'We bought a fixer-upper together, just over a year ago, and then he pissed off and left me with it, so that was fun.'

Awkward part over, my mum re-joins the conversation, seeing her opportunity to help defuse things.

'Her house is stunning now,' she gushes. 'Just phenomenal – and she did it all by herself.'

'Well, mostly,' I reply. 'I still needed electricians and plumbers and carpenters.'

'Oh, my!' Mum jokes.

Tom practically melts. He's so charmed by her. I get it, though, because while she may have transformed herself into this blonde bombshell who doesn't look a day over thirty, she's still the same sweet, caring, mumsy mum on the inside, and there's a great comfort in a personality like that.

'You really have done such a fantastic job, my darling,' Mum says, wrapping an arm around me. 'It's going to be so wonderful, the two of us living together.'

'You two are going to be living together?' Tom asks curiously. He has a cheeky glint in his eye, I'm not quite sure why. Perhaps he's imagining us having sleepover parties, painting our nails and talking about boys. That may not be that far off the mark.

'Yes!' Mum beams. 'We're going to be each other's wing-woman, and have such a magical Christmas in her beautiful home. Oh, you really should see it.'

'I'd love to,' Tom replies quickly.

'Oh, shit, did you hear that?' I interrupt. 'Is that... is that your friend calling for help? He sounds hurt!'

'Back in minute,' Tom announces heroically as he dutifully dashes inside.

'I didn't hear anything,' Mum says with a casual shrug as she smooths out her coat.

'That's because I made it up,' I insist plainly. 'Stop flirting with the movers!'

Mum laughs.

'You're such a grump,' she teases. 'I am not flirting with the movers, I'm just proud of what you've done with your lovely home, everyone needs to see it. When did you get so uptight?'

'Sometime around all the stuff we just talked about,' I reply, stating the obvious. 'Please don't invite random men over, Mum. I don't care if that makes me seem uptight.'

She wraps an arm around me and pulls me close for a half-hug.

'I'm just proud of you, and what you've done – and all without a bloody man,' she tells me. 'I just want everyone to see.'

I smile.

'Well, I'm proud of you too,' I tell her.

Even if living with Mum for a while is going to drive me slightly crazy, I love her to bits, and we do have a great relationship.

'We're better off without men,' I insist, just as Tom arrives back. His face falls, like I've just told him there's no Santa Claus.

'We really are,' she eventually replies. 'A man-free Christmas is just what we need.'

Mum is absolutely right about a man-free Christmas being a good idea, but my plans were about so much more than that. Still, it will be nice to have some company – a break from living alone might be good – it's just not the Christmas period I had in mind.

'So, what time shall I come over?' Tom asks her quietly, but not so quietly I don't hear.

'Erm...'

Mum looks over at me expectantly, like a kid asking if their friend can come over for dinner after school.

I – without a doubt, without even trying, in fact – can manage a man-free Christmas.

I don't think my mum can, though. And that definitely isn't on my Christmas list.

2

There's something about the last day of term that makes everyone a little crazy.

One of the great things about teaching in a private school is that we finish for Christmas much earlier than most schools. Still, we do all down tools the days before the last day of term, so today is just about having fun, allowing the children to celebrate together and swap presents before going off to their country mansions or winter sun holidays.

I'm an English teacher at Perstead School – one of the top private schools in Canterbury. I do really enjoy it but, at a certain point, teenagers are just teenagers and, to put it plainly, you can get them to give a shit about *Othello* or you can't.

It's funny because we all remember what it was like at school, anticipating the holidays, looking forward to those weeks off. As a teacher, I still feel that way. I can't wait because, for the first time since I bought the house, it will be the first holiday I have with it finally finished. I can actually enjoy it. No tradespeople, no painting, no eating beans so that I can pay the electrician.

The staff room at Perstead is more like a trendy café meets a

WAG's living room. You know when you see influencer houses on Instagram and they're just a swatch of shades of grey? That's what this room is like. I suppose it's supposed to look high-end and classy but there's something kind of cold about it – almost clinical, too. It's so clean you're almost scared to eat your lunch here. The staff room does have its perks, though. There's a coffee machine that would put a Starbucks to shame – which I get a lot of use out of – and the different seating zones make it a great space for working or relaxing, either alone or with other members of staff.

Speaking of which, Angie, my best friend, is sitting on one of the sofas with two gigantic chocolate muffins in front of her. Angie is a maths teacher and it's funny because we both think the other person has the harder job. The thought of tackling trigonometry makes me feel physically sick. I want to say that after my GCSEs I dumped it from my mind, but I would be lying if I said I ever felt like I had an understanding of it in the first place. The kids here definitely know more about maths than I remember. Angie, on the other hand, is intimidated by all things English. Anything much more than a casual message and she will often run it by me before she sends it. I often point out to her that English must be easier because even the text box where she composes messages can check her spelling and grammar, which she will counter with the existence of calculators, but I *still* wouldn't know how to do trigonometry, even with a calculator, so I think that settles it.

'I got you this,' she tells me, pushing one of the muffins my way as I take a seat next to her. 'Chocolate, orange and cranberry.'

That's another great thing about working here – when it comes to Christmas, they go hard. Festive menus, multiple Christmas trees, decorations everywhere you turn.

'You angel, thank you,' I reply. 'I need it today.'

'Had enough of the festive fun?' she asks through a knowing smile.

Why is it that work is so much harder, and drags on for so much longer, when you're not doing any actual work?

'No one is interested in playing games,' I say with a sigh as I slump back in my seat. 'They're running out the clock, the same way we are. Half of them are just sitting, chatting, messing around on their phones. The other half are dancing for TikTok. I'm politely declining their invitations to join in.'

'You would almost certainly go viral,' Angie says through a snort. 'With your crap "dad at a wedding" dance moves.'

'I can't even be mad at you for saying that,' I reply. 'This muffin has more sense of rhythm and grace.'

'And yet you're an amazing skier,' Angie says, leaning back next to me. I feel her body tense up as she realises she has potentially put her foot in it.

'Shit, sorry,' she says quickly. 'I'm not trying to remind you of it, or try to convince you to come with us but... are you sure you won't come with us?'

Just before last Christmas – before Declan walked out on me – we booked a Christmas skiing holiday with Angie and her husband Bill, and our other couple friends Ari and Brian, and Anne and Jules.

I shake my head.

'I've got Mum with me now,' I remind her. 'I don't fancy leaving her home alone in my house.'

Angie laughs.

'Are you sure?' she asks again.

Initially, when Declan and I broke up, I couldn't think of anything worse than still going on a cosy couples' holiday, being the only one who was single. I know it's not my friends' fault, and no one ever tries to make me feel bad for being single – in fact, they work overtime to make me feel better about it, and ensure that I know how much better I am without Declan – but inevitably it would have been a problem sooner or later. Whether it was sharing ski lifts or playing boardgames where you're in teams of two, my single status would have made things slightly off.

'*You're* our friend, not Declan, he's not coming, but you still could,' she persists. 'It won't be the same without you – and if the whole squad is away all Christmas...'

'I know you think I'm making this up, but I promise you it's true,' I insist. 'I really am looking forward to a nice, quiet Christmas mostly alone in my newly completed house. I've cleared my calendar, I don't have any work, no social obligations of any description. Mum is a surprise but I'm sure she'll behave. Honestly, it's going to be great. I'm just going to relax and appreciate all my hard work.'

'Well, you've certainly earned it,' Angie insists. 'But it won't be the same without you. Declan, on the other hand, would have made the whole thing less fun. His chaotic energy was exhausting. I wonder what he's doing now. Surely he can't last long without someone to sponge off? I'll bet you anything he still doesn't have a job.'

I smile. You've got to love a supportive friend who will badmouth your ex forever.

Declan was chaotic, she's right. I mean, the proof is in the break-up. Talking me into buying a fixer-upper, putting all *my* cash into it, getting a big, fat mortgage and then abandoning me with the lot. We haven't interacted in months now. He's vanished. At first, I was worried sick, terrified that something horrible might have happened to him. These days, for his sake, he would be better off if something horrible had happened to him, because if I ever see him again... I'm the mug who spent years propping him up, while he was trying to make a living as an artist or a writer or whatever his latest creative whim was – I think one of our last arguments was about him wanting to buy a double bass.

After the initial shock of him abandoning me wore off, honestly, all I felt was relief. We may have bought the house together, but I am so much happier living in it alone. It would have been so easy to stay with Declan forever – well, not easy, he was actually quite difficult to live with, but you know what I mean, when you're with a person for a long time, it's hard to make a change. Being alone has allowed me to create a space that is me through and through, and I couldn't be happier with it. Would it be nice to have a boyfriend? Well, yeah, in theory. I miss the idea of a boyfriend; someone to hang out with, cuddle up to when it's cold, go on holidays with, take to family parties and friends' weddings. I don't miss Declan, though, not now that I can see what my life is like without him, versus what it was like when I was with him.

'I'll be honest, it does sound lovely, having the house mostly to yourself, having no obligations, no work-work or house-work,' Angie enthuses. 'Just think, you can get home this evening, jump into your pyjamas, and leave them on until next year if you feel like it.'

'That's the plan,' I reply with a smile. 'Although I'll probably dress for a shopping trip here and there. Otherwise, it's a home alone Christmas for me. Well, with my mum, of course.'

'You'll probably enjoy having her around,' Angie says. 'She's a fun mum. She's not like my mum.'

'I love your mum,' I insist.

'I love my mum too but, you've got to admit, she's an old bag compared to yours,' Angie jokes. 'She's snooty and narrow minded. The only thing she enjoys more than knitting is scowling and judging people. Your mum feels more like a cool older sister.'

'Never tell my mum that,' I say with a playful seriousness but, also, I really hope she never tells her that.

'I commented it on one of her Instagram photos last week,' Angie admits through a giggle. 'She was over the moon.'

'I bet she was,' I laugh. 'When we were emptying her house, she was chatting with one of the removal men, and she told him she was my wingwoman – or that I was going to be hers. Either way, imagine going out on the pull with your mum, and it's not just that she's my mum, it's also the fact that we really could pass for sisters. It's great that she looks younger than her age, and that she's so happy, but inviting that comparison somehow ages me up.'

'Oi, you are gorgeous,' Angie insists. 'You look like Florence Pugh's only slightly older sister. People would kill for that long blonde hair. And your face always looks so fresh. Me and my black hair dye are losing the battle against my greys, and I've got a face like I've always just been given bad news.'

I snort.

'You have, maybe, three grey hairs, because you can't be arsed dying them, and you can't even see them – and even if you could, grey hair is cool,' I remind her. 'And your permanent expression is a sort of cool but warm kind of thing.'

'Cool but warm?' she repeats back to me with a teasing smile. 'And you're an English teacher, yeah?'

'I mean you look cool, like you don't need to give a damn, but you also still look so warm and friendly and approachable – I'm trying to pay you a compliment,' I remind her. I place my hands over my cheeks. 'I have chubby cheeks and overprocessed hair.'

'My goodness, it's no wonder our young ladies have self-esteem issues, if you two are shaping their minds,' Fee, one of the more senior teachers, interrupts us, having blatantly been eaves-dropping on our conversation.

'Erm, my girls have more confidence than me,' I point out. 'One of them reminded me that her car – which she can't even legally drive yet – was worth more than mine. Another gave me her mum's surgeon's Instagram username. It still keeps me up at night, wondering which part she thinks I need fixing.'

'Your bum,' Angie teases, causing Fee to cringe at her use of the word bum.

Fee, hilariously, is head of pastoral care. If you asked her what this involved, she would probably brag 'a few extra thousand a year'. You've got to feel sorry for them, with Fee in charge of their wellbeing, because I feel like kids today have so much more to contend with than I did when I was at school. I don't want to sound like I'm a thousand years old, but we didn't have social media, which must have made all the difference. I would say we didn't have influencers, but we did, in a sense. I remember watching *The Simple Life* and being obsessed with Paris Hilton and Nicole Richie. I loved everything about them, from their style to their dogs to their confidence. Looking back, it's easy to see that they probably weren't the best role models – at least not with the way that they portrayed themselves in the show. Of course, all this manifested as was me cutting the top section of my jeans to be lower and begging my mum to let me have a chihuahua. Nothing like cosmetic surgery and sports cars.

The toughest thing about Fee being head of pastoral care is that she isn't only out of touch with youth, she's out of touch with the times too. Issues like sexuality and gender are pretty black and white to her, which means the rest of us have to work over-time to support the kids. It's pretty much known, throughout the school, that you don't talk to Fee about things like that.

'Clocked off for Christmas already?' Fee asks. Pretty ironic, given how I was just thinking about how little she does for her wage.

'Not quite yet,' I reply through a forced smile.

'We're going to our Patricia's for the Christmas period,' she tells us. 'She's just had another baby, you know.'

Oh, we all know. It's almost all she talks about.

'Nice,' I say, simply.

'She's a year or so younger than you two, you know,' she points out. 'You know' ought to be her catchphrase.

'Good for her,' Angie replies.

'You two ought to start thinking about having kids,' she tells us.

'Together?' I blurt, purposefully misunderstanding her point.

'Oh, my God, we'd make such cute mums together,' Angie sings. 'Imagine how cute our baby would be?'

'Cute and a genius,' I point out. 'With my words and your numbers.'

'Erm, that's not what I mean,' Fee interrupts, clearly not amused.

'We've already got fifty kids between us,' I remind her.

'So long as you're happy,' she says with a shrug. 'If you're happy with your lot.'

'Oh, look at the time,' I say, probably looking at my watch a little slower than my words come out. 'We need to go get set up. Our classes are doing a TikTok thing together.'

I say this knowing full well that as little as saying the word 'TikTok' gives Fee a headache.

'Oh, for goodness' sake,' she replies. 'I shall be encouraging mine to revise.'

'Well, good luck,' I tell her as I stand up. 'And if we don't see you, have a lovely Christmas.'

'Yes, and give our love to Patricia and the baby,' Angie adds politely.

Once we're out in the corridor, away from prying ears, Angie hooks her arm with mine.

'Have you seen photos of Patricia's baby?' she asks. 'It looks like an egg with blusher on.'

I laugh.

'You're going to have to start talking more maternal than that, if you expect me to have a baby with you,' I point out. 'And you'll have to get Bill on board.'

'Well, if I know Bill, and I like to think I do, given that I married him, I can say with confidence that the idea of the two of us trying for a baby is something he wouldn't object to,' she jokes.

I snort. That one caught me off guard.

'Oh, my God, Angie!'

'Seriously, that man's browser history would have made Hugh Heffner blush,' she adds. 'Another perk of not having to live with a man, there you go.'

'It's starting to seem like a long list,' I say with a smile. 'Thanks.'

'Are you sure you won't come on holiday with us?' Angie says again. 'It really isn't too late, there's room in the lodge – I'll even share a room with you, Bill can have ours – again, he'll be delighted.'

I laugh.

'Thanks for being such a brilliant friend,' I tell her, squeezing her arm. 'But, honestly, I've never been more excited to have clear calendar and an almost empty house.'

'Well, okay, then,' she replies. 'Perhaps we can have a girls' weekend away, in the new year?'

'I'd love that,' I sat with a smile.

'Ooh, you don't still use Matcher, do you?' Angie asks enthusiastically.

I pull a face.

'I think I still have it on my phone, but I have to be feeling pretty existential to venture onto dating apps,' I reply. 'Sometimes I get a notification – but not from a person, from the app, trying to encourage me to use it. I usually log in, start up a couple of conversations, someone fast says something that reminds me why I'm much happier being single, and then I close it again.'

'You know Catrin, my classroom assistant? She's obsessed with dating apps – to the point where I can't imagine her ever having a boyfriend, because she enjoys the process too much. Anyway, she was telling me about this thing they're doing for the festive period, where users submit events, and it creates this calendar of stuff for singles to do, so if you get really bored with us all being away, perhaps you could give that a go.'

'I don't think I'm that desperate yet,' I reply through a chuckle. 'That sounds like a nightmare.'

'Yeah, I suppose you're right,' she replies.

I know it might seem sad but, honestly, I am genuinely looking forward to a nice, quiet Christmas in my finished house, just relaxing and appreciating all my hard work. And Angie is right, I probably will enjoy having my mum around, so long as she doesn't actually expect me to go out on the pull with her.

I just need to get through this last afternoon and then quiet Christmas can begin. Perhaps my luck is finally about to change. It may not be the Christmas I thought I was going to be having until recently, but I honestly can't wait. Just me, Mum, and the house. No men needed. Let's just hope she agrees.

3

It's bloody freezing out this evening, so I only stand on my driveway, admiring my house, for a moment.

I remember the first time Declan and I viewed the place, standing out here, gazing up at it. I couldn't get over how wide it was, it seemed massive. Even if it was a tired, ugly red brick thing, I could see the potential in it. It doesn't even resemble its former self now, since I've had the garden landscaped, fitted with contemporary lighting, and having the house rendered and painted white has made all the difference. What stands before me now is a sleek, modern house – something I never would have been able to afford had I bought it already renovated. It took years of saving, the money my grandad left me when he died, and a lot of hard work, but I finally feel like now I have my dream house.

The light from inside beams through the white wooden venetian blinds I have in all the windows. The warm glow spills out into the garden, dragging me inside. I have to admit, it is nice coming home from work on a cold, dark evening, to be greeted by a house with someone in it, with the lights shining, the heating on – and now that I'm inside, the smell of something cooking filling my nostrils. Perhaps I could get used to this.

Inside the hallway, I have a large floor-to-ceiling mirror with a shelf that sits halfway across it. I drop my key in the jar and take my coat and shoes off before placing them in the cupboard. I never used to be so organised and tidy. In the flat I was living in before, I felt like I was always in a mess. I always seemed to have a floordrobe on the go, where I would pick up and drop off clothes in a hurry on a morning and an evening, and I would let dishes pile up in the sink sometimes – but, in my defence, we didn't have a dishwasher, and you forget just how big a part of your day washing dishes actually takes (although that could be a by-product of letting them pile up first). Declan never really did much about the place, even though he had lots of free time, which was infuriating. I try not to read too much into things (although I so often do anyway) but in hindsight, his general atti-tude, lack of care and attention, and unwillingness to work as a team with me should have signposted the fact that he was going to abandon me.

It was hard at first, moving into a project of a house like this one on my own, but I decided to start as I meant to go on, to get everything absolutely perfect and then work overtime to keep it that way. It's actually quite easy to keep up with, when you have pride in what you've done, and you can feel the benefit of keeping the place tidy. I clean up as I go along, I have all the gadgets and potions recommended to me by 'cleanfluencers', and I have a place for everything. One of the best things about renovating this house from scratch is that I've been able to create spaces for everything, inside and out, to better organise my day-to-day life. Do I think that in suddenly losing my relationship and not having much else going on I have potentially gone all in on house stuff, making it my entire personality, the thing that I focus on? Yes, probably, but it's given me something to throw myself into over the last year, something to care about – and I feel like I'm good at it. I have a well-organised pantry, colour-coded cleaning products, and I'm even our street's binfluencer. Now it's time to enjoy it.

I follow my nose into the open-plan living space. A wood-burning stove is all that separates the lounge from the dining room, and a long kitchen island does the same for the dining room and the kitchen. The long room is in three sections, but still one big open space, which is exactly what I wanted. The wood burner is the only thing that remains from when we viewed the place. Knocking down walls and modernising the space was the first thing I thought to do, and I couldn't be happier with the result.

Of course, having an open-plan space means that I can see the kitchen the second I step into the room, and the first thing that catches my eye is Mum, chaotically dashing around like she's in a hurricane.

'Chicken stew and dumplings,' Mum announces.

My God, that sounds good. I could definitely get used to home cooking waiting for me when I get in.

Mum might be a blur, but the kitchen around her is in focus and, wow, it looks like a bomb has hit it. There are pans on the hob, vegetable peelings all over the island, various dishes and pieces of cutlery everywhere.

I feel my face drop and my heart sink.

'And there's wine, by the fridge,' Mum adds as she begins violently mashing the potatoes. 'I hope you don't mind, I already got started on that.'

'Wow, Mum, the food smells amazing,' I tell her sincerely. It really does, and it's so nice of her to cook for me, but genuinely this room was less of a mess when we knocked the wall out. But I just need to look at it for what it is – a genuine gesture from someone who loves me, and an amazing-smelling meal that I can't wait to get stuck into. And if Mum cooked then I am more than happy to clean up after dinner. Nothing I can't fix.

'I just wanted to do my bit, to say thank you for letting me move in for a few weeks,' she says. 'Even though I did let you live with me for most of your life.'

I laugh. I love my mum's sense of humour. I like to think I inherited it from her, even if I have been a bit uptight recently. It's just the stress with work, and the anniversary of Declan walking out on me, and all the blood, sweat and tears (and basically every penny I had) that I've put into this place over the last twelve months.

'Are you settled into your room now?' I ask her.

'Yes, all unpacked,' she replies. 'It's such a beautiful guestroom – nicer than any bedroom I've ever had.'

'Well, we can change that with your new house, if you like,' I suggest. 'I'm an expert at panelling now.'

'Oh, that would be wonderful,' she replies. 'Nip upstairs and get washed up and changed. Dinner will be on the table by the time you get back down.'

'Okay, will do,' I reply. 'The table mats are—'

'Just go and get changed,' Mum demands.

I think she can tell that I'm worrying about my table.

Clearly this is all about so much more than mess and the surface of the table. I've made this place my fortress, my world, I need to try to loosen up a little. It's just my mum, she's just trying to help.

'Okay, sorry,' I reply, with a slight laugh. 'I'll go get changed.'

'Oh, but where are the table mats?' she calls after me.

'In the sideboard, under the window,' I reply, smiling to myself as I head up the stairs.

The house has four bedrooms. There's my room, the guest

room Mum is staying in, a third room that is set up as another guest room, and then finally there is the smallest bedroom, which is an office space, but with a sofa bed in there. I loved the idea of my friends being able to stay over, if they came here for dinner parties or if it got too late and they'd had too much to drink. That was the idea with downstairs too, to make it a social space, although granted, I'm seeming relatively anti-social at the moment, but this was supposed to be a quiet Christmas. I was mentally on track for peace and tidiness and doing my own thing. I can make space for the stew and dumplings, though, and the woman who gave me life, of course.

Mum used to wear her dark curly hair on the shorter side. She was never one for taking her time with her make-up, despite Jess's and my best efforts with her when we were younger (and we obviously thought we were the teenage UK answer to Paris Hilton and Nicole Richie). I in no way mean this offensively, but she had quite a mumsy sense of style. Function over fashion. Substance over style. Bold looks and bright colours really weren't her sort of thing at all.

You know the paradox, about the Ship of Theseus, that questions whether or not a ship is still the same ship if you replace enough parts? My mum is genuinely a whole new woman. She looks so different, she has sleek, straight, blonde shoulder-length hair, and her fashion sense is less cardigans and more Kardashian but, honestly, she's so classy with it. I know it sounds like a strange thing for a daughter to say, but breaking up with my dad has been the absolute making of her. She's a much happier person, and a constant reminder to me that it's never too late to turn it around. I think that's why I try not to fret about being suddenly single. It rattled me at first but there's plenty of time for me to meet someone new. For now, all I can think about is my nice, quiet Christmas. I'll worry about finding a new love in the new year.

'Here you go, my darling, dinner is served, just the way you like it,' Mum says as I join her at the dining table. 'Chicken stew, because I know you prefer chicken to beef, dumplings, and rosemary mash. And don't worry, I'll clean and tidy the kitchen once we've eaten – I saw your face when you walked in.'

She smiles, acknowledging that this is just classic me and that I don't mean anything by it. I – confusingly and ironically – relax about my uptightness, just a little.

'Sorry, I'm just coming down from a seriously hectic term,' I tell her. 'But obviously I will do the cleaning up. You cooked, let me clean.'

'I like to earn my keep,' Mum tells me. 'Can I give you a piece of advice that someone gave me that I've found invaluable in recent years?'

I freeze, my fork hovering just in front of my lips. I wasn't expecting her sentence to take such a drastic detour.

'Erm, sure,' I reply cautiously. I dare to continue eating, mostly because I am starving and this is delicious, but how bad can what she is about to say really be?

'Have you ever considered that you apologise too much?' she asks me.

'Well, yeah,' I admit, like it's the most normal thing in the world. 'At work the other day, someone dropped a hole-punch on my foot and I apologised to them. Given half the chance, I would have apologised to the hole-punch too. Isn't that just human nature?'

'I used to think that,' she replies. 'But someone told me to try saying thank you instead. It doesn't always apply but, more often than not, you can give it a go. Not to the hole-punch, obviously, but when I told you to leave dinner to me – thank you, not sorry.'

I can't help but laugh. That's kind of brilliant, although I don't know how easy it will be. Mum finds everything easy, since her glow-up.

'That's actually, maybe, good advice... I think,' I reply. 'I'll give it a go, but apologising is second nature to me.'

'I know,' she replies. 'I would hear you apologise to Declan all the time.'

'Noted, but this is a Declan-free zone now,' I remind her. 'In fact, it's an ex-free zone.'

I think for a second.

'Actually, no, it's a man-free zone,' I insist.

'Let me know when you get where you're going with this,' Mum teases.

I quickly pick my fork back up. Dinner really is delicious. Well, doesn't home cooking always taste better when you are not the person who has been slaving away in the kitchen for hours?

'I am declaring this Christmas man-free,' I state.

'Okay, darling,' Mum replies. It's not that she doesn't sound convincing, there's just something in her voice, I can't quite put my finger on what it is, though.

'I'm serious,' I insist. 'No exes, no dates, no nice young men who move your furniture. No one. And no talking about them, either. It's Christmas. Dwelling on the existence of men is not what Christmas is all about.'

'I thought Christmas was about showing good will to all men?' Mum dares to joke.

'Well, I don't know any that have earned it,' I reply with a smile, to show her that despite coming across as aggressively feminist, I'm absolutely fine. 'Okay, to clarify.' I put my fork down, to show her that I mean business. 'If there's one thing I am going to insist on this Christmas, it's that this house – from this moment on, until at least the new year – is officially a man-free zone.'

The front door opens and closes with a bang, causing us both to jump, before we're joined in the kitchen by a familiar face.

'Bloody men!' my sister, Jess, announces as she drops most of her bags down on the floor. She keeps one in her hand. A white paper bag. It looks (and smells) like a takeaway.

Jess always looks cool, no matter what she's wearing – even when she looks kind of scruffy, it looks like a style choice. Her latest dye job is fading, revealing previous dye jobs as it retreats, which you would think would look awful, but it gives her this unique iridescent hair colour that suits her. She's wearing skinny jeans and a black leather jacket and, as she sniffs the air, the stud in her nose catches one of the spotlights above her, causing it to twinkle. The piercing is new, since the last time I saw her, and I noticed on her Instagram that she has a new tattoo somewhere too.

'Oh, Jess, princess,' my mum says as she jumps to her feet, running over to her daughter to give her a hug.

Jess has always been known as princess, which sometimes kind of makes it seem like Mum loves her more, but it's a nickname that started when we were younger, when Jess was a bit of a brat. She always had to get her own way, she was quite possibly the fussiest eater known to man, and she absolutely did not do anything she didn't feel like doing. So we started calling her a princess, because she clearly thought she was one, and even though over time she isn't quite so fussy (although she still only does what she feels like doing), the nickname has stuck.

'This is such a lovely surprise,' Mum says after she's given her a thorough squeezing. 'I didn't think we'd see you until Christmas Eve – if at all. I thought you and Armie were spending the holidays in Prague.'

'Did you not hear me say "bloody men" as I walked through

the door?' Jess asks through a laugh. 'Me and that clown are over. He was a prize weirdo. Aren't they all, though?'

She directs this question at me as she hugs me.

'You're not wrong,' I say with a sigh. 'Also, hello, it's been a minute.'

'I know, I know, things have been mad,' she replies. 'If I'm being honest, I kind of lost my job a few months back, so the funds weren't really there for travelling back from Edinburgh. Honestly, Armie was so tight. I would ask him for money and he would be like "no way, you've already spent enough money on plants this month, the house is like a jungle" but I let him keep them when we split. I don't get his problem. Anyway, since then, my Etsy started popping off, given that it's Christmas, and I sold all the wreaths I've been making, so I thought I'd use the money to come and stay with my mum and my favourite sister.'

'Your only sister,' I remind her.

'Right. That's why I saved you a wreath, I swapped the one on your door for it on my way in. That's just the empty bag it came in. That bag is washing, the other one is clean enough stuff for now.'

She directs the comments about her dirty washing to my mum, as though it's her problem.

'And this... this is a Chinese banquet for four.'

She places the white paper bag on the worktop and starts unloading containers.

I glance at my empty dinner plate.

'You should have said you were coming,' Mum tells her. 'I would have made you some extra, without peas.'

'Well, I brought Chinese for everyone,' she exclaims proudly.

'You should have called, to say you were coming,' I point out gently.

'Oh, okay, fine, if you don't want any Chinese...'

Jess wraps her arms around the containers set out on the worktop in front of her and pulls them closer to her. As she does this, she grins, like she knows me too well.

'Well, obviously I'm going to have some,' I reply through a laugh. 'Second dinner is practically a tradition in this family.'

Second dinner is a bit of an in-joke we have. It stems from Jess's fussy eating habits and how, when we would have to go somewhere where we didn't like the food, like a particular restaurant or a family event, Mum would bribe us into eating a little bit, or at least pretending to, by saying she would make us something special when we got home.

'Shit, I always forget how many cupboards you have,' Jess exclaims as she starts opening and inadvertently slamming doors (which is quite the feat for a soft-close cupboard) in her search for plates.

I wade through the mess in the kitchen, where Jess is causing even more chaos, to grab some plates and help her serve up all the Chinese food she's brought.

As we all sit back down at the table together, Jess tucks in, like it's the first thing she's eaten in days.

'Armie never let me eat Chinese food,' she says through a mouthful of noodles. 'He said if we got fat before we were thirty, that would be it. We also had to keep a chocolate-free house, so that he could avoid temptation, but that just made me sneak it all the more. I was putting it away on the sly left, right and centre, I've put like half a stone on, but it's gone straight to my chest, look.'

Jess grabs her boobs in her hands and sort of pushes them together. In doing so, she gets sweet and sour sauce on her top. She shrugs it off.

'It sounds to me like you're better off without him,' Mum says.

'I've always thought that, although I never would have said anything. It was the same with Dec—'

'Erm, let me stop you there,' I interrupt her.

'You're not seriously going to try and defend Declan?' Jess asks in disbelief.

'It's not a competition,' I point out. 'And if it were, I'm not sure if you would win by having the best or worst ex, but that's not what I'm getting at. Mum and I were just chatting and we agreed this is going to be a man-free Christmas. Even the mention of exes is strictly prohibited.'

'That's cool, I can sign off on that,' she replies. 'Well, if it's chill, I thought I'd stay until the new year.'

A quiet Christmas is slipping slowly away from me. With just Mum, I still stood a chance of something close to quiet, but Jess is going to complicate things. But she's my sister, and I love her, and it's Christmas. It will be nice to spend some time together.

'I don't know if this sweetens the deal at all, but I let someone swap me some gift vouchers for that boujee farm shop for a wreath, so the food shopping is on me,' she adds, spreading her arms out in a ta-da kind of way. 'Unless you've already done it?'

'We thought we'd go in the morning,' I reply.

'Oh, it will be so fun, the three of us shopping for Christmas together. Like the good old days, after your da...' Mum stops herself in her tracks. 'Before the two of you left home.'

I smile at her for changing course.

None of the plates are clear, but we've all definitely had enough.

'Cuppa tea?' Mum suggests.

'Maybe something sweet?' Jess chimes in.

I suppose there's always room for something sweet.

'Are you sure I can't help tidy?' Mum asks.

'You go sit on the sofa,' I insist. 'I'm sure Jess will help me.'

Jess looks at the mess in the kitchen and pulls a face.

'Yeah, of course,' she says, without a hint of enthusiasm. 'Everything just goes in the bin or the dishwasher, right?'

Yeah, apart from the hand-wash only bits and the recycling. I've always suspected Jess purposefully does a bad job of things so that you don't ask her again. Unfortunately, because these have only ever been unprovable suspicions, it's always worked really well for her.

'Don't worry, you go help Mum get set up on the sofa with the TV, I'll tidy up,' I insist with a heavy sigh.

'You sure?' Jess says as she heads for the sofa, she doesn't wait for a reply, though. 'Two sugars for me, please.'

I guess I'm making the cups of tea too, then.

I stand in the kitchen, between the island and the worktop behind me, and slowly twirl around, taking in all the mess. Pans, utensils, chopping boards covered in colourful peels from varying vegetables. There's even a bit of mashed potato on the wall, probably from Mum's over-enthusiastic mashing, but thankfully it's only on the splash-back. Then there's Jess's mess. All the take-away containers, all the food that didn't quite make it to the plates, and worst of all, all the leftovers that are looking more unappetising by the second.

I sigh, then get to work. After scraping food into the bin, rinsing plates and sorting the recycling, I grab the binbag with the food in to take it outside to the wheelie bin. It's only on my way back into the house when I notice the wreath Jess has placed on the door. The one I had up – which is currently on the floor propped against the house – was a classic green one with a golden bow. It features dried oranges, cinnamon sticks, pinecones and tiny, delicate gold baubles. Jess's wreath couldn't be more different. The dark green of the wreath is almost completely covered, the dried orange slices are swapped for grapefruit (with extra synthetic pink colouring to make them pop) along with a chaotic barrage of pink fluff, gigantic sparkly baubles in everything from peach to fuchsia, and then there's all the mad details, like plastic flamingos, and mini replica cocktails dotted around. I don't have the energy to even think about how I'm going to deal with this right now, so I go in and close the door behind me.

Mum and Jess are curled up on the sofa, cackling at reruns of *The Royle Family*. It's nice to see them both smiling, I must admit. The women in our family don't have much luck with men. I already knew it was true, but it's good to confirm that we don't need them to be happy.

So quiet Christmas has turned into mini-family Christmas. I'll just have to make the most of it – it really will be good, to spend time with them both – so long as they don't make any more mess, that is.

4

Our local branch of Wilson's, the boujee farm shop chain, isn't somewhere I shop often, but it turns out it's one of the few stores that isn't hell on earth to visit in the run-up to Christmas time. The aisles are wide, the place isn't rammed with frazzled shoppers, and they have so much delicious-looking food that you can't get in the supermarkets. However, things didn't go exactly to plan when we arrived there earlier today.

First of all, other than boasting a healthy (but actually quite unhealthy) array of snack foods, it turns out that if you're wanting anything for your Christmas dinner, then you have to pre-order it.

The second issue was that Jess's gift voucher was only for £30. When I say only, don't get me wrong, there was never any expectation that Jess should pay for the food over Christmas, but she definitely made it sound like the voucher was going to cover a lot of it. She hyped up a sort of Supermarket Sweep spree on the drive there. In the end, we spent the whole amount on extortionately priced snacks – and we don't even have much to show for it, just a bottle of apple juice, a few bags of crisps, some sweets and a couple of tins of biscuits. The crisps and one packet of biscuits had gone by the time we reached a supermarket in town.

Someone bumps their trolley into mine before giving me a dirty look and storming off. See, this is more like what I expected shopping for Christmas supplies to be like. It doesn't matter which supermarket you go to; everyone is in holiday mode. We're all stressed, over-shopping – picking up enough food to feed a thousand people – and rushing around like the world will end if we don't secure six different snacking cheeses by the time the shops close on Christmas Eve. I'm no different. In fact, with Christmas Eve being this time next week, this is probably the earliest I've ever done my Christmas big shop. I really have got my organisational skills together over the past year – well, compared to before, at least. Neither my mum nor Jess is a naturally organised person, they've both kept marvelling at how early we're doing the food shop, but my mum is the kind of person to be zooming around the Co-op on Christmas Eve because she forgot to buy potatoes four hours earlier when she was doing her shopping last-minute, and Jess is the kind of person to do absolutely nothing, and just turn up at someone's *something* to spend the holidays – whatever was going on, that would suit her if it was free and easy.

Mum grabs two bags of nuts – the net ones full of a variety of nuts in their shells, the kind you only really seem to see at Christmas.

'Does anyone actually like those?' I ask curiously. 'I know one of the things we aren't mentioning used to, but I'm pretty sure he was the only one.'

The thing we're not mentioning being my dad. Mum would always put out a basket of nuts at Christmas and Dad would be the only one who ate them. She would leave a fancy nutcracker in the basket and Dad would be back and forth to it all Christmas break, cracking nuts, leaving bits of shell everywhere. No one else would touch it, though.

'It's Christmas, Billie,' Mum insists, as though I'd missed the memo.

She used this same excuse when she put a bag of clementines and two bottles of sherry into the trolley too.

Another thing she keeps saying is 'just in case', as a reason to buy extra items, or random things that would be good for people dropping by. I politely reminded her that no one will be dropping by. Auntie Jane has taken Grandma to Australia with her for Christmas, to spend it with my cousins, and when she mentioned inviting my next-door neighbour around for a drink (because apparently you have to keep your neighbours on side, if you want them to call the fire brigade so you don't die in a fire) I had to break it to her that Kenny, the divorcee who lives next door, would happily watch my house burn to the ground, as I would his. We definitely don't love thy neighbour on this street.

I'm going to stop complaining and just let Mum and Jess do whatever they want. It's easier that way. At least we have a good system. Mum grabs what we need, Jess scans it on her phone using the shop's app (which is fantastic, because the queues to pay are long), and I place it in the trolley – which I regret offering to push, because I've managed to pick one with a dodgy wheel, so half the battle today is trying not to take out all the shoppers on my left, although lord knows I'd like to with some of them. What is it about Christmas time that makes everyone so selfish? People keep ramming me, others block the aisles, and I'm pretty sure I saw a woman lean into someone else's trolley and take her gravy, rather than heading back to the aisle where the instant stuff lives.

We're nearly done now – thank goodness. I'm currently hovering by the trolley, behind my mum, while she deliberates between buying legit Rennies or the off-brand ones. Either way, antacids are the cornerstone of a decent May family Christmas. We're all prone to a bit of reflux – apparently something passed down from my grandad's side – and there's nothing like a double dose of my mum's Christmas cooking to fan the flames.

'Won't you move out of the way,' a delightful old dear in her seventies says as she shoulder-barges me out of the way with a strength that will make me think twice about labelling people an 'old dear' again.

'Sorry,' I reply, as Jess and I move out of the way.

'Honestly, the youth of today,' she rants to herself. 'Pathetic.'

'She thinks she's insulting me, but I'm pretty jazzed to be thought of as a youth,' I joke to Jess under my breath.

Sadly, there's nothing wrong with the lady's hearing, because she stops in her tracks, turns around and approaches me. Jess, my darling sister, steps out of her line of fire.

'What did you say?' the lady asks me.

I look to my mum, who is still comparing antacids, oblivious to the fact that I've regressed back to being a child and clearly want my mummy to come and shout at her.

'Oh, no, nothing,' I insist. 'I was just joking with my sister. I wasn't talking to you. Sorry for the mix-up.'

Wow, I'm babbling with fear, like a ticked-off child. Tragic.

'You can't even stand up for yourself, can you? How do you think your generation would have survived during the war, hmm?' she asks, pausing, as though she expects an answer.

I'm briefly distracted, glancing over her shoulder, trying to work out what Jess is doing. Eventually, I realise. She's placing boxes of condoms in the woman's trolley.

'Nothing cheeky to say in reply to that, have you?' she asks me, leaning closer for a second. 'Spineless.'

The woman turns on her heel, grabs her trolley and marches off.

I smile and laugh at Jess as we reconvene.

'Oh, my God, I can't believe you just did that,' I say quietly.

'No one is rude to my sister and gets away with it,' she replies.

Mum eventually joins us.

'Right, that's it, I think we're done,' she declares. 'Let's go pay. I went for proper Rennies in the end. I didn't want to chance it.'

'Probably for the best,' I joke.

Mum hands Jess the box to scan with her phone. Jess angles it carefully, lining the barcode up with her camera.

'Oh,' she says softly.

'Oh?' I repeat back to her. That doesn't sound good.

'What's the matter?' Mum asks her.

'I think I just accidentally wiped all the shopping from the app,' she says. 'Well, everything but the Rennies.'

'You think?' I say.

'Well, no, I definitely have,' she replies sheepishly. 'But it wasn't on purpose. The scan button is right next to the button to start a new shop.'

I sigh.

'Does that mean we need to queue and scan it all?' Mum asks. 'Because I need to get home. I've got a delivery. A surprise.'

'Oh?' I say nervously.

'I need to get back and, to be honest, I could do with Jess's help,' she says.

'If you guys want to get a taxi, I can queue with this stuff, and bring it back in the car?' I suggest helpfully. The last thing I want to do is queue here, but if Mum has arranged some kind of surprise, then I don't want to stop her.

'Are you sure you can manage?' Mum replies.

I look down at the overloaded trolley.

'Yeah, definitely,' I reply.

It won't be easy, but I'm sure I'll be fine.

Once Mum and Jess are gone, I consider whether I can rescan all the items in the trolley myself, but there's just no way that's going to be possible, there's too much in there, and I doubt anyone would appreciate my laying it all out on the floor. I'll just have to suck it up and join the queue. At least there's a surprise waiting for Mum when I get home. Let's just hope it's a good one.

5

The first thing I see, when I pull up on my driveway, is the wreath that Jess put on my door.

I know she's just trying to be nice, and it's not like it isn't well crafted, she's done a really good job, it's just not my style at all.

It's dark out now, but the lights from outside my house and in the garden shine bright and ping off the glitter, drawing even more attention to it.

My own wreath, which is more my style, is currently upside down on the floor, having blown onto the lawn. I go to retrieve it. Maybe I'll suggest we move hers to the backdoor where we'll see it more? I mean, we won't, but it's worth a gentle try.

'Nice wreath,' I hear a voice call out.

I glance over the fence to see Kenny, my neighbour, escorting a twenty-something woman into a taxi.

I look at the wreath in my hand.

'Not that one,' he says. 'That one.'

He's got this cheeky look on his face, like he's taking the piss out of me.

'Have you had the local school choir over singing carols for you?' I quip, nodding towards the younger woman in the taxi, as he closes the door for her.

'Ooh, good one,' he replies.

If I'm being honest, there are a few reasons why I dislike Kenny, and the more I get to know about him, the more I dislike him. He seemed fine, when we first moved in, but Kenny was newly single pretty much from the get-go (I think I only saw his wife, Beth, a couple of times before they split – and she wasn't very nice either) and looking for someone to hang out with, so he started taking Declan on nights out with him. Declan would come home with all the gossip for me. He told me that Kenny and his wife had got divorced, and that he was dating a constant stream of young women (and it would infuriate me, that Declan would say this as though it were something to be proud of) and these days he could do whatever he wanted, and that he seemed like the happiest person in the world, and blah blah blah. To be honest, it just made him sound like a total clown to me, and I can't help but wonder if everything Kenny said about his new life could have contributed to Declan deciding that he was disenchanted with his own, and subsequently taking off so soon after we moved to the area. You've got to laugh, that it was another man who turned his head (to a 'better life' at least) and not a woman.

'Run along, Kenny, the other ones might be trying to escape,' I say as I start unloading my shopping.

'You look like you could use a hand with all those bags,' he points out. 'Good luck with that.'

Kenny heads back inside and closes his door behind him. As if I'd want any help from him, I'm surely too old for him to waste any time on.

I notice my mum's face in the living room bay window before she and Jess join me outside. They both have huge grins on their faces.

'Did you get it all sorted?' Mum asks.

'Yep, all here,' I reply. 'We officially have enough food for fifty people, most of which needs eating in the next few days.'

I'm exaggerating, but we do have a lot of fresh food that needs eating in the coming days. I could be tempted to make a list, on the home hub that sits on the kitchen worktop. I use that screen for everything from displaying recipes to setting timers for my cooking to organising my calendar and to-do list, it's great. Although it's probably not worth the amount of teasing that Jess will sling my way, for something so dorky.

I whizz back and forth between the car and the front door, while Mum and Jess carry the bags inside. With everything unloaded, I lock up and head inside.

It's so lovely and warm indoors. I feel it the second I close the front door behind me. And then there's that tell-tale smell, that they've got the log burner going, which I love. It's such a homely and welcoming smell. The diffusers must be on too, because the other thing I can smell is the sandalwood oil that I like to use in them. Perhaps now that I'm home, everyone is here, and the shopping is done, that quiet-ish Christmas can finally begin. Just as soon as we put all this shopping away, of course.

I don't know if it's the familiar smells that lull me into a false sense of security, but when I walk around the corner into the living room, I am stunned into a state of shock. I freeze on the spot, staring into a room that is not only unrecognisable from the one I left earlier today, but could not be less me if it tried.

'Surprise,' Mum and Jess sing at the same time, holding their arms out, smiling widely.

'What do you think?' Mum asks. 'Do you love it?'

'It's...' I don't know what to say. 'It's... wow.'

When I put my Christmas decorations up earlier in the

month, I decided on a colour scheme, and I went for a definite 'less is more' approach. It looked great, though, and I loved it.

Now the room is a barrage on the eyes. My Christmas tree is decked out in entirely new decorations, my usually clear sideboards and tables are covered in red tablecloths with gold doilies. There are so many different colours and shapes and textures, it's hard to truly take in any one thing. It looks like someone threw a Christmas grenade into my living room and this is the fallout.

'I know you had your decorations up and it did look beautiful,' Mum starts. 'But with all mine being in storage, and all the family bits and pieces I usually put out every year, I thought, well, why not put them all out here?'

Mum's heart was definitely in the right place with this one, and I'm sure that when I look closely, I'll see all the little details and individual items that make me feel nostalgic, but it's just all way too much. It's just so messy, and distracting, and cluttered and… and she looks like she's really happy with it.

'I love it,' I lie. 'It's so much better than what I had going on.'

'Yours was a bit soulless,' Jess points out. 'Don't worry, I put out lots of pink sparkly bits to match the wreath.'

Oh, Jesus Christ, I can't even see them. I don't know if that's a good thing or a bad one.

'Let's get this shopping put away then,' I say, changing the subject. 'Oh, have you done it?'

'No, no, it's all here, behind the island,' Mum replies. 'I didn't want to overstep the mark, I'm sure you know exactly how you like your cupboards to be.'

Oh, the irony.

'Thank you,' I reply.

Well, at least it's the 16th today. I got to make the most of my decorations the way I liked them for a few weeks. With a week to go until Christmas, they'll all be coming down again soon anyway, and Mum does seem really happy, having all her traditional decorations around her, so that's nice, I guess. Even if I do feel kind of claustrophobic just looking at it all.

'Oh, I almost forgot,' Mum says, hurrying over to one of the windows to grab a small remote. 'There we go.'

With one push of the button, the windows in the living room all spring to life with small twinkling lights, hanging down in front of them like curtains.

'The finishing touch,' Jess says as she plonks herself down on the sofa. 'What's for dinner?'

I just laugh quietly to myself. In just over a week, Christmas will be over, I'm sure Jess will take off before New Year's Eve, because she's one of those people who can't acknowledge a new year without throwing a booze-heavy wake for the previous one, and Mum's house will be ready before you know it. And then I'll have my house back – back to the way I want it.

And it can't come soon enough.

6

I am woken up by the sound of Wizzard's 'I Wish It Could Be Christmas Everyday' blasting through the house. I can't quite figure out if the song is on repeat, or whether it's just so much longer than I remember it being.

I thought I was being so smart and sophisticated when I had speakers fitted throughout the house that all linked to the home hub in the kitchen. The main pro of doing this, other than being able to ask the smart device for music, is that it doesn't matter which room in the house you are in, your music follows you around. The major con, it turns out, is that when someone asks for a song to be played (without knowing to ask for a specific room) it just plays everywhere. I grab my phone from my bedside table, open the app, and tell the music to stop playing in my bedroom.

Peace at last? Nope, I can still hear it playing downstairs (stupid century-old house), and as 'I Wish It Could Be Christmas Everyday' transitions into 'Merry Xmas Everybody' by Slade, it only seems louder. I swear, Noddy Holder's voice actually permeates the floorboards.

I guess I'm getting up then.

I head into my en suite, where thankfully the white marble tiles dampen the music a little. It's a shame I can't stay in here all day. I wash my face, brush my teeth and moodily shrug on my dressing gown – livid to be out of bed before 10 a.m. on not only a Saturday, but the start of my time off from work. I usually like to decompress by sleeping in for the first few days, to offset all the early mornings throughout the term – something I can't do on a normal weekend, because throwing off my sleeping pattern makes those Monday mornings all the harder.

By the time I find Mum in the kitchen, already dolled up to the eyes, all wrapped up in a festive apron, she's listening to Lady A's almost aggressively cheery cover of 'A Holly Jolly Christmas'.

She dances over to meet me in the dining room, singing into a wooden spoon to serenade me.

I allow her to flap my arms a little, like a moody kid, but I can't help but smile.

'Crêpe?' she says.

'You're telling me,' I reply.

'No, *crêpe*,' she says again. 'You cheeky little girl.'

'That would be great,' I admit, pulling up a stool at the island.

'You'll be pleased to see I'm serving them with Chantilly cream and clementines,' Mum points out. 'Making use of the clementines already, see.'

'Well played,' I reply.

'Cuppa tea?' she asks. That really should be Mum's catch-phrase. It's definitely her cure-all answer to everything.

'I might have a coffee,' I reply.

Bon Jovi's 'Please Come Home for Christmas' starts playing. Mum pulls a face.

'Not a fan of this one?' I ask.

'It's not a real Christmas song, is it?' she replies. 'There's all sorts of songs on this playlist that shouldn't really be on a traditional Christmas playlist. I noticed the bloody Cheeky Girls on the list. They're yet to rear their heads.'

God help them when they do.

'Alexa, skip,' Mum says.

'It's not an Alexa,' I tell her.

'Right,' she says with a bat of her hand. 'Hey, Silly. Hey, Silly!'

'Silly?'

'The one you talk to on your phone,' she points out.

'Siri?' I say back to her.

'Siri? Is that what she's called? Well, that is silly. Okay, Google, Simon, Baby Jesus – help me out, Billie. Skip this one.'

'It's a Smarty,' I remind her – I talked her though it yesterday. 'Smarty, skip this one.'

Bon Jovi is replaced by Chris Rhea, with 'Driving Home for Christmas'.

'Much better,' Mum says. 'I did try to figure out your coffee machine. I gave it a good go.'

Not too good a go, I hope.

'I didn't break it,' she insists. 'Blooming hell, look at your face.'

'Sorry, sorry,' I reply. 'No one tells you how expensive it is, having a house. Well, they do, but all they talk about is mortgages and bills. No one tells you how expensive it is or all the things that can break, like appliances, and all the stuff that gets destroyed just because it's windy and all the neighbourhood trampolines decide to congregate on your garage roof.'

'I know all too well, darling, why do you think I'm downsizing?' she replies.

'And, of course, I didn't think I'd be doing it all on my own, but then bloody—'

'Oi,' Mum snaps, brandishing her wooden spoon at me. 'No men allowed, remember, not even by name.'

I laugh.

'Sorry! Thank you,' I reply. 'You're absolutely right.'

Mum takes her phone out of her apron pocket, glances at it, and then drops it back in.

'You get that coffee machine fired up, I'll go wake your sister, see if she wants any breakfast,' Mum says. She wipes her hands before heading upstairs.

Yeah, okay, good luck getting Jess out of bed on a morning for anything.

I feel my own phone vibrate in my dressing gown pocket. I assume it's going to be from Angie, checking up on me, but it's just an app notification. It's from Matcher. Ha! The last thing I need right now is a dating app.

Single all the way this year? We've got you covered. Click here.

Curiosity gets the better of me, so I take the bait. The app looks the same as it always does. No new messages, just a series of old ones with people I grew tired of messaging with, but when there's no spark, there's no spark. What's the point of forcing conversation for the sake of it, if you know it's not going to go anywhere?

One thing that's different is a red banner at the top which reads: Mingle All the Way. Oh, this is that thing Angie was talking about.

I browse the page. It's a user-generated calendar of events for groups of singles to mix. I guess in somewhere like London it would be packed with events. Here, where the pool is much smaller, by the time you consider the fact that most people are only on here for quick hook-ups, or to meet one person (like I naively used it for), there's not a ton going on, but there's at least something organised by someone once a day.

There's a red button at the top which simply says, 'Feeling brave?' – I'm not, but of course I click it anyway, just to see what it is.

Do you want to mark yourself as attending all events, and add all events to your calendar?

Oh, no. No, no, no. I quickly retreat. That's the last thing I need.

I fill the coffee machine with water in one part, milk in another, and pop in one of the pods. It's Christmas, so I pour a dash of cinnamon syrup into the bottom of my cup before letting the machine do all the hard work. When it's ready, I remove my cup and hold the button to blast steam through the milk nozzle to clean it. It's pretty noisy, so I don't hear my mum walk up behind me. Eventually, I hear her talking to me.

'What?' I ask loudly over the machine.

'I said your dad needs to talk to you,' she shouts back. The machine stops halfway through her sentence, so she screams the latter half at me. I imagine her words would have echoed in my ears either way.

'What?' I ask softly.

'Your dad is on the phone,' she tells me again, holding out her phone for me to take from her. 'Talk to him, I'll go wake up Jess.'

Oh, God. This can't be good. This can't be good news at all. Is he dying? People don't just ring up people they don't speak to very often in the days before Christmas to deliver bad news, do they? Then again, his timing has always been off.

Needless to say, I am not Rowan May's biggest fan. Sometimes, even having his surname feels like an emotional burden. It always baffles me that my mum kept his name, but if you ask her about it, she just shrugs, says that it's been her name for years, she likes it more than her maiden name, Turner, and that she'll be damned if she's going to let him take everything from her. Of course, she doesn't say that last part much any more. Mum doesn't dwell on her split from my dad. They're not close, they don't speak or see each other – at least, I didn't think they did. Obviously he's called her today.

Jess and I were teenagers when Dad left Mum for someone else, so we were old enough to know what was going on, and to remember everything that happened in real time. Mum never encouraged us, but neither of us wanted anything to do with Dad after that. He'd been distant for a while; we all knew something was up. He was shouting at us all more and obviously the affair he was having cut into our father-daughter time. He gave us space after the split – perhaps a bit too much, because we were never really able to get our relationship back on track. We're a bit more grown up about things now, I guess, which is to say we're all just politely going through the motions. We swap cards on birthdays and stuff like that. He didn't invite us to his wedding, to Gail when he married her last year, but they did have a sort of spur of the moment Las Vegas wedding (at least, that's what he told us) so we haven't even met Gail yet. Obviously we're not in a rush to do so. She might not have been the 'other woman' who broke up our family, but if she thinks my dad is worth marrying, you've got to question her judgement.

I swallow hard as I take the phone from my mum.

'Hello?'

'Billie, love, hello,' Dad replies.

'Hello,' I say again.

'How are you?' he asks brightly.

'I'm okay,' I reply. This is like pulling teeth. 'How are you?'

'Not good, I'm afraid,' he says. Okay, here it is. 'Things have been a bit chaotic.'

I pause, waiting for him to say more. Mum is upstairs with Jess, so I can't even get a read on the situation from her.

'They say everything happens in threes,' Dad starts. 'First of all, we found out Gail's boys can't make it for Christmas. They're both married.'

He pauses for a second and I can't help but wonder if this is a dig or a hint of something. Well, Dad, sorry Jess and I aren't married, but we didn't exactly grow up around the best example of marriage. Even though you couldn't fault my mum, that only makes things worse. Even if you throw everything you've got into a marriage, it's all for nothing, if the other person decides to throw it all away.

'We though Michael and his wife and kids might make it, but they live in Carlisle, and Michael's father-in-law had a heart attack yesterday. It's awful,' Dad insists. 'We bought so much food.'

Yep, that's the travesty. I feel like he's bombarding me with small talk, stalling for time, maybe...

'Gail was running a bath, when she went to take Michael's call. She forgot about it and, long story short, the bath overflowed, soaked through the floor, and the bathroom is now in the kitchen.'

'Wow,' I blurt. Well, take it from someone who has spent the past year doing house jobs, that one is going to be expensive. 'Will your insurance cover it?'

'Ah, that's the thing,' Dad starts. 'Last night was fine, we went out for dinner, someone was over from the insurance company first thing this morning and it seems like we're going to need the dryers in for a few days. Which would be fine, except the bloke who came to check it out reckons we might have asbestos in the old floor tiles, that were under a second layer of flooring someone put down before we moved in. So that's going to need testing and removing very carefully.'

'Yeah, definitely,' I reply, allowing myself to get a little more into the conversation, now it's something I know about. I might not be married, but I had my own little patch of asbestos removed, shortly after we bought the house. What a weird thing to try to bond over.

'The problem is, so close to Christmas, we're having trouble finding somewhere to stay,' Dad says.

I hear his words. Then I hear them again, when I realise what he's about to say. No! Don't say it, please don't say it.

'And then I remembered I have a daughter with a big, beautiful house that I haven't seen,' he says in a bright and breezy tone that he has absolutely no right to adopt. 'I thought perhaps—'

Dad's voice cuts off. I glance at Mum's phone. The battery has died. I search the island drawer for a charger as Mum and Jess join me. Jess looks half asleep still, her dressing gown belt trailing on the floor on one side of her. My mum grabs it and starts threading it through for her.

'Did you speak to your dad?' Mum asks.

'Yes,' I reply. 'Do you know why he called?'

'Wait, Dad called?' Jess says, suddenly a lot more awake. 'What the hell did he want?'

'He did mention it, yes,' Mum says softly.

'Oh, brilliant, so he asks you instead of me – and I imagine you told him he has to ask me himself,' I say.

'Obviously,' Mum replies.

'And, now that I think about it, he was chatting about his new family, and I thought he was just stalling for time, but now I feel like he was buttering me up, trying to garner some sympathy and—'

'Erm, can someone please tell me what's going on?' Jess asks, interrupting me ranting.

I grab my coffee and hand it to her. I can't face it now, and they say sugar is good for shock, right?

'Drink this,' I insist.

'Come on, Billie, tell me,' Jess replies. She does take the coffee, though.

'His bathroom has fallen through to his kitchen, he needs somewhere to stay,' I tell her.

'Right, well, obviously he can't just turn up and expect to stay here, this isn't a hotel,' she points out ironically. I smile for a split second. It's different, obviously, because Jess is welcome here.

'He sounded pretty desperate,' Mum says softly. 'Good will to all men, remember.'

'I thought we were only doing good will to all *wo*men this year, though?' I reply.

Mum's phone eventually has enough to restart. It makes a noise as it powers on again.

'A polite reminder that he abandoned us in our time of need – when we were kids and needed a dad,' Jess points out.

'Yes, but Billie isn't like her dad,' Mum says with a smile.

'Ugh, she's right,' I say with a sigh.

I grab Mum's phone and call Dad back.

'Hello, Billie?' he says as he answers, after not even an entire ring. 'What happened?'

'Sorry, Mum's battery died,' I tell him. 'You were saying?'

'Oh, that's a relief,' he says, and I can actually hear the relief in his voice. 'I don't know how long I was talking for before we got disconnected, but can we stay with you, if you have the space for us, that is?'

What am I supposed to say? I mean, obviously my mum has been there for me much more than my dad ever has, and I have an actual relationship with her, but how can I help my mum but not do the same for my dad? No, I'm actually asking. Because I really, really don't want to do this.

I glance over at Mum and Jess. Jess's eyes are wide and she's shaking her head. Mum looks strangely proud of me. I think that's the reason I do what I do next.

'Of course you can,' I reply simply. 'When do you need to come over?'

'Today, if that's all right,' Dad says.

Bloody hell. I am in no way mentally prepared for this. Physically I am, the house can take more guests, but this is the last thing I wanted.

'Yeah, of course,' I insist as best I can. 'I'll get your room ready.'

If it's possible, Jess's eyes widen even more.

'They're getting my room, aren't they?' she says to Mum.

'Don't worry, there's a sofa bed in Billie's office,' Mum whispers back.

'Why can't they sleep on that?' she replies.

Dad is talking but I'm listening to Mum and Jess. I start listening again.

'... if that's okay,' he says.

'Yeah, that's fine,' I reply. 'So you're staying until...?'

'That's what I mean,' Dad says. 'It's going to be after Christmas, at least, but like I said, it's just the two of us, we've got lots of food to bring with us. Gail would love to bring her Christmas tree.'

I blink a couple of times. I didn't hear that right. Any of it. Surely! He wants to stay until after Christmas and Gail wants to bring her tree?

'We've got a Christmas tree already,' I tell him. 'Tell Gail it's okay. But thank you.'

I roll my eyes at myself for adding on that lame thank you at the end.

'It's no trouble,' he replies. 'She's really quite fond of it. She's already wrapped it in clingfilm, for easy transportation – she saw a video online, it's really quite impressive.'

By all means, spend extra time in the house with asbestos in it, wrapping the Christmas tree in clingfilm.

'Well, okay then, I'll send you the address from Mum's phone,' I say. 'And we'll see you soon.'

There isn't an ounce of enthusiasm in my voice. You would think Dad would be able to detect it but he's oblivious, as usual.

I hang up the phone.

'Two more for Christmas,' I announce with a sigh.

'No!' Jess blurts.

'I'm proud of you,' Mum says, rubbing my shoulder. 'I raised you right.'

'Yeah, you did, he didn't, that's why this sucks,' I point out. 'They're bringing their own Christmas tree, apparently. Wrapped in clingfilm.'

I glance around the room. Lord knows where they'll put it.

Jess hands me the now empty coffee cup.

'Well, I guess I'll go vacate my room,' she says, angrily.

'Sorry, sis,' I tell her.

'It's not your fault,' she replies. 'He could have guilted me into doing the same.'

'I'm proud of you both,' Mum tells us. 'I'm going to make you both the best crêpes of your life.'

Mum heads to the kitchen, to resume making breakfast, and Jess plods upstairs to move bedrooms.

That's quiet-ish Christmas out the window. Quiet, comfortable, cosy, calm – all over. Ah well, I suppose it's a relief. It's like when you get a new phone, and you're terrified of scratching the screen, but then you do and from that moment on you never worry about it again. My dream Christmas is over. At least now things can't get any worse. I hope.

7

I rub my hands together, to warm them up, for all the good it actually does.

I'm standing at the end of my driveway, keeping an eye out for Dad and Gail, who should be here any minute, with the food that was originally bought for Gail's married sons and their wives and kids, that I have no idea where I'm going to store, and the cling-film-wrapped Christmas tree that I have no idea where I'm going to put either.

I hear Kenny's front door open. Brilliant, that's just what I need, my usual sparring with my unfriendly neighbourhood shagger man. Admittedly not my best work, but give me a break, I'm stressed.

Obviously he has a younger woman with him, again, I can't tell if it's the same one, but this one is being picked up by another girl. She hops into the car. As Kenny makes his way to the back car door, he gives me a wave – a sarcastic one, if such a thing exists – as he goes to get inside too.

'Aww, Kenny, I didn't know you were fostering,' I say, in an entirely put on, sickly-sweet voice. Okay, that is my best work.

He just sticks his tongue out at me, gets in the car and they all drive off together. It's as I watch them drive away that I notice a black Range Rover driving in this direction.

I take such a deep breath; the cold air hurts my lungs. I cough and splutter right as they pull up next to me. I'm effortlessly cool like that.

'Hello, Silly Billie,' Dad says warmly as he hurries around the car to give me a hug.

I suppose it should be cute, that he calls me the nickname he did when I was little, but it only reminds me that our relationship got sort of suspended in time.

I'm a little taken aback when I clap eyes on him. Dad always had a thick head of black hair that he would wear very neatly styled backwards. He looks so different now. His hair is softer, and shorter, and grey, just like his short beard, and he wears a pair of round tortoise-shell glasses. It's a shock to see him looking so much older.

'Hello,' I say politely.

'You're our hero,' he tells me. 'Isn't she, sweetie?'

Ugh, sweetie. He never called Mum sweetie.

'Thank you for letting us stay with you,' Gail says as she approaches me for a hug.

Gail is probably in her mid-sixties. Her light brown hair goes to just below her shoulders before flicking outwards – too perfectly to be something she isn't styling that way on purpose. Her brown eyes are dark, made darker by the heavy kohl eyeliner she's wearing on her upper and lower lids. She looks nice, like she's dressed up to meet us all for the first time.

I glance down at the men's joggers I'm wearing that I bought indiscriminately from TK Maxx to do decorating in (but found them too comfortable to mess up by the time I got home and tried them on) paired with a cropped T-shirt – not that you can see that under my oversized puffer coat. Perhaps I should have dressed nicer, to meet my dad's new wife for the first time.

'So wonderful to finally meet you. Your dad has told me so much about you and your sister. Go on, Rowan, get the tree.'

She turns to my dad and hints towards the car with a strange movement of her head.

'Yes, of course,' Dad says with an enthusiasm I don't remember him having.

He hurries to the boot and begins unloading two suitcases, bags for life full of shopping, and then finally the Christmas tree. Well, I think it's safe to assume it's the Christmas tree, it's a large green and blue something tightly bound in clingfilm, looking like anonymous leftovers you forgot were sitting at the back of the fridge for God knows how long.

'Come inside,' I say, as warmly as I can. 'Cuppa tea?'

God, I sound just like my mum.

'That would be lovely,' Gail replies. 'Can you handle all those bags, Rowan?'

There's an uncomfortable stiffness to Gail. Obviously Dad can't carry all those bags and that mouldy sausage Christmas tree on his own.

I take my phone from my pocket and punch a message to Jess.

Help!

'I can help him,' I say. 'Jess is on her way out too.'

'There she is,' Dad says brightly as Jess joins us. Jess's reaction is more of a dull one.

'Yo,' she says, very much like an angsty teenager. I find this especially funny because I've never heard Jess say 'yo' in her life.

Dad hugs her. Gail is up next.

'I've heard wonderful things about you, Jessica,' she tells her.

Erm, she didn't say she had heard wonderful things about me! The stepchild putting a roof over her head. Charming. I give myself a mental shake, reminding myself that I need to think clearly, and only (privately, obviously) dislike Gail if she very clearly says and does things that I don't like, and not just because she's Dad's new wife. I like her more than I do him, so she's got that going for her, at least.

'Wonderful to finally meet you, Gill,' Jess replies.

I purse my lips.

'Can you help us with the bags?' I ask her.

Gail makes a move towards the front door with nothing but her handbag.

'Sure,' Jess replies to me, before calling after Gail. 'The door is open, Gill, head in.'

I slink up alongside Jess while Dad finishes unloading the bags and locks up the car.

I give her a wide-eyed look.

'I know she's called Gail,' she whispers to me. 'I just think it's funny to get her name wrong too.'

'It is, but we need to be mature, if we're going to get through Christmas with our sanity,' I tell her.

Jess frowns for a second.

'You're right, I'll cut it out,' she replies. 'You know how much I hate being called Jessica.'

Years of the kids at school calling you 'rabbit' will do that to a girl. If it were me, now, I would more than welcome the comparison, but anything that makes you feel singled out as a kid is pure torture, especially when every kid in your class runs with it.

'I'll say your name at every possible opportunity,' I tell her. 'She'll soon catch on.'

'Thanks,' she replies. 'Although I think I might not spend

much time in the house, if they're here, I'll go visit friends or something.'

I can't really blame her for looking for places to escape to. I imagine Mum will have friends to visit too, just because it's Christmas time, so here's hoping Dad and Gail won't be in much. I might actually get some time to myself still, in all of this unexpected chaos.

Jess rests her head onto my shoulder for a second.

'Right, girls, come on, let's get all this inside,' Dad commands cheerily.

I sigh – again. Let's get this show on the road.

We find Gail hovering inside the hallway, checking her hair in the mirror.

Dad rummages through a bag to find one of those metal Christmas tree stands with the screws that you tighten to hold it in place. With that in one hand, and the tree in the other, he looks at me expectantly.

'Where is this going?' he asks.

That's a very good question.

'If you want to come through to the living room,' I suggest, 'we'll see if we can find somewhere.'

'Oh,' Gail says as we walk around the corner, into the open-plan living space. 'It's very... festively busy already.'

That's one way of putting it.

'Wow, Billie, this is a stunning room,' Dad says. 'It's so modern, for the age of the house.'

'Yeah, it used to be two rooms, a lounge and a kitchen diner, with old-fashioned arches between them either side of the fireplace, so I opened it all up,' I explain.

'They say open-plan living is on the way out,' Gail says thoughtfully as she takes in the room.

'Well, I live here on my own, so they'll get over it,' I reply. 'And they're just walls. It's much easier putting them back in than it was taking them out.'

'No Declan?' Dad asks curiously.

Oh, fantastic, he's said the D word. I guess I forgot to loop him in on that one, that just goes to show how little we interact.

'No Declan,' I reply. I leave it at that, hoping he'll move on. He does.

'It must be a fun space for parties,' Dad continues. I can tell he does genuinely like what I've done.

Something catches my eye in the hallway: Mum's feet, as she walks down the stairs.

'Mum's here,' I announce, keen to change the subject. We all look to the hallway.

As Mum walks around the corner, I notice Dad's jaw drop and his eyes widen. She's wearing a black leather skirt and a white blouse. Her hair and make-up look flawless, as always, but I don't think Dad was quite prepared for the new Kate May. His entire body stiffens (and now I really wish I hadn't used those exact words). If this were a movie, I imagine Mum would be walking in slow motion, a beam of light behind her, as something like REO Speedwagon's 'Can't Fight This Feeling' plays.

'Katie,' he blurts. 'Katie... what? How is it possible you've dropped twenty years since the last time I saw you?'

'And you've found them,' Mum teases him, gesturing towards his hair.

Oh, God, don't tease him, Mum. And don't call her Katie, Dad. This is beyond weird.

Gail clears her throat.

'Mum, this is Gail,' I say, making the introductions, because Dad still has the look of a man who has just been hit in the face by a brick.

'Lovely to meet you, at last, Gail,' Mum says warmly. 'Cuppa tea?'

Gail looks back and forth between us, as if to acknowledge how similar we are when we say that.

'I'll put the kettle on,' Jess offers up quickly, clearly keen to get out of such an awkward situation, but by the time she reaches the kettle and realises that it doesn't actually get her out of the room, she looks back at me and pulls a face.

'Sorry, I just can't get over how different you look, and yet somehow like you haven't aged a day – in fact, you look younger?'

Dad's sentence almost winds up like more of a suspicious accusation, like perhaps Mum might have some kind of Hocus Pocus deal going on.

It's strange, seeing the two of them in the same room again (I daren't even consider how many years it's been since Jess and I saw them at the same time). It only highlights how young Mum looks, and how old Dad seems all of a sudden. As far as Dad goes, I guess all of my notable memories of him are from when he was much younger, so while he doesn't suddenly look like a sixty-something overnight, it seems that way in my head.

'Oh, stop,' Mum insists.

'Yes, stop it,' Gail echoes her sentiment, although hers sounds like there's a little more to it. 'You're going to make the poor woman feel awkward.'

'Sorry, sorry,' Dad says, although he still can't take his eyes off her. 'You know, we were feeling quite disappointed that it was going to be a quiet Christmas without Gail's boys and their families, but now we get to spend it here, with my girls – and Katie, of course – in this beautiful house. All the fun activities, the crafting Gail had planned, the festive movies and the games we were hoping to play – well, we can all do it together, isn't that fantastic?'

That doesn't sound fantastic at all. It sounds like my own personal hell. I need to think of something.

'I'm actually pretty busy,' I lie.

'Oh, no, with work?' Gail asks.

'No, she's a teacher,' Dad reminds her. 'She'll be finished for the term already.'

'I have social plans,' I insist.

'Do you?' Mum can't help but reply in disbelief. She isn't trying to drop me in it, I think she's just surprised.

'Yep, stacked,' I insist.

Dad and Gail stare at me. I can't quite put my finger on the mood, whether things are awkward, or they're suspicious, or they feel like I'm avoiding them – which I am, but things really will be awkward if they realise that.

'Would you prefer us to make other arrangements?' Gail asks.

Dad made it pretty clear they had no other options. So as much as I would love them to...

I grab my phone from my pocket and, without really thinking it through, I open up Matcher and hit that button – the 'feeling brave' button that adds all events to your calendar.

'Here, see,' I say, as I quickly switch from Matcher to my calendar app, and hold up my phone for them to see how stacked my social calendar really is. The calendar events will show up on the smart hub in the kitchen too – only as little dots, though, so no one will know where I'm actually going to be – but it will just go to prove how 'busy' I am.

Okay, so stacked is an exaggeration, the uptake here is still reasonably low, but there's still at least one thing a day I can take myself off to, to get out of the house. I suppose, just because not many people have organised events, doesn't mean there won't be many people at them. Hopefully.

'Wow, you are a sociable girl,' Dad says.

'Yeah, well, single girl in my thirties,' I remind them. 'I've got to keep myself out there.'

I don't believe that for a second.

'I didn't realise you had plans,' Mum says with a smile that looks almost optimistic for me. 'What are you doing this evening?'

I hold my phone up and point to the day with my finger, as if to show everyone while I tell them, but it's going to be news to me too.

'Bingo,' I announce, unable to hide the surprise in my own voice.

Jess leans in, to look at my phone.

'Oh, wow, boozy bingo,' she says.

'Yep – do you want to come?' I ask her.

'No way,' she replies. 'That sounds even more lame than regular bingo.'

'Well, anyway, let's show you guys to your room, because I'll need to start getting ready soon,' I tell them.

I guess I really will.

I'm impressed that I managed to pull something out of the bag, and find somewhere for me to escape to, but I'm not jazzed at the thought of having such a hectic social calendar – yes, even one event a day is hectic to someone like me, who has spent pretty much all her free time over the past year in her house.

I've never played bingo before, never mind boozy bingo, so that will be interesting, at least. I'd prefer a night on the sofa, watching a movie, eating my weight in Quality Street, but this is my only other option.

Stupid open-plan house. All that time and effort taking the walls down – only to leave myself with nowhere to escape to. I really stitched myself up with that one.

8

Never, in a million years, under any circumstances, did I think I would be spending my Saturday night at a bingo hall. But here I am, dressed in my best (the best I could be bothered with, at least), trying to pluck up the courage to head inside.

I've driven past the House of Bingo many times – it's the only bingo place in town – but never been inside, obviously. It's a large old building with insides (as far as I can tell, from glancing inside the lobby) that do not match its classic exterior. Well, classic apart from the big blue sign, surrounded by lights, with the name of the place in big gold lettering.

I walk towards the entrance, careful not to get too close, so that I keep up the pretence that while I might be here, I'm not actually here. I'm walking past the bingo, not into it. That sort of thing.

I'm lingering around the entrance when I notice a guy appear. He's a twenty-something, dressed to impress – well, in that way twenty-something lads who are going out-out do, in a pair of tight jeans and a clingy T-shirt with a neckline that looks way too low.

Is he here for boozy bingo? He must be, surely? Eventually a girl approaches him. I watch as they greet one another. Okay, they've got to be here for the bingo.

I feel strangely nervous, like I'm on a first date, which is daft. I try to find my confidence as I approach them.

'Hello,' I say, all bright and breezy. 'Matcher?'

Best to be direct.

'Erm, yeah,' the guy replies. His cheeks flush slightly.

'How did you know?' the girl asks. She seems kind of embarrassed too. It's nothing to be embarrassed about – going on these Matcher nights out – I don't think... it's only as embarrassing as we make it. I need to find a little more confidence, to channel the teacher in me, to take charge and help these two feel less uncomfortable about the whole thing.

'It's bingo,' I say simply, all smiles. 'Come on, let's head inside.'

The couple glance at each other before following me through the big double doors, into... the lobby, I guess? There's a woman sitting behind the desk.

'Three for bingo, please,' I say. I don't really know what you're supposed to say.

She taps on her computer keyboard a few times. I look back at my new friends and smile.

The guy approaches the woman behind the desk.

'It's Callum,' he tells her. 'I called earlier.'

She glances at her screen.

'Yes, Callum, I've got your request here,' she replies. 'So, three, is it? That's okay. Follow me, I'll show you to your seats.'

'Exciting!' I say, turning to my new friends. 'I'm Billie, by the way.'

'Callum,' he replies, even though I'd already worked that one out.

'Alice,' the girl says.

'Quiet as we walk through the bingo hall, please,' the

employee instructs us. 'I don't know if this is your first time, but the other customers take this very seriously, so keep noise to a minimum.'

'Sorry,' I say quietly.

The doorway she walks us through leads us straight into the bingo hall.

It's a huge room, about three quarters full, with an average clientele age of about sixty-five, but only if you factor the three of us into the equation.

We're shown to a table that is different to all the rest. There are helium balloons attached to one of the chairs and a bottle of prosecco in an ice bucket.

Alice turns to look at Callum and smiles in acknowledgement. Aww, I guess it must be her birthday, and these two must have spoken before. How sweet of him, to call ahead and ask them to make it special.

We all take our seats. Bingo cards and dabbers are already laid out for us. I pick up my dabber and look down at my card. The bingo caller is in full swing, with a game or a round or whatever you call it obviously well under way, and he's clearly going at full speed, but no one at any of the other tables seems to have a problem keeping up with him.

I try to get the knack of marking my card, but it takes me so long to find each number that at least two more get called before I've checked my card. I'm surprised it isn't digital, although, given how many seats there are in this massive room, that would be a lot of tech, and a lot of maintenance. Everyone else here looks old school, like they've been coming here for years, and wouldn't welcome the change to something techy.

I can't believe we're the only three here. I didn't think the events would be packed, but I expected more than the three of us to be attending them. Perhaps the fact that it's bingo has put people off? Anyway, I thought it was supposed to be boozy bingo, that made it sound like it was going to be way more fun than a bottle of prosecco in a bucket of melting ice.

I smile at Callum and Alice before grabbing the bottle. They haven't even opened it for us, so I take charge and wiggle the cork free with my thumbs.

It all happens so quickly. As the cork finally budges it flies out of the bottle, up into the air, where it hits one of the balloons and pops it. It's so loud – and the fact the room was so quiet before that only seems to amplify the volume. I place my hands over my mouth and giggle into my hands.

'Oh, my God, how embarrassing,' I whisper to Callum and Alice as I pour each of us a glass of prosecco. There are two wine glasses and a plastic cup, so I give myself the plastic one. 'I thought boozy bingo would be more fun.'

'What do you mean?' Alice asks me.

'Boozy bingo,' I say back to her. 'Boozy bingo.'

Saying it again doesn't make things any clearer to them.

'It said the event was called boozy bingo,' I remind them. 'In the app.'

I sip my drink. It's not very good. I don't know if it's cheap prosecco or if the plastic cup has an off-putting smell to it. Either way, I doubt I'll be getting too boozy on it, I can hardly stomach it.

'What event?' Alice asks me. 'Wait, do you work here or what? I assumed you were like an events coordinator or something?'

I cock my head and stare at her for a second.

'You're here from Matcher?' I say to them, stating the facts, but my voice shoots up at the end like it's more of a question.

'Yeah, we're on our first date,' Alice replies. 'But how do you know that?'

I take my phone from my bag and open the app. As I cast an

eye over the event details, I see that it's not being held here at all, it's something they're doing at a pub in town.

I glance around the room. This isn't boozy bingo; this is just bingo-bingo. Oh no. Oh, God. How have I done this? I've crashed their date. I'm drinking their prosecco – that explains why there were only two glasses and I'm drinking from (what a quick glance around the room reveals to be) a pot for extra dabbers. I'm not only ruining their date but I'm ruining non-boozy bingo for everyone. I am absolutely mortified.

'I am so sorry,' I tell them, although I'm more embarrassed than I am self-aware, so I say this at a normal volume, which only angers the other bingo-goers.

'Shh,' I hear someone behind me tick me off.

'Sorry,' I say, turning round to face them. 'So sorry.'

Someone else shushes me.

I bite my tongue. It's probably best if I stop talking – even if it is to apologise profusely. Even if I knew what to say to explain this, I don't think anyone would appreciate me saying another word.

I grab my bag and make a dash for the door.

So that's why the whole thing felt awkward, like a first date, because it was a first date, and I've certainly given Callum and Alice one they can tell their grandkids about.

9

'Were you always this good in the kitchen?' my *dad* asks my *mum*.

Ew. For some reason, it makes me really uncomfortable. I say 'for some reason' like I can't quite figure out why – it's obvious why, it's because it's my *divorced* parents, and because my dad's new wife is upstairs, working from home – well, from my spare bedroom, while my parents are down here, getting on like a house on fire. Setting the house on fire might actually be the only way to defuse this.

'I was always great in the kitchen,' Mum replies.

Please make it stop.

There are a few moments of silence. I'm sitting at the dining table, facing the TV above the fireplace. Last time I looked, Dad was sitting at the island and Mum was standing behind it, making French toast. I'm too scared to turn around, anything could be happening right now.

'Billie, you need to try this,' Dad insists.

I don't have the heart to tell him that I've eaten Mum's French toast a thousand times, because I've actually been around, unlike him. It's not worth getting into at Christmas, is it? Or at all, to be honest, given how long ago it was. You don't need to forgive, or forget, to keep a lid on things, even if it's only for your own sanity.

I get up from my seat to join them at the island. Mum has stuffed slices of brioche bread with Nutella to make her French toast, served with fresh fruit and a dusting of icing sugar, best enjoyed by those who didn't cheat on her.

'That's really good,' I tell her after taking a bite. 'I'm so glad you're making Christmas dinner here. I live in fear of the year I'm expected to make my own, I wouldn't know where to begin.'

Individually, it's not that any one part of Christmas dinner seems difficult to make, it's making all the parts of it, and trying to make them all be ready for the same time that overwhelms me. When I watch Mum do it, it's like a military operation, if not an art form.

'We were just talking about that,' Dad tells me. 'We're going to do it together, like old times.'

I look at Mum. She gives me a smile as if to say, look, I know it's weird, but it's peaceful.

'Cool,' I reply. I chew my lip for a second. 'I'll go wake Jess up, see if she wants any breakfast.'

'Okay, darling,' Mum replies. 'Just shout if you want me to make another batch.'

I hop down from my stool and head upstairs. As I pass the first guest room, I cross paths with Gail on her way back from the bathroom.

'Good morning,' I say.

'Good afternoon,' she replies.

'Right, it's after twelve,' I say – not that I got to sleep in. 'Did you sleep okay?'

'Yes, it's a very interesting bed, though,' she replies.

'Is it?' I frown. 'It's just a normal king-sized bed.'

'Are you sure it's a king? It feels sort of small.'

Gail narrows her eyes at me, as though I'm trying to deceive her.

'I'm just going to wake Jess up, she's sleeping on a sofa bed – I could ask her to trade with you, if you like?'

It's a good way to remind her of Jess's name, so she doesn't call her Jessica again.

'Oh, no, I can only imagine that's worse,' she replies. 'I'd best get back to work.'

I don't actually know what Gail does for a living. To be honest, I don't want to ask, I don't want to get into conversation, but it must be something that doesn't stop just because it's Christmas because she makes it sound like she's really busy all the time.

I knock on the door, to give Jess a chance to object to me walking in. Growing up, we were always in and out of each other's rooms. One of the best things about having a sister is having an in-house best friend. The worst thing, if you're interested, is having someone who steals your clothes and then tries to pretend they didn't. We're still putting the great lilac halter-neck theft of 2003 down to a petite, kind of slutty burglar.

'You awake?' I ask quietly as I approach the sofa bed.

'I'm trying not to be,' she replies sleepily. 'Unless I just had a nightmare in which Dad and his new missus showed up for Christmas. If it was a nightmare, then I'm glad to be awake.'

I climb into bed next to her.

'Not a dream, unfortunately,' I tell her. 'He's downstairs now, with Mum, chatting over brunch, talking about how they're going to make Christmas dinner together like some sort of Instagram couple goals account.'

'Gross,' Jess groans.

I think for a moment.

'He seems really quite taken with her new look, although I suppose it's a good thing that they're both being so mature about being in the same house together for Christmas. How would you feel if Armie came to stay?'

'I'd be cooking *him* for Christmas dinner, not cooking it with him,' Jess mumbles into her pillow. 'How was bingo?'

'Oh, fine. Bingo was bingo, you know?'

'Sometimes I'm amazed that you're an English teacher,' she teases, finally rolling over to face me, her eyes still half-open as they adjust to the light.

I smile.

After what happened last night, I'm pretty baffled myself, that people let me teach kids. I couldn't have felt more stupid. Actually, I suppose it could have been worse, I could have tried to go home with them.

'Mum seems really happy, doesn't she?' I point out.

'Mum is always happy,' Jess reminds me.

'She is, but she's got a real sparkle about her today – I suppose it's her easy confidence, and seeing her around Dad for the first time in years, she's nothing like she used to be,' I think out loud.

'What are your plans tonight?' Jess asks curiously.

I take my phone from my pocket and check my calendar.

'Disco bowling,' I reply simply.

'Wow, okay, sis,' Jess says through a snort. 'Boozy bingo one night, disco bowling the next – you're definitely up to something. Whatever you're really doing, I hope you have fun. Be safe, etcetera.'

'Thanks, Mum,' I tease. 'Speaking of Mum, she asked if you want something to eat.'

'If the two of them are playing all nicey-nicey, I'd rather starve,' she says firmly.

'It's French toast.'

'Then I'll have it in my room,' she replies.

I knew that would change her mind.

As I head back downstairs, willing to play waitress to Jess to save her from bearing witness to our suspiciously mature parents, I think about the decidedly immature evening I've got ahead of me: disco bowling. We only have one bowling place in town, but I won't make the same mistake as last night, I'll double check.

Disco bowling, though – that's not exactly up my alley, no pun intended. Do I really need to go to some random event, just to avoid being at home with my family?

As I turn the corner into the living room, I see that my dad is on the same side of the island as my mum now, leaning in close as she shows him how she cuts the pockets into the thick slices of brioche bread. He has the biggest smile I've ever seen on his face – I hope it's because he's impressed with her cooking skills, and nothing more.

Well, that makes my mind up about that one. Disco bowling it is.

10

As I deliberated over what to wear this evening, I wondered whether the 'disco' part of disco bowling referred to the disco era, or just a general party vibe, like a school disco. In the end, I decided that leaning in to the disco era would be more of a miss, if it turned out to be the latter, and I hustled into the room wearing flares and pink tinted sunglasses.

Thankfully, for once in God knows how long, I made the right decision. There's nothing seventies-themed about tonight, it's just more of a party vibe than usual bowling, so I don't look out of place in my black skinny jeans and nice top. I'm glad I made the effort with my hair and make-up, though. I feel like everyone, generally, got way more attractive while I was off the social circuit.

As bowling alleys go, this is just, well, a bowling alley. I'm surprised they haven't changed more over the years, moving with technology like everything else has, although I don't know what more I'm expecting. It's busy here, but in a good way. There are plenty of people around, lots my own age, and no rules about needing to stay silent that I'm aware of – but also there are no balloons, and drinks are served behind the bar, so there is no danger of me making the same faux pas tonight anyway. I suppose I could walk into a Christmas tree, or accidentally string myself up in tinsel, so I'd best not speak too soon, had I?

One thing about tonight that's better than last night is that the organiser of this event, a girl called Leila, told us whereabouts in the place to meet, and that she would be wearing a bright yellow dress. I'm relieved when I head to the seating area at the left side of the bar and spot a tall, red-haired girl in a gorgeous bright yellow dress.

I head over there, kind of nervously (but can you blame me for worrying, after last night?), and hover awkwardly beside her. Thankfully she takes charge of the situation.

'Hello,' she says brightly. 'Are you one of our Matcher lot?'

'I am,' I say, loosening up, now that I know I'm in the right place. 'I'm Billie, nice to meet you.'

'Lovely to meet you, Billie, I'm Leila, as you've probably worked out from the loud dress.'

'It's a beautiful dress,' I tell her. 'You look gorgeous.'

'So do you, hun,' she replies through a big smile. 'That's you secured your place on the same lane as me. We're just waiting for everyone to arrive. In the meantime, go to the bar, grab yourself a drink – everyone in this section is one of us, so mingle away. And then it's time to disco bowl, baby.'

I smile.

'I can't wait,' I tell her.

I've probably only been bowling a handful of times, and they were all when I was still at school, but while this may not be my scene, there's a really fun vibe here. Tonight might actually be okay.

I take a seat at the bar. Eventually a bar man, who seems like he's already juggling at least three other drinks, asks me what I want.

'I'll have a Fig Lebowski, please,' I say, laughing to myself at the name of the fruity gin cocktail I fancy.

'Coming right up,' he replies.

'Isn't it great here?' the man to my left says.

I turn to face him. He's a thirty-something blond with chiselled cheekbones and blue eyes.

'It is,' I reply. 'Really cool.'

'You're here with this lot too, I take it?' he says, nodding towards Leila and the rest of the Matcher squad.

'I am,' I reply. 'This is my first one, actually. Have you been to many?'

'Quite a few,' he admits, pausing briefly while I pay for my drink. 'I went into London for a couple of days at the start of the month – there are hundreds of events to choose between. Here, not so much, but enough to keep you busy. It's mostly the same crowd, though. It's good to see some new blood.'

'I'm Billie,' I tell him, introducing myself, eager to make a friend.

'I'm Sid,' he replies. 'Let me buy you a drink.'

'Oh, that's okay, I've just got this one,' I reply.

Sid gestures to the bar man.

'Two Dirty Donnies, mate,' he says. Then he turns to me. 'It's not a drink, it's a shot.'

'I am not great with shots,' I insist politely.

'It's sweet, I think you'll like it,' he insists. 'And you'll need it, to get through one of these events, with some of this lot. They can be majorly dull. Everything is easier with a drink in you.'

'Oh, hello,' a male voice interrupts us.

I turn around to see that the man is talking to us – talking to me.

'Erm, hi,' I reply.

'You don't remember me, do you?' he replies through a big smile.

I don't, but I'm pretty sure I would remember him, if I had met him before. He's tall, at least six foot three. If I stepped down off this stool, with almost a foot between us, my head would probably only just pass his shoulders. His brown hair is long on top, blown back, but not perfectly, and he has that trendy, attractive style of facial hair where you can't quite figure out whether or not it's a short beard or just overgrown stubble, but it's definitely intentional. He's got a little bit of the Andrew Garfields about him, apart from the fact that underneath his thick dark eyebrows he has the greenest pair of eyes I've ever seen. The more I look at him, the more certain I am that I would definitely remember him.

'Erm...' I stare at him for a moment, then back to Sid, to see if he has any idea, then back to the mystery man.

'It's Rocco,' he tells me, holding his hands out to the sides, as though the revelation of his name is going to click everything into place. 'You went to school with my sister, Angela.'

I honestly would welcome any sort of link to this man. He's gorgeous, instantly charming, and clearly very friendly. But I don't remember going to school with anyone called Angela.

He must realise I have no idea what he's talking about because he takes his phone from his pocket. He taps the screen a few times before holding it up for me to see.

'Here's a photo of her,' he says.

I notice his marked effort to hold the phone in a way that I can see it, and Sid can't, before I realise that he isn't showing me a photo at all, it's a message typed in his notes app.

Every night this guy tries to get girls drunk so he can take them home.

My first feeling is a sick, twisty sensation in my stomach. I've been out of the dating game for so long, being with Declan for years, and then keeping myself off the market ever since we split, that I forgot what it's like out here. I didn't even consider that not all men's actions are completely genuine, and that some might even be acting maliciously – even if they don't see it that way, but surely that makes this guy even more dangerous? Imagine if I'd accepted his drink, then had another, then another. I would have thought we were getting on like a house on fire – I might even have gone home with him, willingly or without even realising. It's scary, and it kind of makes me want to go home, but this gesture from a stranger quickly calms me down, enough to encourage me to stay. Not all men are up to something.

'Oh, my goodness, yes! Angela!' I say enthusiastically. 'How is she doing?'

'You know what, not great,' he replies. 'It's a long story, if you'd like to hear it before we start bowling? I'm sure she would appreciate you reaching out, actually. It's been a really difficult time.'

'Oh, no, that sounds awful.' I turn to Sid. 'Sorry, I'd better go find out.'

'But your shot is coming,' he protests.

'I'm really not a shot person,' I insist. 'You have it. Thanks anyway.'

I grab my cocktail, hop down from my stool and follow Rocco. I wait until we're far enough away from Sid before I say anything.

'Oh, my God, thank you,' I tell him. 'If you hadn't stepped in, who knows what could have happened?'

'I've been keeping an eye on him,' Rocco replies. 'He's tried a few times now, I'm wise to his tricks. These aren't private events, for the most part, so there's no actual way for me to stop him being here. All I can do is keep a close eye on him, and warn anyone off him, who he starts to play his games with.'

'Well, I really can't thank you enough,' I tell him.

We naturally gravitate towards a sofa, back over where Leila and the rest of the Matcher gang are busily sorting teams, ready for the bowling to begin.

'To be honest, it's put me off staying,' I admit. 'I'm starting to think I shouldn't have come. None of this is me.'

'I know what you mean,' Rocco replies. 'But don't let one clown put you off. The rest of us are... well... fine, I guess? No predators, but a real mixed bag.'

He laughs and it's contagious.

'It's just given me a bit of a scare,' I confess. I shift uncomfortably in my seat. Allowing myself to be vulnerable in front of a man, even one who seems okay, makes me feel uneasy.

'These things can actually be quite fun, I've been to a handful now,' Rocco tells me. 'If you want to stay, I'll have a word with Leila, make sure you're on our lane, and that Sid is as physically far away from us as possible. We're playing in groups, with teams of two on two. We can team up if you like?'

'Are you any good at bowling?' I ask him, relaxing a little. Rocco is right, I shouldn't let one person ruin this for me. The world is crawling with guys like Sid. I just need to be more careful. Now that I'm single again, when I do set about trying to find love, I'm certain there's going to be plenty more where that came from, unfortunately.

'Absolutely not,' he tells me with a very straight face.

'Me neither,' I reply. 'Let's do it.'

The smile quickly returns to Rocco's face.

'Nice. Well, given that you didn't in fact go to school with my sister,' Rocco says in hushed tones, leaning closer, 'I should probably ask you what your name is.'

I laugh.

'It's Billie.'

'Okay then, Billie, let's do this,' Rocco insists.

I spring to my feet.

'Rocco, there you are,' Leila says. Her eyes light up the second they land on him. 'Ready to rock... o.'

She laughs at her own dorky joke. Rocco laughs in a way that I'm sure is just polite.

'And you found Billie,' she adds. 'I put us all on the same lane, along with Tobias.'

'I was wondering if Billie and I could be on the same team?' Rocco asks. 'Otherwise she's going home.'

Rocco laughs. Leila laughs too, until Rocco turns around to pick up a scarf someone walking past him just drops. When it's just the two of us, for a few seconds, Leila's expression changes. She doesn't look happy, but she turns the smile back on as Rocco turns around. Oh, God, am I stepping on her toes? I'm not trying to. I'm under no illusions about Rocco and the reason he's taking me under his wing. He so very clearly feels sorry for me.

'I'm honestly not that bothered for playing,' I quickly insist.

'Nonsense,' Leila says, her voice actually breaking for a second mid-word. 'It can be you and Rocco versus me and Tobias. Mixed doubles. And may the best man and the best woman win.'

Wow, I can even hear the competitiveness in her voice. Yep, I'm definitely stepping on some toes here.

'Great, let's get to it,' Rocco says excitedly.

It isn't long before the lanes are ready for us. We all make our way over there, led by Leila, who – as event organiser – is taking her role very seriously. She's doing a great job, though. As a teacher, I could definitely learn a thing or two from her, for managing the kids.

Leila keys our names into the machine. Eventually we're joined by a man in his late twenties/early thirties. He's got mousey-brown hair that is short and neat – but not neatly styled, like he spent time crafting his look, instead just too short to possibly be messy.

'This is Tobias,' Leila tells me. 'Tobias, this is Billie.'

'Oh, hello?' he says as our eyes meet. He poses his greeting almost as though it's a question, I don't think he's expecting to see me here. 'A newbie.'

'Hi,' I reply. 'Yep, this is my first one.'

'You've been missing out,' Tobias replies. 'Boozy bingo last night was fantastic.'

'I'm not a big bingo fan,' I reply. I'm really not now.

'I bet,' he replies, although I'm not sure what he means by that. 'Has anyone ever told you that you look like Margot Robbie?'

I snort. Oh, wow, he isn't joking. He might not be joking but he definitely can't be serious.

'Never,' I reply simply.

'Come on, it's almost starting time,' Leila insists.

I'm not really sure what we're waiting for until it happens. The lights drop to nothing, plunging us into darkness for what is probably only a couple of seconds, but feels like much longer. My senses are heightened. Rocco must only shift on his feet but as his arm brushes mine, it feels almost electric.

The lights come back on but in a completely different way. So different the place doesn't even resemble the room we were in a few seconds ago. Now I understand the disco part of disco bowling. It's a full-on party. Dancing colourful lights, a disco ball, and now the music is pumping. The mood has totally shifted into something way more fun. I'm so glad I stayed.

As 'Believe' by Cher fades in, I feel a warm wave of comfort wash over me. This disco might be just what I need tonight.

'Are you on my team?' Tobias asks me.

'She wants to be with Rocco,' Leila tells him.

Everyone is having to raise their voices now that the music is playing but there's something extra in Tobias and Leila's exchange, a look between them perhaps.

'No worries, we'll thrash them,' he reassures her.

I sidle up to Rocco.

'I don't really know what I'm doing, to be honest,' I confess. 'And I'm up first.'

'I'm not that competitive,' he replies. 'Just pick up a ball, roll it down the middle, and knock over as many pins as you can.'

There's a really comforting casualness to Rocco. I like it. It somehow makes me feel more laidback, just by being in his orbit.

'Come on then, Billie,' Leila calls out. 'Show us what you can do.'

I select a sparkly pink ball from the rack.

'That's a kids' ball,' she sings, lightly teasing me.

I put it back down and pick up a yellow one. It's much heavier, so I cradle it with my other hand as I approach the lane.

For a moment, I just stare at it.

'How do you do the sides?' I call back.

'What do you mean?' Tobias asks.

'The sides,' I say again, not that it makes it any clearer. 'The things that stop it going down the sides.'

'Ahh, the bumpers,' Rocco says, helping me out.

Leila practically cackles.

'They really are for kids,' she calls back. 'Go on, you'll be fine.'

I take a deep breath as I step up to the line. I swing the ball backwards and then launch it down the lane. I don't think it's much surprise to anyone when the ball veers left into the gutter and promptly disappears.

'Oh, hard luck,' Leila calls out.

Rocco grabs a ball and joins me.

'Do you want to watch me? I don't have many skills, but I can pass them on to you, if you like?'

'That would be great,' I reply. 'I clearly need all the help I can get.'

'So, you take your ball, you stand like this, pull your arm back and...'

Rocco releases the ball. We both watch it travel down the lane. It reaches the pins, veers left, and takes two pins down with it.

'And that's how it's done,' he says with a playful proudness. I have a feeling he knew that was going to go down like that and it's completely charming.

We head back over to the seats together.

'I think our lane might be wonky,' Rocco jokes. 'It's pulling all our balls to the left.'

'Let me show you both how it's done,' Leila insists.

She struts over to select a ball. I do watch her, until Tobias asks me a question.

'How old are you, Billie?' he asks.

'You're not supposed to ask a woman her age, are you?' Rocco says with a smile.

'It's just a number, nothing to be ashamed of. I'll be twenty-nine on Christmas Eve,' he replies. 'I'm all for equality. How old are you, Rocco?'

'I'm thirty-six,' he replies.

'Wow, you're a proper grown-up,' I blurt.

Rocco laughs.

'Are you not?' he asks.

'I'm thirty-two,' I tell him.

'I hate to break it to you, kid, but thirty-two is a grown-up too,' he replies.

I sigh.

'Don't make me existential so close to Christmas,' I say with a laugh.

'Didn't you see?' Leila asks angrily. 'I got a half strike!'

'I can beat that,' Tobias says as he springs to his feet.

Leila sits down opposite us.

'Tell us about you then, Billie,' she says. 'What's Billie all about?'

I hate being asked questions like that. Mostly just because I draw a complete blank and forget everything interesting about myself. I'm sure there must be some things but none of them are at the forefront right now.

'I'm a teacher,' I start.

'What and where do you teach?' she enquires.

'English, at Perstead,' I reply.

'Is that the snooty private school?' she asks.

'It's the *private* school,' I correct her, but in a gentle, friendly way.

'Oh, nice,' she replies. 'I manage Cea and Toffee, in town. I've got four people under me.'

'Lucky you,' I joke. It doesn't land with Leila but Rocco snorts.

'What do you do for fun?' she persists. 'Not bowling, obviously.'

'No, not bowling,' I reply. 'To be honest, I've been quite boring for the last year. I bought a house and decided to do the world to it.'

'You're up,' Tobias tells me.

Again? Already?

I puff air from my cheeks.

'I'll come with you,' Rocco says.

'Tobias, let's go get some more drinks,' Leila says. 'While these two take their turns. I don't think we'll miss much.'

Rocco and I slowly make our way over to the ball rack again. 'Toxic' by Britney Spears is playing. I might suck at bowling but it's hard not to enjoy disco bowling, even if I am embarrassingly bad.

'Being a teacher and owning a house are both pretty grown-up things,' Rocco says with a smile.

'What do you do?' I ask.

'I'm an architect,' he replies.

'Oh, come on, that's way more grown up,' I say, giving his arm a playful shove. 'What a—'

My feet vanish from under me. Stupid bowling shoes, they're like glass underneath.

Rocco extends his arms and catches me, pulling me close. We both laugh – mine is mostly one of relief.

'You were saying?' he asks me while I'm still in his arms.

'I was saying... What are you working on at the moment?'

'You,' he replies, and it's the single sexiest thing I've ever heard. A static-like shock ripples through my body. My breath catches in my throat.

Rocco laughs as he steadies me on my feet again before releasing me.

'I've always wanted to say that,' he tells me with a laugh. 'Come on, take your shot, and then I'll go buy you a drink, and we can whisper about them. Do you fancy a soft drink, or another drink-drink?'

'Oh, it's going to need to be a drink-drink,' I tell him. 'If I'm going to get through any more turns of this.'

I grab a ball and throw it with all the confidence I can muster. It's another gutter ball.

'Have another go,' he tells me with a smile. 'Throw mine for me while no one is looking.'

I shrug, grab another ball, and throw. Another gutter ball.

'If the goal was to hit the fewest pins possible, we might have a world champ on our hands,' he says with a smile. 'Drink-drink it is. Look at this.'

Rocco sticks his tongue out as far as he can. It's bright purple.

'Erm...' I laugh.

'Being here made me feel really nostalgic,' he explains. 'I used to love bowling when I was a kid and I would always have a slushie. Long story short, there's a girl behind the bar who will stick a vodka shot in them for the *grown-ups*.'

He says 'grown-ups' in a funny voice.

'Consider me a grown-up then,' I reply. 'Let's go.'

Leila and Tobias return with their drinks, so Rocco and I head off to get ours.

'You two are really bad at this,' Leila muses as we pass her.

'Thanks,' Rocco replies. 'And we're only going to get worse.'

11

I can't quite decide what hurts more, my aching neck or my throbbing head, and the only thing drier than my eyes is the inside of my mouth.

The only thing that makes accidentally falling asleep on the sofa even worse is doing so after you've had too much to drink – and waking up with one hell of a hangover.

I don't drink much these days, so my hangovers are few and far between. Perhaps I'm just not used to them any more and that's why I feel so rotten. The alternative is that I'm obviously not wearing them as well as I'm getting older, but I'm not ready to accept that idea yet.

It takes everything I've got to pull my eyes open, but it's a good start. I'm just lucky no one has come downstairs and woken me up yet. I can't think of anything more mortifying (actually, I'm sure I can, I did crash a couple's first date a matter of days ago) than my mum or dad finding me asleep on the sofa. I'm a grown woman and this is my house... but I'd still rather slink off to my room than be caught here in last night's clothes.

I feel quite warm. I realise this is because I've been sleeping in a dressing gown around the same time my eyes adjust to the light and I discover that I have absolutely no idea where I am. I don't know this sofa, or this room, or where the hell I am. It's not that I'd put it past my mum and Jess to surprise remodel my house, it's just that I don't think I'd had enough to drink, and having first-hand knowledge of how long these things take, it seems unlikely they did it in a night.

I sit up quickly, leaning back on my elbows as the blood rushes to my head. Okay, where am I? It's a contemporary room decked out in tasteful, earthy colours. I'm lying on a sofa next to a coffee table that faces a large wall-mounted TV. Behind me there's a large window. Perhaps looking outside will tip me off to where I am?

I sit up properly, now that all the blood in my body has redistributed from my head, and swing my legs around. When I'm facing the coffee table, I notice a glass of water with a note that reads 'drink me'. Next to it, there's a packet of paracetamol with a note that reads 'eat me'. I notice the small print on the second note, telling me not to 'eat' more than two and I can't help but take a brief break from being freaked out to laugh. I feel calmer for seeing the branding on the note paper. Both pieces say 'The Edgerton Hotel' at the bottom. Did I check into a hotel? I must have. I've never stayed at the Edgerton Hotel before, given that it's in my hometown, but I know it's seriously expensive, otherwise I wouldn't be checking out until 2023.

I sip the water. Curiouser and curiouser.

The room has two doors. It's obvious which one leads out into the hallway – although it would be a very 'me' thing to do, to accidentally walk out there in my dressing gown, and probably lock myself out there. The other must go to the bedroom, and ultimately the bathroom. I imagine that's where my clothes are (I only have my underwear on beneath this dressing gown) because there isn't a thing out of place in here.

I open the door and head inside. I must be hungover because I can't believe I didn't consider for a second that there might be someone else in this hotel room with me, until I walked in on him just now.

'Oh, God,' I blurt.

Rocco was asleep, and probably wouldn't have woken up, if I hadn't said anything. You can always count on me to make things worse.

Rocco jumps out of bed and onto his feet. He isn't wearing anything but a pair of boxer shorts. Oh, for goodness' sake, why does he have to have a body like that? I think they call it 'skinny fit' – imagine being skinny and fit. I'm neither.

I avert my eyes.

'Sorry – for at least a hundred things, I'm sure,' I say as I stare at the floor.

As soon as I hear Rocco laughing, I dare to look at him.

'How's the head?' he asks me.

'Somehow full and empty,' I reply. 'Why are we in a hotel?'

'I'm staying here,' he replies.

My mind suddenly clears of everything apart from one question.

'Don't you live round here?' I ask.

'My last gig was in Dublin,' he tells me. 'But my family are from round here.'

'So, you're only here for Christmas then?' I can't help but ask. I try to sound like I don't care but I think I do. Just a bit.

'Yes, well, until I line up my next job,' he explains. 'The world is my oyster until then. But not until after Christmas, obviously. You know what families are like, with their festive demands.'

Boy, do I.

'So, last night...'

'Last night,' he replies with a smile.

That smile of his has this way of putting me at ease. As Rocco sits back down on the bed, I allow myself to sit on the chaise at the end of it.

'You were adamant that you weren't going home,' he reminds me.

Even if that didn't sound familiar, it's not exactly hard to believe.

'We all went to the bar, next door to the bowling alley,' he continues.

'The karaoke bar?' I reply. It comes out like a question, but it isn't taking much to jog my memory.

'Don't tell me you don't remember doing karaoke?' Rocco replies, astonished.

'No! Tell me I didn't...'

'You didn't,' he chuckles. 'We just sat and laughed at the people who did.'

'So we got absolutely destroyed at bowling, obviously...'

'Obviously,' he echoes.

'And then we went to the karaoke bar, had more to drink...'

'You had quite a bit at bowling,' he tells me. 'You were addicted to the boozy slushies. You bought a few rounds.'

'So, in the end I spiked myself?' I reply. 'No man required.'

'Something like that,' he laughs. 'You're a good feminist. At the end of the night, when I tried to book you a taxi home, you said you couldn't go home.'

I remember that now. I remember all of it, now that he's triggered my memory. I also remember...

'No!'

'What?' he asks.

I look down at the hotel-branded dressing gown.

'I didn't do that,' he quickly insists. 'I gave you the dressing gown, but I didn't undress you.'

'No, I know, *I did*,' I reply.

I remember feeling tired, wanting to go to sleep, and trying to wrestle off my dress. I don't remember waiting for Rocco to leave the room before I did this.

'Well, I never would have reminded you, if you hadn't remembered, but I just chucked you a dressing gown and then went to bed. You didn't have an audience.'

I sigh a huge gust of relief.

'Is everything okay?' he asks me seriously. 'You really didn't want to go home.'

'I don't know what got into me,' I insist with a smile. 'Just being drunk and daft.'

A couple of things are abundantly clear to me, and one doesn't seem to sit right with the other. The first is that Rocco is only in town to spend Christmas with his family and will be taking off soon after so, despite being on a dating app, he's only looking for a good time, for a short time. If that's true, then you would think that something casual would be a welcome distraction to him, but last night Rocco didn't so much as touch a hair on my head.

I suppose I should be grateful – no, I am grateful – but there's something kind of tragic about not making the cut for a casual fling. It's good, though, because while Rocco is looking for a Mrs All Right for the Night at these Mingle All the Way events, he can be my Mr Right Hand Man, someone to buddy up with, someone fun to hang out at all these stupid events... if he'll have me.

'Are you going to the cooking thing this evening?' he asks me, reading my mind.

I glance down at his body before dragging my eyes back up to his – stop it, Billie!

'The cooking thing?' I repeat back to him.

'There's another event this evening,' he explains. 'Some kind of cooking class/competition. It's not my usual scene but I thought it might be fun.'

'Are you going to many of these events?' I ask curiously.

'Only the ones I fancy,' he replies. 'You?'

'Same,' I reply. 'Do you fancy buddying up? It would be good to have someone to go to these things with.'

I instantly regret asking him. He's not going to agree to saddling himself with a saddo like me, not when he's on the pull.

'Buddying up?' he replies curiously. 'Like a wingman?'

'Like a wing*woman*,' I reply.

'Sure,' he replies. 'We can do that. You'll be surprised how many of these things require a partner. I suppose it's genius, really – given that we're all from a dating app. It forces you to partner up.'

'Well, until the girl of your dreams turns up, you've got me,' I reply. 'But, until then, I'm going to go and ride out my wave of embarrassment in the shower.'

'There's a clean towel on the rail,' he replies with a smile. 'Last night was fun, honestly, and you didn't do anything embarrassing. Fun, yes. Low-key violent, maybe.'

'Violent?' I reply.

'Leila,' he prompts.

'Oh, God, I was hoping I'd dreamt that part,' I insist, placing my head in my hands as the words trigger a memory of a very Billie faux pas. 'I thought I was stepping on her toes – that's nothing compared to literally dropping a bowling ball on them.'

'She was fine,' Rocco insists. 'What do you mean you were stepping on her toes?'

'Oh, nothing,' I say. 'Right, bathroom, then home, then cooking later?'

'That sounds like a good plan to me,' he replies. 'I might get an extra fifteen minutes' shut-eye, if you don't mind?'

'No, no, go for it,' I reply. 'This is your room – your rooms.'

I head for the bathroom and glance back just as Rocco is getting back into bed, snuggling down into his pillow. I can think of nothing I would love more than to climb in there with him right now – well, not with-him with him. I just mean that I'm knackered and the bed looks so comfortable. I have a comfortable bed at home, though, and thanks to my stupid open-plan house, it's the only place I can avoid everyone, so a disco nap might be the best course of action.

I have my phone with me, so I peep at my calendar. I'd already put my name down for cooking later. It's good to know I'll have a partner. Even if it is one who isn't remotely interested in me.

It's after midday by the time my taxi pulls up outside my house. Midday on a Monday, what would the neighbours say?

'Walk of shame?' Kenny calls out as he checks the post-box at the end of his driveway.

'Just a normal walk,' I call back. 'Just been out for lunch with the girls.'

A lie, but I'm not going to give him the satisfaction.

'In last night's dress?' he replies. 'I saw you leaving.'

'What an unhealthy level of obsession to have for a neighbour,' I tell him, keeping my game face firmly on, but my knotted hair and the ropey remains of my make-up probably tell a different story. 'Maybe try getting a hobby. Or a girlfriend who doesn't have a curfew.'

'You'll have to let me know where you go out,' he calls after me as I head for my door. 'Somewhere where the girls like to stay out all night sounds perfect.'

Oh, how I hate him. I resist shouting anything back because I'm finally at my front door, and what I really need is to get inside, and up to my bedroom, without anyone noticing. The front door opens easy enough, and closes silently too. The biggest problem I've got is that, to get to the bottom of the stairs, I have to walk through the hallway, past the open double archway into the living room. Stupid, stupid open-plan house.

I dare to peer round the corner and see Dad sitting in the living room, thankfully facing away from me. I take off my shoes, to make it easier for sneaking, but I pick them up to take them upstairs with me because nothing will give me away like last night's shoes suddenly discarded in the hallway.

As I tiptoe through the hallway, as I approach the bottom of the stairs, I realise my mum is walking down them. With nowhere to go, I retreat towards the living room. I hear my dad clear his throat as he starts moving around. I practically pirouette, as I try to work out which way to go. Eventually I find myself stuck in the hallway, my mum on one side of me, my dad on the other. For a second, they both just stare at me, taking it all in, putting all of the pieces of the puzzle together.

'And what time do you call this?' Dad asks.

I begin to smile but I quickly pull it back. He's not joking.

'What?' I reply, stalling. 'It's, erm...'

I hold up my wrist to check my watch, but the battery is dead. That doesn't look great.

'Those are last night's clothes,' Dad points out.

I guess that doesn't look great either.

'I've just been out,' I say. I glance at Mum, then back at Dad.

'Out all night,' Dad adds.

I snort. He chooses now to be a parent.

'Dad, I'm thirty-two years old,' I point out. 'I'm a grown woman, I'm allowed to stay out all night.'

'Just because you're older, doesn't mean we stop worrying about you,' he insists. 'Tell her, Katie.'

'We'll never stop worrying about you, darling, obviously,' she replies tactfully.

I ditch my shoes and my bag on the hall floor.

'If you must know, I stayed with my friend Angie last night,' I lie. 'We went out for a drink, and her husband is away so, when she asked me if I fancied a sleepover, I thought she might appreciate the company.'

'Well, that was very sweet of you,' Mum says. 'Angie is lucky to have you.'

Dad narrows his eyes at me.

'A text would have been nice,' he concludes, before heading back to the sofa.

Mum moves to let me pass before following me up the stairs.

'Unbelievable,' I say to her once we're out of earshot. 'Who does he think he is, interrogating me? I'm allowed to sleep over with a friend when I'm in my thirties.'

'Your dad is just being a dad,' she replies.

I roll my eyes.

'Better late than never, I suppose.'

Mum gives me a knowing smile.

'You know you already told me that Angie and the gang are all skiing,' she reminds me. 'Wherever you really were, I hope you had fun.'

I half-cringe, half-smile. I can always count on Mum to cover for me.

'I'm going for a shower,' I tell her. 'And maybe a nap.'

'Oh, it was a good night then,' Jess chimes in as she walks from her bedroom to the bathroom. Her hair is all stuck up and some of yesterday's eyeliner has relocated to her cheeks. She looks like she's had a wilder night than me.

I just shake my head as I go into my bedroom, closing the door behind me. This is my only sanctuary in this house now.

Last night was not like me at all. I don't know how it happened. I suppose I had all this pent up... something in me. Something that needed to be released. A year of being wound tight, slogging my way through DIY jobs and not having much fun. Going out-out for the first time in a long time, I dare say, has done me the world of good.

And then there's Rocco, who might not be interested in me, and I'm not really interested in him. It's not that I don't fancy him, it's just that I can't imagine he'll be around for long.

But he's a great distraction for the holidays, and I'm weirdly looking forward to cooking with him later.

Let's just hope we're better at it than we are at bowling.

13

Two things that don't mix are hangovers and families. I haven't even seen any of my lot today yet (well, since my nap, technically) but I already know that my headache and my hangover aren't going to complement one another – and, yes, I am referring to my family as a headache.

I'm a little ticked off today, after my dad decided to start being a dad, decades too late. Thankfully, as I join him in the kitchen, he doesn't mention it. In fact, he doesn't say anything, he's too busy staring at his phone with a big, dumb grin on his face. Eww, everyone knows what it means when someone looks at their phone like that, it means they're messaging someone they're into. I'd say get a room, but they have one and it's one of mine so, just, no. Gail is up there working. She's always working, and I wonder if her workload is as intense as she makes out, or if perhaps she's just doing everything she can to avoid us all. I would do the same if everyone didn't know I was a teacher. Well, I'll clearly do anything to avoid being home, attending events submitted by users of a dating app just goes to prove it.

'Good morning,' I say, loudly, to drag his attention from his phone.

'Oh, hi, Billie love,' he replies, still looking at his screen. 'I think the morning ship has sailed, though.'

It may not be actual morning but it's morning to me.

'Good afternoon, then,' I correct myself. 'Where's Jess?'

'She, er...' He laughs quietly at something on his screen and then starts tapping away.

'Dad!' I say, raising my voice again.

'What?' he asks through a chuckle. 'Ask your mum.'

I narrow my eyes at him.

'Fine,' I say, happy to leave the room, if whatever he's doing on his phone is more important than talking to me.

I drag myself up the stairs, my headache briefly intensifying for a few seconds, reminding me of all the reasons why I shouldn't drink so much. As I pass Gail's room, I can't tell what she's saying, but I can hear muted murmurings coming through the door, so she must be on a call. I knock on Mum's door quietly. Eventually she calls me in.

'Good morning, party animal,' she teases. 'What time do you call this?'

It's funny, no one says a word to Jess when she sleeps in.

Mum is fully clothed, with a perfect face of make-up, sitting on her bed, her phone in her hand – sort of how you would expect to find your teenage daughter in her room.

'Nap time,' I reply, climbing on the bed next to her.

As Mum scoots up a little, to make room for me, I could swear I notice her try to subtly angle her phone screen away from me. Before I have chance to figure it out, she locks it and places it face down on her other side.

'Everything okay?' I ask her.

'All good here, darling, how are you?'

'Oh, you know,' I say with a sigh. 'All the things.'

'Christmas will be over before you know it,' she replies, giving my shoulder a meaningful rub.

'I know but, that's the thing, I don't want it to be, I want to be able to enjoy it – I want the Christmas I originally planned,' I explain, right as Mum's phone dings with a message.

'Do you know what I mean?' I prompt.

Her phone dings again.

'Mum?'

'I'm listening,' she insists.

'Do you need to check that?' I ask, vaguely annoyed.

Mum picks up her phone, still careful to make sure only she can see it, and then she smiles that same big, dumb smile Dad had on his face and I feel like I've been kicked in the stomach. No! They're not messaging each other... are they? They can't be. It must be a coincidence. Still, I need to tell Jess.

'Where is Jess?' I ask her. She's still grinning at her phone. 'Mum, Jess?'

She looks at me for a second or two, while her ears inform her brain of what she hadn't quite been taking in for the last minute, before eventually answering.

'Oh, she said she was taking the bins out,' Mum replies casually. 'A little while ago, actually.'

I narrow my eyes.

'And that didn't flag as weird to you?' I ask her.

'Well, nothing Jess has done has ever really surprised me,' Mum replies. 'Lord knows she's given it her best shot, though.'

I head downstairs where I grab my shoes and my coat, quickly hurrying them on, to head outside and check Jess's last known location.

I am momentarily surprised to find her by the bins at the side of the house, not just because it's so unlike Jess to do one of the less desirable chores, but because from what Mum said, it sounds like she's been out here for a while now.

All becomes clear when I approach her and realise that she isn't alone. She's talking to Kenny.

'A lawyer? That's so sexy,' she tells him with a wiggle of her shoulders.

Scratch that, she's not talking to him, she's flirting with him.

'I can get almost anyone out of trouble,' he replies. 'Or into it.'

Oh, my God, no, gross, he's flirting back. I pick up the pace, hurrying over to join them. There's already a fence between them but still, I insert myself in the space between Jess and the fence.

'Jess, can you come inside, I need you,' I tell her firmly.

'I was just saying similar,' Kenny jokes. I shoot him a look. 'Jess was just telling me she made that gorgeous wreath on your front door. I was saying I didn't even have my artificial tree up this year, she's appalled.'

'It's Christmas,' Jess protests. 'You can't not have a tree up.'

'Well, you are talking to a regular Ebenezer Scrooge,' I can't resist pointing out.

'Jess is going to help me see the light,' Kenny informs me.

I look over at Jess, who can't control her grin. Jesus Christ, what is it with this family, being so thirsty? It's embarrassing.

'Actually, she's going to help me with our parents,' I inform her. 'I think Mum and Dad are flirting.'

'Ew,' she replies simply. 'You must have that wrong.'

'Go in and see for yourself,' I tell her.

'I'd better go sort this lot out,' Jess tells Kenny in a tone that suggests she's often solving problems, whereas anecdotal evidence would suggest she's more likely to cause them.

I notice that Jess is holding the plastic bins from inside the island, where the recycling goes, but that she's standing next to the general waste bin.

'Which bin did you use?' I ask her.

'Er, this one, I think,' she says.

'You think... Was it just recycling, or the black bag from the bin too?'

'A bit of both,' she says with a sigh. 'Why? Don't tell me I've put the bins out wrong.'

She says this with a tone that suggests there is no incorrect way to put things in the bins.

'You've absolutely put the bins out wrong,' I inform her. 'The different coloured lids are for different things.'

'Oh,' she says simply. 'I thought you were just being extra, with the jazzy colours.'

Unreal.

'Let's go see Mum and Dad then,' she continues, unbothered by the bin situation. 'And Kenny, I'll see you later.'

'I'll catch you up,' I tell her. 'I need to sort these bins, or I'll get fined.'

Jess just rolls her eyes.

'See you around, Kenny,' she says as she walks off.

'Yeah, I'll see you later,' he calls after her.

While it is true that rules about what can go in what bin are strict, that's not the main reason I'm hanging back, there's a different kind of trash I need to get rid of first.

'She seems great,' Kenny tells me once we're alone.

'She seems like none of your business,' I tell him, sort of confusingly, but he knows what I mean. 'I'm warning you, Kenny, stay away from my sister.'

'I could try and stay away from your sister, but I can't promise she'll stay away from me,' he tells me with a wink. 'Have fun with your bins.'

Once he's gone, I grab the general waste bag that Jess put in one of the recycling bins, lean over the fence, and drop it inside

Kenny's recycling bin. I instantly take it back out, though – it's not the environment's fault he's an arsehole. Instead, I put it in *his* recycling bin because, ha! That will show him. He'll be sorry, when his recycling fills up over Christmas, and he has to find somewhere else to put it. Then again, he does live on his own, and he doesn't appear to be doing much to celebrate. Petty revenge isn't what's important right now, not when it comes to Kenny; my issues with him aside, I can't watch Jess become another notch on his post-divorce bedpost – if there's any post left. Kenny must have so many notches by now it must seem like he has a termite problem, and I'll bet that's not the only sort of bugs he has in there, and... and I need to calm down. I can only tackle one randy family member at a time, so my priority has to be making sure there's nothing going on between my parents.

Just when I think things can't get any worse, there's always a horrific development that proves me just how wrong I am, and my parents getting back together would most definitely be horrific. I haven't asked for much this Christmas but if my parents could stay divorced, I would really appreciate it. I wonder how many kids put that on their Christmas list?

14

After swapping phone numbers with Rocco before I left his hotel this morning, I feel a lot more confident about turning up to this evening's event, knowing that I'm not walking into a room of strangers, with no idea what I'm getting myself into.

Location noted. At least now I can tell the police where to find your body. x

I roll my eyes at Jess's message. Since I didn't come home last night, she has decided that, to make sure I'm safe, we should share our locations with each other over the Christmas period. To be honest, it's not a terrible idea, so I'm happy to do it. Although I do hope she doesn't turn up anywhere I am, just to be nosy. She would never let me hear the end of it if she knew I had populated my Christmas calendar with events from a dating app. Not only would she find it hilariously sad, but she would probably want to come along for a laugh, and the last thing I need is competition from a younger, prettier, more outgoing and easy-going version of myself.

I'm hovering outside the building in town where tonight's event is taking place. It looks like nothing more than an office block, but apparently the cooking competition is taking place in here – even if we're in the wrong place, this is where Rocco and I said we would meet. It's another cold evening. I can see my breath in the air and the end of my nose is starting to feel numb.

A few people walk past me and head inside. They're chatting loudly, having a laugh, their excitement clearly visible. I think I recognise one or two of them from last night's event. It seemed like a shame, that there aren't many Matcher users in this area, so not many people creating and attending the events but, realistically, how many men do I really want to be *not* fancied by, all in the one room, at the same time? It's actually quite nice that we aren't a huge group. Seeing the same faces at the same things feels a bit like school, in a very strange way, although no one really fancied me at school either, so perhaps it isn't that strange that I'm getting a similar vibe.

'Hello, Billie,' Leila says as she greets me.

'Hello, how are you?' I ask brightly.

Other than Sid (who hopefully won't be coming this evening, if it's a drink-free event), Tobias and Leila are the only people (apart from Rocco, of course) who I've spoken to, so it's nice to see a friendly face.

Leila stands next to me for a moment. Her face doesn't look that friendly today.

'You know what, I'm not doing great,' she replies.

'What's the matter?' I dare to ask – I instantly wish I hadn't because something about the look on her face makes me think it might be my fault.

'I liked you when I met you,' she begins.

Oh, boy, it's going to be like that is it? She met me less than twenty-four hours ago. I didn't think I was interesting enough to have turned someone off me so quickly. Then I remember dropping the bowling ball on her foot.

'I know what this is about,' I interrupt. If I can get ahead of the issue, and show her that I'm sorry, and that it was a genuine accident, perhaps she'll come around. 'I didn't mean to do it.'

'You didn't mean to do it?' she repeats back to me. 'I'm supposed to believe you did it accidentally?'

'Come on, look at me,' I say, resorting to self-deprecation to get Leila back on side. 'And you saw me last night. Is it really a surprise?'

Leila glares at me.

'You know, Billie, I thought you were a girls' girl,' she tells me through a scowl, her jaw so tight her voice doesn't sound like her own. 'I was wrong.'

She turns on her heel and walks away, without waiting for a reply, not that I would have known what to say to that anyway.

I pull a face to myself. A girls' girl? What does that even mean? Does she really think I'm the kind of girl to drop a bowling ball on someone's foot on purpose? Surely no one is that bad. I would feel worse about it, if I had actually hurt her, but it just slipped through my fingers, landed on the floor and sort of clipped her foot – she's clearly unharmed, though, because she walked away from the incident absolutely fine and she marched away from me pretty fiercely just now.

'That looks like the face of a woman who knows I'm not very good in the kitchen,' Rocco says as he approaches me.

'Oh, it's just Leila,' I tell him. 'I don't think she's very happy with me after last night.'

'She'll be fine,' he replies. 'Oh, look, it's Tobias.'

'How about you call me Toby and I call you Rocky?' Tobias replies as he wraps an arm around Rocco. He shakes him excitably. 'The boys, the boys!'

'How you doing, buddy?' Rocco asks him, politely ignoring his request.

'I'll be better if Billie will be my partner tonight,' he says, looking at me optimistically.

'Oh, I'm sorry, I already promised Rocco I'd be his partner,' I reply through gritted teeth.

'Are you not pairing up with Leila?' Tobias asks him.

'No, we haven't spoken about it,' Rocco tells him. 'Go for it.'

'Come on, let's head inside, I am freezing,' I insist, defusing a semi-awkward situation.

Inside one of the units, there's a room full of large square tables. Not unlike the tables in the *Great British Bake Off* tent, each one is fitted with hobs, sinks, ovens and fridges – one of each on either side of the table.

A small woman in her fifties hurries around the room, counting heads by tapping each of us on the shoulders as she passes us.

'Right, okay, hello,' she calls out. She might be small, but her voice is loud and powerful. I suppose it needs to be, when you're managing rowdy groups of people at this sort of thing. 'My name is Margarita; I'll be hosting today. It seems like everyone is here so get into your pairs and make your way to a table, please.'

Rocco and I naturally gravitate towards the nearest table to where we're standing.

I notice Tobias chatting with Leila before the two of them join us, on the other half of our table. Fantastic, working opposite them, just what I wanted.

'Okay, okay, settle down,' Margarita shouts. If I thought things felt like school earlier, you can multiply that feeling by a thousand now. Margarita has big food tech teacher energy, for better or worse. I never really enjoyed food tech at school. I feel like it should have been a fun break from lessons like English, maths and science – and one that included food – but it always felt like more trouble than it was worth, for something underwhelming like a fruit salad that would be all brown and mushy by the time you got it home. My mum, God bless her, would always dutifully try whatever I made.

'This evening we will be making scones,' Margarita announces. 'And then you'll be judging each other's, so it isn't me you need to worry about impressing, it's your worktop mates.'

Rocco gives me a subtle nudge with his elbow, as if to say we've got no chance, if it's Leila and Tobias we're supposed to be impressing.

'You will find all the ingredients at your station,' she tells us before running us through the rules and the time we have.

'Scones should be easy,' Rocco whispers to me.

'Anyone who thinks scones are easy to make is wrong,' Margarita announces, in a spooky coincidence. 'There's a lot that can go wrong. Your ingredients need to be right; your timing needs to be right. Do not over or underwork them. Do not over or undercook them. As we like to say here: the proof is in the pudding. Okay, get to work.'

Leila and Tobias spring to action – you would think it was a race, not a competition.

'We beat you guys at bowling and we're going to beat you at baking too,' Leila smack-talks us.

'Yeah, may the best team win,' Tobias adds.

Rocco and I talk between ourselves for a second, not rushing into action at the same speed as our rivals. It's a big work area, and the room is quite noisy now, so we can talk quietly without anyone else hearing us.

'Obviously we should try and beat them,' I tell him.

'Obviously,' he replies. Rocco takes the instructions and casts an eye over them. 'All the ingredients are in front of us. What about, I tell you how much flour and butter we need, and you measure them out?'

'Sounds like a plan,' I reply.

I take the electric scales, and a bowl, and set things up.

'First up, 225 grams of self-raising flour,' Rocco instructs. 'Do you say scone, as in gone, or scone, as in cone?'

'I'm team "gone",' I tell him, although our host has been saying it the other way. 'Although I'm the kind of pathetic where I'll say it the other way if other people are, so I don't embarrass myself.'

Rocco laughs.

'I'm team "gone" too,' he replies. 'But I don't really worry about what people think. You should try it, it's liberating.'

'My mum says I apologise too much,' I reply. 'She told me to try saying "thank you" instead – although I don't think Leila would have appreciated me saying that after I dropped that ball on her foot.'

'It rolled into her foot at best,' he reminds me. 'Next is fifty-five grams of butter.'

With the flour and the butter ready to go, we swap roles again. I read out the instructions while Rocco begins combining them.

'What's your go-to dish, if you're cooking to impress?' I ask him.

'Pasta alla Deliveroo,' he jokes. 'Honestly, I'm hopeless. I know women find it really sexy, I do try.'

'If you had to go on *Come Dine with Me*, and you obviously couldn't get away with takeaways, what would you do?' I ask through a smile.

'I definitely don't think I could pull off three dishes,' he replies, as he rubs the flour and butter together with a confusing confidence. 'I once tried to make my parents an anniversary dinner and I burnt the prawn cocktail.'

I snort.

'How do you burn a prawn cocktail?' I have to ask. 'Even I know you don't even cook them.'

'I accidentally put the bowl with the prawns in on the hob,' he confesses. 'I hate to reinforce stereotypes, but I'm hopeless at multitasking.'

'I can't say anything, I once set a barbecue on fire,' I confess.

'Aren't they supposed to be on fire?' he replies.

'Yes,' I say. 'This was, somehow, an additional fire to the intentional one.'

'I can make pizza,' Rocco offers proudly. 'Vague Italian heritage. Something lurking in my DNA must help with that. My mum says I make the best pizza she's ever tasted, and if you can't trust your mum, who can you trust?'

'Are you close with your mum?' I ask curiously. He makes it sound like he is, which is an excellent quality for a man to have.

'Oh, my mum is the best,' he replies. 'I know it's not necessarily cool, to love your mum, or whatever, but she's great. We lost my gran last year, it hit us all pretty hard, but my mum did everything for her when she was alive and there's clearly a real comfort in that. I try to do right by my mum, when I'm not serving her blackened prawns with a plastic reduction. Are you close with your mum?'

I smile. It might not be cool, but it's endlessly charming.

'I am,' I reply. 'She's been cooking for me a lot recently, in my kitchen – it's nice to see it being used by someone who knows what they're doing. I'm getting quite used to it, actually. No one beats your mum's cooking, do they?'

'Erm, if I were you, I'd reserve judgement until I'd tasted these scones,' he replies. 'Have you seen this rubbing technique?'

'Yes, you look like a man who has spent years practising his rubbing technique,' I reply.

Rocco laughs. There's something so attractive about the way he laughs. His face is so animated. He somehow finds a way to make everything he thinks and feels come across as so authentic. Although, let's be real, there's something so attractive about Rocco's everything as far as I'm concerned. He's 'my type on paper' as they say on *Love Island*, which I watched in lieu of a summer holiday this year.

A loud clatter grabs my attention.

'You idiot, Tobias,' Leila shouts. A surge of red flushes through her usually pale complexion. 'Look what you did.'

It appears as though Tobias has managed to drop their tray – with their *oven ready* scones, *what*? – on the floor, scone side down.

'It's all good,' Margarita reassures them, springing up from nowhere. 'We allow lots of extra time, for accidents like these. In this kitchen, we don't call them accidents, we call them first drafts. Your second batch will be even better.'

'I would suggest we throw ours on the floor, if they might be better the second time, but looking around the room, it seems like we're miles behind everyone else,' I whisper to Rocco.

'Then I guess we had better just make these ones extra special,' he replies. 'The first time's a charm, as they say. What's next?'

'Next is twenty-five grams of sugar,' I reply. 'It needs measuring.'

'I'm on it,' Rocco replies.

I take a moment to watch Leila and Tobias, working together at double speed, to get their second attempt at scones ready in time. It's funny, we've made one batch in the time they've made two. It levels the playing field slightly, giving us both just enough time left on the clock to cook our attempts. I can't believe how competitive Leila is. I occasionally notice her looking up, glaring at us, before throwing herself back into her work.

I turn my attention back to Rocco.

'Oh, and 150 millilitres of milk,' I tell him. 'Imagine if we forgot the milk.'

'We wouldn't be winning anything with those,' he replies.

'Is it bad that I really want to win, just because I can see how hard they're trying to beat us?' I ask.

'I want to win too,' he says. 'So get that milk measured, quick.'

For a few moments, we concentrate. We divide our mixture onto the baking tray, we wash the tops with a little milk, and then we head for the oven – carefully, of course.

Two ovens sit side by side at the end of our table. As bad luck would have it, Leila goes to put theirs in at the same time as I bend down to put ours in.

'You can wait your turn,' she ticks me off. I hang back for a second. 'And may the best scone win.'

I mock her voice in my head. May the best scone win. God, I want to win even more now. Competitiveness is contagious.

After placing our scones in our oven I head back around our side of the table where Rocco is straightening up.

'You know what, I only got a quick peep, but ours actually look much better than theirs,' I tell him excitedly.

'And that, my friend...' Rocco lightly sucks his index finger before dipping it in the bowl of leftover sugar, '... is how it's done.'

I smile as Rocco pops his finger in his mouth but then I see his expression change and my smug grin drops. His face goes on a real journey, scrunching and stretching every facial muscle he has, practically in slow motion. He looks like he's going to be sick.

He does well to keep a lid on it, while I quickly grab one of the glasses we were given, and refill it with fresh water. Rocco must drink for a solid two minutes before he regains his composure.

'What's wrong?' I ask him. 'Are you okay?'

'Yeah, we fucked up,' he says immediately, in a very matter of fact way, despite his voice still sounding a bit funny from... well, whatever it was.

'Oh, God,' I blurt softly.

Rocco inspects the ingredients on the table. As he turns the small red bowl around, it slowly reveals the label on the other side: salt.

'We used salt instead of sugar,' he says.

'What?' I reply. 'How?'

'I guess *I* used salt?' he says.

'But I think it was *me* who passed you the wrong bowl, or left the wrong one near you, at least,' I insist.

'Let's just say neither of us checked it,' Rocco reasons. 'No point assigning blame – we've both got previous, this was never going to go well.'

I roll my eyes as I nod in acknowledgement.

'*Obviously*,' I say. 'Can we quickly make some more?'

'Just ten minutes to go,' Margarita calls out.

Ten minutes is about the time left on the oven.

'I guess not,' Rocco says. Eventually he laughs. 'We're so bad at everything. I thought you said I was a real grown-up?'

'You said I was one too,' I playfully protest.

'You're a teacher, so it's maybe worse that you're so bad at these things,' he jokes.

'Says the man responsible for keeping buildings *standing*,' I reply. 'Are we just going to have to take this one on the chin? Ugh, but they're so smug, look at them.'

Leila and Tobias are whipping their cream, ready for serving with their scones. Now that the hard part is over, they look like they're having a joyful time.

'We're tasting each other's scones, right?' Rocco asks.

'Correct,' I reply. 'And as much as Leila is getting on my nerves right now, I wouldn't feed her a scone laced with salt. Why, do you have an idea?'

He has a look on his face like he does.

'We're not going to win, that's a given,' he starts. 'But I would rather they didn't know that we had messed up. They'll be smug if they've won but they will be ten times worse if they know we messed up so badly they're the winners without any competition.'

'You're right,' I reply. I chew my lip as I wonder how we get ourselves out of this mess. 'But what can we do?'

'If we can swap our scones with theirs then they will eat their own and we'll have ours,' he suggests. 'I'm not suggesting we cheat to win. We can just pretend we tried them and rave about how good they were.'

'Ah, so we get to save face, maybe seem like they only won because we laid it on really thick, going on about how amazing theirs are,' I reply, nodding along with my words.

'Exactly... but we need to swap those scones first.'

Rocco looks around for inspiration, so I join him. My eyes eventually land on the worktop.

'We need a distraction,' I tell him.

'We do, but what?' he replies.

'Anything goes?' I ask him quickly, because we're running out of time.

'Why not?' he replies. 'Do you have something in mind?'

I grab the bowl of cream from the worktop, followed by the electric mixer, which I promptly turn up to full blast. As cream sprays everywhere, I angle the bowl so that Rocco bears the brunt of it. Then I let out a girly squeak, so that all eyes are on us.

'Okay, stand back, people, we've got a cream incident,' Margarita announces.

'Oh, my God, Rocco, it's all over your shirt,' I point out, and while I won't be winning any Academy Awards for my seriously wooden delivery, it does seem to get everyone's eyes on him.

'Quick, take your shirt off,' I say loudly, which definitely ensures all eyes – including Leila and Tobias's – are on him.

'In slow motion, if you can,' I whisper playfully.

With all eyes on the cream incident, and the impromptu strip-tease, I grab an oven glove and crouch down at the end of the counter, swapping our scones with Leila and Tobias's, before quickly standing up, grabbing a tea towel, and heading back to Rocco.

Margarita is already there, rubbing his chest with a damp cloth. As I watch the whole room watching him, I regret not selling tickets. But then I join them. My eyes lock onto Rocco. Why have I wound up locking myself into a festive friendzone with someone so dreamy? I suppose it's because, even without a romantic relationship, I like the way he makes me feel. I like the calm vibes he gives off, the unexplained familiarity in his face. It's the friendly warmth, I think, that makes him feel like an old friend, even though I only met him a couple of days ago.

The alarm on our oven – and Leila and Tobias's going off at the same time – snaps me out of it.

'Thank you,' Rocco tells Margarita. 'I can take it from here.'

'Right, yes.' Margarita comes to her senses too. 'Oh, the scones. Time to judge. Everyone, scones out, set them to cool, it's time to taste.'

'I'm sorry,' I whisper to Rocco.

'That's okay,' he replies through a cheeky smile. 'At least I can say I got some action through Matcher this Christmas, hey?'

I should probably laugh but the words stick in my mind. He's probably just making a joke, right? The whole point of that sentence wasn't intended to confirm to me that things have been so far so platonic for him. This is just me wishful thinking.

'I guess I'll wear my coat?' he suggests.

'Yeah, I probably would,' I reply. 'I hadn't realised everyone would be quite so... stare-y.'

'I'll clear the floor once we're out of the woods,' he whispers.

Eventually, the four of us take our seats around our table, each with our own scones in front of us.

'Ours look so much better than yours, it has to be said,' Leila points out.

I wonder if that means ours do genuinely look more appetising than hers (even if they're spiked with salt and will probably taste disgusting) or if she would have said that regardless.

'Shall we do this then?' Rocco suggests. I think he's keen to get this over with. So am I. We're both terrified we're going to be rumbled. Hopefully we're almost home and dry.

'We have to wait for Margarita,' Leila points out. 'She's going to tell us how to taste them, and what points to consider.'

'She's what?' I reply, casually as I can.

'She talks us through how to rate them,' Leila says again.

'Do we really need to wait for that?' Rocco says with a casual snort.

'Yeah, I've been eating scones my entire life,' I say playfully. 'I'm sure we know how to do that bit at least.'

'We're up now anyway,' Tobias points out as Margarita approaches us.

'Oh, wow, look at these ones,' Margarita gushes. 'This is going to be a real clash of the titans. Have you swapped scones yet?'

Yes.

'No,' Leila tells her, in full-on teacher's pet mode.

'Okay, come on, guys, swap your plates,' Margarita instructs us.

I exchange a glance with Rocco before pushing our plate across to Leila, and pulling her plate closer to us.

'You guys can go first,' Margarita tells our opponents. 'We'll call you Team One. So. First of all, how do they look?'

'Good,' Tobias says simply.

'Yeah, they look all right,' Leila adds. 'Not as visually appealing as ours, and I am a really visual eater so it's a bit of a stumbling block.'

I can't help but roll my eyes. If only she knew that she was talking about her own scones.

'Okay, next, you want to smell them,' Margarita instructs. 'Then break a piece off and feel the texture.'

'A little harder than I'm used to,' Leila reasons. 'The smell is good, but I could be smelling all of the ones in the room, to be fair.'

It is hilarious that she's talking about her own.

'And finally...' Margarita pauses for dramatic effect. 'Taste.'

I look at Rocco. He looks so funny in his coat, his bare chest clearly visible at the top. I widen my eyes at him, as if to say: how are we going to get away with this one?

'Not bad,' Tobias says.

'Yeah, they're okay,' Leila adds. 'A bit drier than I make them...'

You're talking about your own, dummy.

'A good effort,' Tobias summarises.

'An effort,' Leila adds. 'Of sorts.'

'Okay, well, that's positive,' Margarita says. 'Now, time for you two – Team Two – to do the same, follow the same steps.'

Perhaps if we follow through with our plan of hyping these scones up so much they couldn't possibly lose, tasting them might not even be necessary?

'Well, they look incredible,' I say to get the ball rolling.

'Maybe the best scones I've ever seen,' Rocco adds.

'And the smell,' I continue. 'They smell unreal, they feel perfect – you guys have seriously outdone yourselves.'

'These are clearly better than ours,' Rocco says. 'Without a doubt.'

'Finally, the taste test,' Margarita prompts us.

'I already know they're the winners,' I insist.

'Taste them,' Margarita says again.

I look at Rocco again. It feels like we stare at each other for an age, but it's probably only a couple of seconds. Without a word, or even an expression, it's like we both know what we need to do. We raise our scones, clink them together, and then take a bite. I wonder how bad it can actually be. I eat salty foods all the time.

The answer, however, is bad. Really bad. Bad from the second it touches my tongue. It sends a sensation from my tongue, into my gums, my teeth, right down into my throat. As my tonsils burn, I feel tears forming in my eyes. Rocco doesn't fare any better. I watch him swallow hard, forcing his small bite down, then he clears his throat as delicately.

'So good,' he says, using minimal words – I imagine because that's all he can get out.

'Just... the best,' I add. 'So nice. Really—'

Oh, God, I just threw up in my mouth a little. I'm glad my mum bought the real Rennies in the end, I'm going to need them.

Leila in particular looks baffled. Margarita, on the other hand, narrows her eyes at us.

'Ah, I see what's going on here,' she replies. 'You guys are friends, and you don't want to say anything bad about their scones, but I am here to push you out of your comfort zone, to help you improve your cooking skills, and to get you talking critically about the things you eat. You say they're amazing, but I've been doing this for a while. I can tell from the looks on your faces that you're not being completely honest. So, I'm sorry, Team One, but Team Two have clearly made the superior scones today.'

It takes everything I've got in me to suppress my smile. I know, this is awful, we didn't deserve to win, but Leila didn't have to be so harsh about our scones – that were *her* scones anyway.

'I just... I don't understand,' Leila says. 'Pass them here, let me try one.'

I take the plate in my hands and do what I need to do. I 'slip' on the cream and land on the floor. It's all over my clothes, my hands, my hair as I push it behind my ear. But most importantly, the salty scones are all over the floor, so no one else ever has to eat them again.

Rocco sits down on the floor next to me. He's already covered in cream; he has nothing to lose.

'So... we really are quite terrible at cooking,' he muses through a cheeky smile.

'We really are,' I reply, unable to control my grin. 'I don't actually think this could have gone worse.'

'But we did win,' he points out. 'And we definitely had fun.'

We really did. And now I'm going to be counting down the minutes until we meet again.

15

Lying in my bed, thinking about the events of the evening, smiling to myself about what a good time I had with Rocco – honestly, I don't think I've lain awake at night daydreaming about a boy since I was at school.

I love that even though everything couldn't have gone more wrong, it all worked out well in the end, and we both had such a blast making such a mess.

Naturally, ending the night covered in cream meant that I needed to have a shower when I got in. When I arrived home, Mum and Dad were sitting at the island, chatting, eating bowls of cereal for supper – something they used to do, so it made me feel especially uncomfortable. Gail is away for a work thing so she wasn't around, and Jess had decided to get an early night. So I had a nice long bath, instead of a shower, and now I'm in my bed. I feel squeaky clean and I can still smell all the products I used on my hair and my skin. General life stresses aside, I feel like I'm on cloud nine right now, lying in my bed, thinking about Rocco.

I let out a sigh of contentment as I snuggle down into my bed.

I pull a face when it sounds like the bed reciprocates. Obviously that didn't happen.

I listen carefully for a few moments. I'm about to get back to daydreaming when I hear it again. A sort of 'mmm' sound.

I jump out of bed and follow my ears to my bedroom door. Is that laughing I can hear? I dare to head out into the hallway where my worst suspicions are confirmed. Oh, my God, it's my mum I can hear, giggling. Chatting quietly, letting out little sounds, in her bedroom with the door closed.

I forget my feet and step on a creaky floorboard. I hear a hushing sound before Mum's giggling quickly stops. The house falls so silent the only thing I can hear is my own heartbeat, banging inside my chest. Is that my mum... and my dad... in her room? No. No, no, no. They can't be, can they?

I continue to Jess's room, light on my feet, before slowly opening her bedroom door. I feel bad, waking her up if she's having an early night, but we've got ourselves a worst-case scenario on our hands here.

Jess isn't in her bed, though, which is odd. I take my phone from my pocket and check her location – turns out this was an excellent idea. It says she's in the house. I wonder if she's downstairs watching TV. Perhaps she heard the same noises as I did and wanted to get as far away from them as possible. I smile at the idea of drinking tea, eating biscuits and watching a festive movie with my sister late at night, like we used to do when we were kids. It's not quite the silver lining of whatever is going on tonight but it's a great excuse to be downstairs.

I walk down the stairs into darkness. As my eyes adjust, in the living room, which is illuminated by both Christmas trees, I see that the room is empty. Very odd. She wasn't in her room, the bathroom door was open – oh, could it have been her up late with Mum, having a giggle together in Mum's room? I grab my phone again, to message Jess, to check before I knock on the door to join them, but as I do, Jess's location gets more accurate, and the flashing circle around my house tightens up, getting smaller, until it shows me exactly where Jess is. She isn't in this house at all. She's next door, at Kenny's house.

I let myself outside, walking a few steps down my driveway until I can glance back at Kenny's house, to see if there are any signs of life over there. As though it isn't bad enough that the only light on in his entire house is his bedroom light, he's got his colour lightbulbs set to red, and I doubt it's red to signify Santa Claus's uniform.

I slink back inside and creep up to my bedroom. All seems quiet now, but I don't want to take any chances. Inside my bedside table there is a pair of ear plugs, back from when I was having building work done, and the noise was so loud no matter where you were in the house. I wedge them tightly into my ears to block out any potential bumps in the night. This bloody family, I can't figure them out at all. I don't know who to speak to first in the morning but clearly everyone needs a talking to. You would think I would be used to it, being a teacher, but telling off your parents and your grown sister, for having the hormones of teenagers, is just too much.

I need to get back to daydreaming, to thinking about Rocco as I drift off to sleep, but instead the thought of my divorced parents potentially getting it on in the next room is all I can think about.

It's a difficult one because, as much as I just wish I could fall asleep right now, I'm definitely going to have nightmares if I do. Let's just hope they're about something less traumatic, like a monster eating me alive, or standing up to do a speech and realising I'm naked. At this point, anything is better than the reality.

16

'Someone must've got in late,' I just about make out Jess say.

I roll over to see her sitting on the bed next to me. I pull out my ear plugs one after the other before grabbing my phone from the bedside table.

'Oh, my God, it's lunchtime,' I say. 'When did that happen?'

'Well, if you will stay out into the wee hours,' she teases.

'Except I didn't,' I point out. 'I must have slept through my alarms or maybe just having ear plugs in kept me even more zoned out and stopped me waking up naturally.'

'What's with the ear plugs?' she asks.

'You would know that they were to block out the noise last night, if you had been here,' I point out. 'You also would have known that I wasn't out all night, if you were here, but you weren't. You were the one out all night.'

Jess smiles, sort of guiltily, but in a cheeky, proud sort of way.

'Okay, I will tell you where I was,' she starts.

'Oh, I know where you were,' I interrupt. 'You were next door, with Kenny.'

'I was, but you've got to admit, he's hot, he's funny, he's charming, he's—'

'He's ploughing through women, since he threw his wife out,' I tell her.

'Kenny?' she squeaks in disbelief. 'I find that hard to believe.'

'You find it hard to believe that the man you've only known for a couple of days tops might not be the great guy he makes himself out to be?' I reply sarcastically. 'You're really out-Jessing yourself today, sis.'

'And how would you know better?' she asks me. 'God, that arguing between the two of you, that's not sexual tension, is it? Eww, you haven't already been there, have you?'

'Hell no,' I quickly insist. 'Declan used to go out drinking with him, after he threw his wife out of their house, and he would come home banging on about how cool Kenny was, how he was starting his life again because he wasn't happy, how he could have a different girl every night if he wanted to. Declan idolised him – I'm pretty sure it was these happiness pep talks from Kenny that led to Declan leaving me. And then there's all the girls coming and going since his wife left. So, yeah, great guy.'

'He is cool,' Jess says, echoing the one part of my rants that she didn't need to take away. Then she laughs. 'I know what I'm doing, sis, and Declan was a scumbag, you're better off without him. Anyone who could abandon their partner is trash, whether someone convinced them to do it or they decided to do it themselves.'

She's not wrong there. I just don't want to see her getting hurt by someone like Kenny. Of course I see the appeal. He's a good-looking guy with a nice house, he's worked hard to build a career for himself, he can be charming, and he is funny, I guess – it's just infuriating, given that I'm usually the butt of his jokes.

'Blergh,' I say, sticking out my tongue in disgust. 'I really wanted to keep this a Declan-free Christmas. I hate talking about him, or even thinking of him, because it makes me feel like he's still relevant, like he still matters.'

'Well, he is irrelevant, and he doesn't matter, and there will be no more mentions of D from now on.'

Jess laughs at her own choice of words.

'Sounds ideal,' I reply. 'I wish I could get all members of this family to think less about D.'

This only makes Jess laugh harder.

'You still think Mum and Dad are up to no good together?' she asks. Her casual tone suggests she might not be convinced but, to be honest, neither am I.

'Something is off in this house,' I say simply. 'That's all I know.'

'You're hardly in it,' Jess points out.

'I could say the same to you,' I reply. 'God, I'm starving.'

'Me too,' she replies, hopping off my bed. 'Come on, let's go get some food.'

I get up slowly and start searching my bedroom drawers for some comfortable clothes to go downstairs in.

'Oh, my God, quick, come here,' Jess demands.

I walk over to the bedroom window where I join her in looking out over the back garden. The garden is nothing fancy – yet. I have all these big ideas but so far all I've managed is cleaning up the stone paths, keeping the lawn nice, and I've painted the summer house at the bottom of the garden. It's a cute wooden thing, with windows, and a little canopy at the front. It's currently stuffed full of garden furniture and tools, not that it would be warm enough to spend time in at this time of year.

All is as it should be in the garden apart from one thing: Mum and Dad are standing outside the summer house, having what anyone with eyes would describe as an intimate conversation.

They're leaning in, Dad has his hands on Mum's forearms and he's rubbing them. Their expressions are serious, then softer, then they're smiling.

'Right, something is definitely going on there,' Jess whispers, even though there's no way they can hear us.

'Definitely,' I reply.

'Shall we confront them?' she suggests. 'Ask them what they're talking about?'

'No, because if it was bad, they would only lie,' I point out. 'We need to be smart about this. We need to watch them, listen to them – try and figure out what they're up to without them notic- ing, just like we used to do when we were kids.'

'Late nights spying from the stairs it is,' she says with a smile.

Jess and I always used to watch what our parents were up to, when really we should have been in bed asleep. They used to throw these dinner parties for their friends and we were fasci- nated by it all. Long after we were supposed to be in bed we would creep back up and sit together halfway down the stairs, spying from the darkness, peering into the dining room through the wrought-iron banister railings. We learned so much by listening to the grown-ups talk, but we were confused by so much more. Well, when we were kids, without the internet, we couldn't just look things up for ourselves and, yes, saying that does make me feel like I'm eighty years old.

'We need to try and trip them up too,' I suggest. 'Normally I'd say you're the best at talking to Dad, whereas I probably know how to chat to Mum more about life stuff. But we don't want that, we need to switch places, swap parents, you talk to Mum – because she tends to try and seem more cool in front of you – and I'll talk to Dad, because frankly I clearly make him as uncomfort- able as he makes me, and it's in that awkwardness where he might slip up.'

'Sounds like a plan,' Jess says. 'I'd be excited, if the whole thing wasn't so gross.'

'It's something to do, I guess,' I say with a sigh. 'Come on, let's go get some food, see if we can find anything out.'

'Okay, but if they are getting back together, then we need a plan for that, to break them up again, because we cannot let that happen.'

'Don't worry, I have something in mind, for a worst-case scenario,' I tell her.

I just really hope it won't come to that.

17

I think that perhaps, because the events we're going to are so varied, and because there don't seem to be any potential romantic couples in any of the groups I've been out in, it's easy to forget that Matcher is in fact a dating app, and the whole point of all of this is achieve something on the spectrum between hooking up and finding love. I don't suppose my motivation for joining the events helped either. Looking for any reason to avoid being in your own home, in the days before Christmas, when all your mates are on holiday probably wasn't written on the white board when the team at Matcher were coming up with the Mingle All the Way initiative.

Rocco and I are here 'together' again but tonight couldn't be more different from the things we've done so far because tonight we're not on the same team at all, and tonight Rocco isn't 'all mine' (in the very loose sense he has been so far, anyway – I know he's not mine-mine, I'm not delusional). Tonight, we're speed dating.

Is it weird that I feel weird? Is it tragic, that I'm having feelings for my wingman? It is, isn't it? What is wrong with me? I should be at home in my pyjamas eating cheese and not even thinking about men. I complain about my mum seeming suspiciously close with my dad, and my sister running around with the boy next door, but I'm just as bad.

Anyway, we're at speed dating, an event where we won't spend any real time together, apart from our allocated minute, of course. We did say we would debrief, afterwards, if neither of us hit it off with someone – the implication being one of us might pull, and I honestly don't know if I led us to that conclusion or Rocco did. I suppose, given that Matcher is a dating app, Rocco must have been on there looking for someone, even if he is only in town for the holidays. My own intentions, the whole reason I'm at these events, was never about romance or anything close to it. I'm not sure I'm ready to even think about meeting someone yet – least of all via speed dating.

I've never actually been speed dating before. Unsurprisingly, it's never appealed. Well, while some might argue that I'm best enjoyed in short bursts, I think I'm what they call a 'grower' – actually, that's something else, but you know what I mean. I'm an acquired taste. To know me is to love me, or something like that. My point is that it takes me a little while to open up, to show my true self – let's not beat about the bush – to be likeable. So, yeah, I don't think speed dating is going to be for me, although women do get to sit still, and men have to do the moving around which I quite like, mostly just because it means I don't have to get up.

My heels aren't helping. I suppose, maybe on some level, knowing that tonight was a 'romantic' event (for a lack of a better term), I probably have tried a little harder to dress up. My heels are high, my black dress is on the shorter side, and I learned how to do my eye make-up from someone on TikTok who was maybe fifteen years younger than me, so hopefully I'm looking like someone you would want to spend a minute talking to – until the bell rings, at least.

So far this evening, my communications with Rocco have been strictly text based. We've been messaging all day, actually, and I suppose it's been strange, making plans to go speed dating together, but there you are.

I'm at the River Bar – somewhere I've been before, but the last time I was here I was probably with Declan. It wasn't as nice then; it must have been renovated since. It looks like we've both gone for an 'out with the old' kind of vibe, although I imagine their ugly old chairs didn't up and leave them while they were working and then send a follow-up text to explain their actions after the fact.

I need to cut that out, right now. My man-free Christmas might be over, but my Declan-free life is something I feel very strongly about. The last thing I need is him in my head tonight – where he's still trying to live rent free – making me wonder what's wrong with me, why he couldn't stand to stay with me in the home we were planning on making together.

'Wow, Billie, look at you,' Rocco says as he greets me with a kiss on the cheek. Ooh, perhaps the outfit is working? He's never kissed me on the cheek before. We have been through a lot together, though. Last night felt like it crammed years of friendship into one really intense mess of an evening.

'Look at me, look at you,' I reply. 'Looking very sharp.'

'I'm wearing the same coat as last night – hastily cleaned in my hotel bathroom, so it probably stinks,' he says. 'But you, you look different, you look like you're about to make speed dating your bitch.'

'Tables, ladies,' a voice calls out.

'Oh, I guess it's starting,' Rocco says. 'I suppose I'll see you at some point but, until then, have a good evening, here's hoping it all goes better than last night.'

I raise my glass.

'To not ending the night covered in cream,' I say, instantly regretting my words.

Rocco flashes me that cheeky smile of his.

'I'll drink to that,' he replies. 'As soon as I get a drink.'

The speed dating event is something put on by the bar, not organised by one of the Matcher lot, so as such there are lots of other people here. Leila is here, obviously, and Tobias. I recognise a few other people but otherwise it's mostly new people and with new people comes the potential for new romantic connections. I don't know if that's a good thing or a bad thing.

I shuffle over to the speed dating tables and find myself naturally ushered towards a particular one. The second my bum touches the seat, I regret it.

'Hello,' the blonde girl on the table next to me says.

In hindsight, it was a dumb move on my part, to take a seat next to the prettiest girl in the room – if not the whole of Kent. Worse than her being Instagram filter levels of attractive, though, is that fact that we're a similar type (in the loosest sense, obviously). She's a blonde in what I'd guess is her early thirties, wearing a black dress, with the exact same fruity gin cocktail on the table in front of her. We look like a before and after picture. But if a ten is sitting next to a seven (if I borrow her surplus points, that is) at speed dating then there can't be any shame in it.

'Hi,' I reply. 'Have you done this before?'

'Oh, God, no!' she quickly insists. 'One of my friends wanted to come. I'm just here for moral support. You?'

'First time too,' I reply.

'Here's hoping it's over quickly,' she says with a smile.

With her sitting next to me, for me, I'm sure it will be over pretty sharpish. I should have sat next to Leila – not because she's unattractive, but because the look on her face when I'm in her orbit would scare away any man.

Men are assigned a starting table and the clock starts ticking. We're actually assigned a few minutes with each man but I'm still sure that's not enough time for me to turn on the charm. Still, I'm willing to try.

First up is Jack. He's tall with spiky brown hair and brown eyes so big I keep thinking something has surprised him.

'So, Jack, what do you do?' I ask him. Stupid, dull question. Is that really the best I've got?

'For work?' he replies.

It would be a very broad question if I didn't mean for work.

'For work,' I repeat back to him.

'I'm a recruiter,' he replies.

'What do you recruit?' I ask.

'People for jobs,' he says simply.

I had already figured that out, I just thought perhaps he might work in a special field, or offer up more information, something for me to bounce off. This is going to be a long few minutes.

'Cool,' I reply. I give him a moment to ask me what I do but he doesn't actually say anything, he just glances next to me, to see who the next person is. Not only has he written me off already but now that he's noticed the hot blonde to my left, Jack is clearly counting down the seconds.

'I'm a teacher,' I tell him.

'Oh, so that means you want kids?' he replies. He seems almost annoyed by the (assumed) fact. I didn't think I could turn him off any more but here we are.

'It means I *teach* kids,' I correct him.

'Never been a big fan of kids, myself,' Jack says with a shrug. 'I don't see what the fuss is all about.'

'Yeah, I suppose, largely, people do it to continue the human race,' I point out. 'Never been a big fan of humans myself, though.'

Jack stares at me.

'Was that a joke?' he asks.

Less so by the second.

'Yep,' I reply simply.

Jack, clearly fed up with talking to me, picks up his full pint and raises it to his lips. He begins slowly chugging it, clearly not stopping until he's had every last drop, but really savouring the process, taking as long as humanly possible until…

The bell. Time to move on.

Next up is Carey. He's blond, he's eager, he's got a notebook with him.

'Ball sports?' is his opening line.

'Ball sports?' I repeat back to him.

'Ball sports,' he says again. 'Ball sports!'

He nods, as though I'm expected to answer some kind of question.

'What, do I like them?' I reply. 'Watching or playing?'

'Playing,' he says, frustrated that I'm only just getting the hang of what I'd imagine are supposed to be quick-fire questions.

'No.'

'Watching?' he asks.

'No,' I say again.

'Chicken or fish?'

'For…' I notice the look on Carey's face. He doesn't want questions, he wants answers, and even though it kind of sounds like he's taking my order at a wedding, answering is probably the best thing I can do. 'Chicken.'

'Pink or blue?' he asks quickly. It doesn't even seem like he's absorbing my answers.

'Pink,' I reply.

Carey narrows his eyes.

'Is that what you think I want you to answer?' he asks suspiciously.

Guy, I have no idea what you want me to answer.

I reel off answers, without giving them much thought, until the time is up.

The bell rings.

The men that follow aren't much better. There's Aaron, whose opening line is to ask me what my deepest, darkest secret is, before telling me his is that he killed a man, waiting blankly for my reaction, and then laughing wildly – implying that he was joking, but not actually confirming it.

Then there was Henry, who was very upfront about the fact that he was currently on a 'break' from his marriage, to explore his options, which (whether sanctioned or not) I find kind of iffy. Even if his wife has signed off on it, say I was interested in him, I would have no idea if the relationship could go anywhere – and if we did get together, I would just be waiting for him to go 'on a break' from me.

One thing all of these men seem to have in common is that once they realise they're getting nowhere with me, they look to see who is up next and start thinking about who they're going to ask to be their best man.

The bell rings.

'One more, then a break to top up your drinks,' a voice calls out.

My glass is empty but I'm sure I can survive one more round.

'Oh, hello,' I say as Rocco sits down opposite me.

'You look pleased to see me,' he replies. 'Is it going that badly?'

'You wouldn't believe some of these guys,' I tell him. 'How are the girls?'

'Nothing traumatising,' he replies. 'I think I'm having an easier time than you. Do the other guys make me look good?'

Crap, they do. He looks great anyway but compared to this lot, he looks like he's easily the most eligible bachelor in Kent.

'They really do,' I admit.

'We might still be on track for grabbing a drink after together, then,' he reminds me. 'But just in case we don't, speed date small talk. What are you doing for Christmas?'

'Just spending it with the family,' I tell him. 'You?'

'Same,' he replies. 'Wow, we're not great at this, are we?'

'I'm not sure this is a good way to meet or get to know people,' I say. 'That or we're not happy unless we're causing trouble.'

'I'm sure we could find a way to cause trouble if we wanted to,' Rocco replies. 'Has Leila spoken to you today?'

'Nope.' I look over at her. She's happily chatting away to the bloke on her table. 'She seems to have some kind of problem with me.'

'She was off with me too,' he replies. 'I've already been to her table. I tried to make a joke about Sconegate but she wasn't interested.'

'I think she was already pretty livid with me about the bowling ball,' I tell him. 'I'll try to smooth things over with her later.'

The bell rings. No! Did I just waste my speed date with the only man in the room I could ever be interested in talking about bloody Leila?

'Stay there, I'll grab you another drink,' Rocco tells me. 'What was it?'

'Like, a fruity gin thing,' I reply, unsure what it was actually called.

'Back in a minute,' he says, grabbing our empty glasses before he heads off to the bar.

'Did he just say he would get a drink for you?' the blonde next to me asks.

'Yeah,' I reply.

'Wow, so there are some good ones here,' she says. 'That's so sweet. How old is he?'

'Erm, thirty-six,' I reply.

'What does he do for work?' she enquires curiously. 'Did you ask?'

'He's an architect,' I say. 'You're talking to him next, save some questions for him.'

I laugh politely but then I notice a look in her eye.

'I will,' she replies. 'He's pretty hot, isn't he? What's his deal? Is he looking for something serious? What does it seem like he's after? Help a girl out, tell me everything I need to know.'

The fact that this woman wants me to give her all the info on Rocco, and has dismissed me as any sort of competition for her, and actually expects me go out of my way to help her pull him makes me feel a whole bunch of things, none of them good. It annoys me that she sees me as little more than a vehicle to get the guy. It messes with my confidence, ever so slightly, but only in that way it would anyone, to be thought so little of. Worst of all, it fills me with jealousy. I don't want to see other girls flirting with Rocco, and I've got absolutely no right to feel that way, no claim over him whatsoever, and yet here we are. I don't want to help her; I want to hinder her.

'He kept going on about buying me drinks, getting me drunk,' I lie. 'He said everything is easier with a drink in you.'

At least Sid's failed attempt to get me drunk was good for something.

'Oh, that seems a bit weird,' she says, pulling a face. 'Maybe he meant it would be easier for him?'

I daren't even consider what she means by that.

'Yeah, I don't know, I wasn't sure at that point,' I reply. 'But then he started banging on about how he hates condoms and wouldn't ever wear one. That was enough for me.'

'Wow, major red flag,' she replies. 'Thanks for letting me know.'

I hear a man clearing his throat behind me. Of course it's Rocco.

'Billie, can I borrow you for a minute?' he asks, pulling me from my conversation.

'Sure,' I reply nervously. He didn't hear any of that, did he?

I walk a few paces away with him.

'There are two drinks on the menu that could be classed as "fruity gin things",' he tells me. 'Was it the one with the lime or the passionfruit?'

'The passionfruit,' I reply.

'Okay, also, did I just hear you telling that girl I don't wear condoms?'

He doesn't seem mad or confused by this – just curious.

I stare at him. So he did hear.

'Yes,' I eventually say.

Rocco laughs.

'It's like that, is it?' he replies. 'You're trying to sabotage me? Well, it's on. That's so funny. I should have known you would come up with a fun way for us to wreak havoc here.'

Oh, he thinks this is some sort of game I'm playing, rather than a crazed act of jealousy. Well, that's certainly preferable, I'll lean into that.

'I thought you might find it funny,' I lie.

'Game on, kid,' he says through a smile. 'Game on.'

Rocco heads back to the bar. I sit back down at my table.

'Is everything okay?' the blonde asks me.

'The pig was actually trying to get me to have sex with him in the toilets,' I tell her, pulling a grossed-out face. 'Can you believe that?'

'Eww,' she replies.

Eventually Rocco returns with my drink.

'Good luck with the next one,' he tells me.

'Yeah, you too,' I reply through a smile.

Why is everything more fun when it feels like we're on the same side?

My next date sits down at my table. I can see from his name badge that his name is Luke. I can see from his face that he isn't really interested in me. At this point in the evening, I don't think I have any self-confidence left to knock so it's water off a duck's back.

'Hello,' I say brightly. 'Having much luck tonight?'

'Not really,' he replies. 'You?'

'Nah,' I say casually.

'To be honest, I'm not actually looking for anything,' he insists. 'I'm just here for a laugh, so I don't want to waste your time, or stop you doing what you want to do, no judgement or anything.'

'No judgement?' I repeat back to him.

'Yeah, you know, you do what you need to do, to get what you want, but I'm not interested unfortunately.'

Weirdly this is the most interested I've been in talking to anyone new all night.

'And what *do* I want?' I ask him curiously.

He leans forward and lowers his voice.

'Sperm,' he whispers.

I chose the wrong time to sip my drink.

'No judgement,' he says again. 'But, if I were you, I wouldn't be hitting up men at a speed dating thing, I'd go to a proper clinic and get a real donation. This is no way to start a family, love.'

I notice Rocco at the next table in the corner of my eye. As I briefly glance at him, he gives me a wink. Oh, my God, he must've told Luke that I'm here to get pregnant! That's hilarious. I love that he gives as good as he gets.

The bell rings – thank God.

'Hello, Billie,' Tobias says with a sigh as he sits down opposite me.

'Hey,' I reply. 'I thought at least you would be pleased to talk to me!'

'Oh, it's not that,' he says. 'It's just that this is speed dating, and I know nothing is going to happen between us.'

'Is this because we had the better scones?' I ask cheekily, trying to lighten the mood. He doesn't laugh. 'Is everything okay? Leila has been funny with me too. I was actually going to ask you if you could help me smooth things over with her. I don't want to let a little thing like my ball-handling skills come between us.'

Tobias's eyes widen.

'Definitely don't say that to her,' he insists. 'Bragging like that isn't cool.'

'Bragging?' I echo in disbelief. 'I'm not bragging. I'm clearly rubbish.'

'I guess she just feels like she could've had something with Rocco, until you stole him away from her,' he explains.

'Wait a second,' I say quickly. 'What are you talking about? Because I'm talking about when I dropped the bowling ball on her foot.'

Tobias starts laughing.

'Right, the ball-handling thing makes a lot more sense now,' he replies through an amused grin. 'No, she's mad at you for taking Rocco off her.'

'Were they together?' I ask him. 'You know the two of us aren't anything more than friends, right?'

'You probably need to take this up with her,' he replies.

That's a great idea.

'Back in a sec,' I reply.

I approach Leila's table and tap the man she's talking to on the shoulder.

'You see that guy over there?' I point out Tobias. 'Could you just go and sit with him for a second please? I just need a quick word with Leila.'

'You want me to speed date a bloke?' he replies.

'I want you to sit at a table with him so I don't get in trouble for standing here,' I tell him. 'But if the two of you hit it off then you have my blessing.'

He frowns but does as he's told.

'And now you're ruining my speed dates,' Leila says. 'Fab.'

'I owe you an apology,' I tell her, cutting to the chase. 'Let me start by saying that, for the past couple of days, we have had our wires completely crossed. I thought you were annoyed at me for dropping that bowling ball on your foot. Tobias just told me I'm wrong.'

'Bloody big mouth Tobias,' she replies. 'This is why I'm not going to mark him as a match, even though we're friends. He's right, though, I'm annoyed at you for stealing Rocco. The two of us were getting close, before you turned up.'

'And that's why I'm sorry,' I reply. 'Because I was so scared when I turned up at that first event – after a spectacularly bad date the night before, which I'll tell you all about sometime – and I clung to the first person who was nice to me. I do really like Rocco but we're just friends. And you and Tobias are my friends too. I'm sorry if you felt like I was stepping on your toes. Or dropping a bowling ball on them, if you are still a little bit mad about that.'

Leila laughs for a second.

'So, when I called you out for stealing Rocco, and you said something like "look at me, it was bound to happen"…'

'I meant me being clumsy and dropping the bowling ball,' I quickly insist. 'Can we please just go back to being friends? All of us.'

'Yes, but one thing is still annoying me,' she starts. 'Stop pretending that there's nothing going on between you and Rocco.'

'There isn't, though,' I insist. 'We're just friends, having a laugh together. We've actually been sabotaging each other's speed dates.'

Leila laughs but in a way that makes me feel like I'm not in on the joke.

'Listen to yourself for a second, Billie. You say there's nothing romantic between the two of you and yet you just told me you are ruining each other's chance of meeting someone tonight,' she points out. 'And not only do you keep looking over at him while you are talking to me, but when he was talking to me, he was doing the same, looking over at you.'

'What?' I reply. I'm not sure that's right although, annoyingly, I did just glance over at him.

'If you're telling the truth, and nothing is going on, then do you think perhaps you're maybe jealous that he's talking to other girls? And that he is jealous that you're talking to other guys?'

'I think we're just messing around,' I insist, without giving it a second of thought. 'I'm going to let your date come back, before—'

The bell rings.

'Ah, it's fine,' Leila says with a bat of her hand. 'He talked about football the whole time anyway. But, in summary, you and Rocco should probably just have sex already. The tension is really starting to annoy the rest of us.'

'Solid advice,' I say through what we'll call a playfully sarcastic smile.

I'm not sure, generally speaking, 'just have sex' is the best advice you can give someone.

My next date is waiting at my table for me before I get back.

'Sorry, sorry,' I say as I sit down opposite him.

'I thought I was being stood up,' the man replies through a smile. 'I didn't think you could get stood up at speed dating, but I'm always open to new and embarrassing ways to make sure I stay single.'

Oh, this one is funny!

'Same,' I reply. 'I'm Billie.'

'Tony,' he replies. 'So, where did you go? Oh, God, unless you went to the toilet, in which case, please congratulate me on what a terrible job I'm doing. Feedback forms are going straight to my mum. Hopefully she'll stop asking me when I'm getting married if she sees.'

I laugh.

Tony is a mountain of a man. He must be nearer seven foot than six, but it's hard to tell with him sitting down. His shoulders are broad and his hair is probably nicer than mine. It's long, dark and poker straight. There's one hell of a shine on it. Would it be weird to ask him what he uses?

'Argan oil,' he says, reading my mind.

I stare at him. I feel like I've just been caught out.

'You were looking at my hair,' he tells me. 'Usually when women look at me like that, it's not because they fancy me, it's because they want to know the secret to my hair.'

'It's honestly a work of art,' I point out. 'You can't blame people for wanting to know your secrets.'

'And yet, when I tell them that I had to be cut out of a child's swing by the fire brigade, when I was twenty-four, they look at me like I'm some kind of freak,' he replies.

Oh, he's really funny. How is this guy single?

It must be some sort of reflex that makes me keep glancing over at Rocco. This time, though, when our eyes meet, he isn't smiling. His eyes are narrowed and his jaw is tight. We look at each other for a second before he turns back to his date. Is Leila right? Is he jealous? I mean, she's right about me, I definitely am. But none of it matters because after Christmas, Rocco will be going back to Dublin or wherever he's working next. I'm really not interested in a fling. I'm sure there will be people out there who think it's what's best for me, to prove I'm over Declan by getting under someone else. It's not that I don't think I'd have a great time with Rocco, and I'm sure it would be really hot in the moment, but I don't *just* want to sleep with him, and that's the problem. It's not exactly going to be difficult, is it? I haven't had sex with anyone since Declan, it's something that's coming embarrassingly naturally to me.

The best thing we can do is keep things strictly friends and keep sex off the table. And now I'm thinking about having sex with him on a table, fantastic! This isn't going to be so easy after all.

18

The good news is that things between me, Rocco, Leila and Tobias are back to being friends again. The old gang (from, you know, like three days ago) is back together again.

What is potentially the bad news, but is something I am also going to file under good news anyway, is that Leila and Tobias have joined us for our post-speed dating drink. It's bad because obviously I want to be alone with Rocco – I want it to be just us, to shut out the rest of the world while we enjoy one another's company. It's for the best that we have company, though, it keeps things strictly platonic. We're just friends. We're all just friends.

We've been here a little while now. The drinks are flowing and so is the conversation. It's not only a lot of fun, chatting about the evening, but it's reassuring to know that none of us had any luck finding someone. If we hadn't all had such a rubbish series of micro dates, I might have wondered if there was something wrong with me.

'Did you speak to the guy who kept going on about how big his downstairs was?' Leila asks me.

I don't know if it's because we've squashed our beef, or

because she's had a fair bit to drink, but I'm finding Leila a lot more fun this evening. She's more relaxed, more outgoing, less hostile – she's actually quite funny too.

'Oh, my God, I did,' I reply.

'He just would not shut up about the size of it,' she continues. 'He was obsessed.'

Rocco widens his eyes.

'Really? Guys talk to you like that?' he asks.

'They can't all be like you,' Leila says, squeezing his arm before grabbing her drink again, and draining the last of it.

'It was weird, because he was so desperate for me to know exactly how big it was,' I add. 'Not by showing me it. Well, no, he wanted to show me it. But it was like, before I filled in my feedback form, he wanted me to know, so that I would consider it when I scored him.'

'Did he ask you to name an item, and he would say if it was bigger?' Leila asks me.

'Yes!' I reply giddily. The reason I'm so happy comes from sharing this experience with her, as odd as that sounds, because once again, it means it's nothing to do with me. It's not the type of men I attract, the calibre of man interested in me, or any kind of vibe I'm putting out. It's just men. Not all men, though, because the two at this table are clearly horrified, but that's reassuring too. It makes it easier to laugh.

'I said a cucumber,' she tells me before lowering her voice and widening her eyes. 'Bigger!'

'I said a baseball bat,' I tell her through a giggle.

'Wow, okay, those are some high expectations,' Tobias says, the colour draining from his face.

'I wanted to make sure I said something ridiculous,' I reply. 'I didn't like the way he was lording it over me, as though I would be powerless to resist it. Like he could be anyone, treat me any way he wanted, and I wouldn't care because he had a cucumber in his pants. He was gutted when he had to say smaller, even though I set the bar ridiculously high.'

'So that doesn't work on girls?' Rocco asks through a relieved-sounding laugh. 'I haven't dated in a long time; I was starting to get worried.'

Well, that's interesting. He hasn't dated in a long time. Neither have I, there's nothing wrong with that, except I want to know everything about him. I can't ask him, though, because it might make me seem interested, and I'm not. I can't be.

'No, that doesn't work on girls,' I confirm, keeping the conversation on track.

'Speak for yourself,' Leila says through a snort. 'I matched with him.'

We all laugh.

'The girls weren't much better,' Rocco tells us. 'There was this one girl who was looking for someone to go to a wedding with her, which I understand, weddings aren't fun to go to alone, it's much better when you've got someone there with you, to have fun with.'

'You should have said yes,' Tobias says. 'You never know, you could have helped her out, and you might have fallen in love with her – she could've been the girl for you.'

'Except eventually I realised I was misunderstanding what she was saying,' Rocco continues. 'She wasn't looking for someone to go to a wedding with her as a plus one, she wanted a wedding – a wedding of her own – she was looking for someone to marry. Not like immediately or anything. She wasn't aiming to marry a stranger next week. But she made it crystal clear that the next person she was involved with needed to be someone she could see herself walking down the aisle with, because she didn't want to be an "old bride" – whatever that is.'

'Who said all that?' Tobias asks curiously.

'The one with the straight dark brown hair,' Rocco replies. 'She had some kind of tattoo running down her back.'

'Oh, *her*,' he replies. 'Well, she never mentioned anything like that to me, all she talked about was her dog, and how much her shoes cost. I didn't match with her. I'm not even sure I want to get married.'

'She sounds like a desperate cow anyway,' Leila slurs. 'I'm a child of divorce but I don't let it change the way I think. I want to get married – although not to someone I met at speed dating – but hopefully one day, if I meet the right person.'

'I totally agree,' I reply. 'And I don't know at what age someone becomes an "old bride" but who cares? Even if I don't meet someone I want to marry until I'm in my seventies, I'll do it when I feel like it.'

'What about you, Rocco?' Leila asks curiously. 'I'm curious to see if all guys think like Tobias.'

Rocco looks slightly awkward at the idea of either siding with Tobias or singling him out.

'Well, yeah, you're all right,' he says tactfully. 'Getting married isn't about ticking some box, or throwing a big party. It's about finding the right person and wanting to marry them because you do, not because you think you're supposed to.'

I can't help but smile. That's a great answer.

'Well, she wasn't even the worst one there,' Tobias says, steering the conversation back to speed dating. 'I heard there was one girl there who was even crazier. She was there to try and get some sperm, to have a baby. Although she didn't want me either. How desperate does a girl have to be to go for Tobias?'

As Tobias wonders out loud about his own eligibility, I am quick to reassure him.

'Oh, no, that was me,' I quickly insist. As Tobias's eyebrows shoot up, I realise what I've just said. 'Well, not actually me. Rocco and I thought it might be fun to sabotage each other's dates, so we were spreading rumours about each other, to put people off.'

Tobias laughs – almost in disbelief.

'That does sound like fun, but the whole point of the evening was to try and find someone,' Tobias points out. 'You two wasted your chances.'

'Oh, look, is that the time?' Leila says, without appearing to check the time. 'I'm thinking it's time we called it a night. Tobias, can you walk me home? I'm not far from here.'

'Yeah, sure,' he replies.

Leila looks at me. I notice the corners of her mouth turn up ever so slightly. Is she... she is. She's doing this on purpose, leaving me and Rocco alone together – she's trying to set us up.

'I should try and get myself a taxi,' I say quickly – too quickly, perhaps. 'It's a nightmare, trying to get home at this time, when it's busy, it's usually a long wait for a car, I'd better make a move.'

Like I even have enough of a social life to know if that's true or not.

'You can always stay in my hotel room again,' Rocco suggests.

This time Leila's eyebrows hit the ceiling.

'On the sofa, again, obviously,' he quickly adds. 'Just to save you trekking home, and waiting forever for a taxi.'

I want to say yes. I really, really want to say yes.

'I'd better get home,' I say instead. 'But thank you, though.'

'No worries,' he says with a smile.

We all say goodnight before Tobias and Leila head off together, Rocco walks off in the direction of his hotel, and I get in my taxi – a taxi that picks me up right away, from outside the bar. It's for the best, though. If there is one thing I can't be trusted with right now, it's being alone in a hotel room with Rocco, if there's even a chance the feelings between us might be mutual, and the taxi arriving right away takes away the opportunity for me to weaken and change my mind.

So I head home, alone, getting dropped off a few doors down from my own house, walking the final stretch of my journey on foot, so that I stand a better chance of making it inside, and up to my bedroom, without waking anyone up. I know, it's pathetic, but I feel like a kid again, one who doesn't want to be in trouble with her mummy and daddy, or to be interrogated about where I've been until this time.

I'm briefly distracted by the red-tinted light that's on in Kenny's bedroom window. Oh, that's so gross. I hope Jess isn't in there with him, but I wouldn't bet my house on her not being.

It's half three in the morning – one of those times that is neither getting home late at night nor early morning and is therefore open to interpretation.

I take my door key off my ring of keys to ensure it turns in the door silently. All the lights are off, so I imagine everyone is in bed asleep (on this side of the fence, at least), but on the off chance my dad is sitting on the sofa in the dark ready to ask me where I've been until this time, it's best I try to be as quiet as I possibly can. I can't believe that after all these years, I am worried about upsetting my dad, but here we are.

He isn't in the living room, thankfully, so I sneak up the stairs. One of the things about an old house is that random steps and floorboards creak when you walk on them, even under the thick carpet, it sounds like walking on snow if you hit the wrong board in the wrong place. I suppose, without even realising it, I've been mentally mapping them all out since the day I moved in, so I know exactly where to stand if I don't want to make a sound.

I make it up the stairs, along the hallway, and into the sanctuary of my room without making a peep. Even with the door closed behind me, the walls in this house aren't the thickest, so I continue to sneak through my dark room before shrugging off my dress and peeling back the covers to climb into bed. At first, it feels like my hand is wet, but there's absolutely no reason my bed should be wet. There's a strange smell in here too. It's only as I sink down into bed that I feel my mostly bare skin collide with someone else's body.

I scream as I jump up. I run for my bedroom door but slip on something – more of the same slippery, smelly substance I found on the bed. I land on the bedroom floor right as my mum, dad and Gail all come running in to see if I'm okay. One of them must hit the light switch.

I scramble to my feet and look back towards the bed. And there he is, naked as far as I can tell, clearly drunk, sitting up in my bed, looking annoyed that we've all woken him up. And the weird substance that appears to be all over the room? A kebab is my best guess.

'Declan, what the hell are you doing here?' I ask angrily.

'Who is Declan?' I hear Gail ask my dad as she yawns.

'Her boyfriend,' he whispers back.

'Oh, I'm going back to bed,' she tells him with a bat of her hand, as though she's above this sort of drama.

'He's not my boyfriend,' I insist, grabbing a hoodie from the nearest drawer and slipping it on. 'I haven't seen him in a year.'

'Declan, what *are* you doing here?' Mum asks him, taking a softer approach, clearly only to get answers. I wish I had her ability to stay calm.

'I'm home,' he announces, laughing wildly. I can smell the booze on his breath from here.

'Get out, right now,' I tell him. 'Of my bed, of my house. Of Kent too, ideally.'

I don't think I've ever been this angry in my life. I was angry when he left me, that's for certain, but I'm absolutely furious that he's back.

'Our house,' he tells me. 'Our bed.'

'The bed is three months old, you clown,' I point out. 'And seeing as though you didn't put a penny into this place, and have never paid the mortgage, you can forget about this being our house.'

I don't know why I'm arguing with a drunk person. Also, he's right, this is technically our house. I feel so stupid now but back when we bought the place, when we were a couple talking about marriage and babies, and even though I was the one with the deposit money, we applied for the mortgage as a couple, in joint names. It didn't occur to me to make a plan for what would happen to the house if Declan were to up and leave me one day. No one makes a plan to break up, do they? It would have been all the same if we had got married, I wouldn't have thought to make him sign a pre-nup, those things are for the mega rich, with all their assets, not me and my fixer-upper. So, yes, it is technically his house, even if he didn't put any money in, and even if he did bail on me right as all the major work started a year ago. The place can't even resemble what it looked like the last time he was here.

'I'll throw him out, don't worry,' Dad tells me.

'It's okay,' I insist. 'Let him sleep it off. I'll sleep in Jess's room.'

'Will you and Jess fit in that bed?' Mum asks.

Declan starts snoring. I want to murder him.

'Yeah, we'll be fine, it's just for tonight,' I reply. Now doesn't seem like the time to say she isn't in there, and I would never throw my sister under the bus, so I don't mention that I'm pretty sure she's next door shagging the neighbour. I can't imagine my parents appreciating that information, or Jess appreciating me telling them it.

'We'll kick him out tomorrow, when he's sober,' I tell them. 'And after he's cleaned this room.'

'Well, I'm awake now,' Mum announces. 'Cuppa tea?'

'I'd love a cuppa,' Dad replies. 'I'll need to calm down, before I can sleep again.'

'Billie?'

I'm absolutely shattered. I really need to sleep. Although Mum and Dad don't know that I've just got in, given that I'd already ditched my night out clothes before they came running in through the door.

'How come you've only just realised he's in your bed?' Mum asks curiously as we head for the hallway.

'Wait, have you just got in?' Dad asks, the pieces of the puzzle finally clicking together. 'Out all night, again?'

'It's not even four,' I protest. 'And, once again, I'm in my thirties. I'm a grown, mature woman.'

'A grown mature woman who stays out until four, a grown mature woman who is covered in garlic mayo, a grown mature woman who is so drunk she got into bed with her ex-boyfriend without knowing he was there,' Dad rants to himself as he walks off.

'Listen, while you're having all your sneaky conversations with Dad, can you ask him to lay off me, please?' I ask Mum once we're alone. 'He's, like, missed the cut-off for entry to Dad of the Year by, like, decades.'

I realise I don't sound very mature right now. And I do sound a bit drunk, but I've only been mildly tipsy all night. And why am I justifying myself? I am a grown woman.

A grown woman with her ex in her bed, though. I'll have to figure out what I'm going to do about that tomorrow.

19

I open my eyes to find Jess staring down at me, like an excitable kid on Christmas morning, or a dog letting you know that it's done a wee on the carpet while you were sleeping.

'Someone was drunk last night,' she sings as she looms over me. 'So drunk that they got in the wrong bed.'

'Well, I did wonder about how you were finding the stomach to sleep with a pig like Kenny,' I say, pushing myself up onto my elbows. 'Great to know booze is the answer.'

'Erm, Kenny isn't a pig, he's a gent,' she informs me.

'He's someone who capitalises on daddy issues,' I tell her. 'And we've got those in abundance.'

Jess just rolls her eyes.

'You trust me, don't you?' I say seriously.

'Of course I do,' she replies.

'Then stay away from him,' I insist. 'I am your sister, I love you, and I only want what's best for you. Stay away from him.'

'Okay, okay, I get it. Anyway, you know I'm talking about you, what are you doing in my bed, hmm?'

'I'm in *your* bed because I came home last night to find bloody Declan in mine,' I say.

'No!' she shrieks. 'Declan? Is he still here?'

'I'd guess so,' I reply. 'He was hammered, naked and covered in a takeaway.'

'Obviously I'm going to go in there and murder him,' she says, pulling herself to her feet. I catch her hand and pull her back down.

'That was my first thought too,' I reply. 'But I think I need to tread lightly.'

'No, you need to tread heavily, ideally on his balls,' she corrects me. 'Why would you need to tread lightly?'

'Because he was banging on about how this is his house too,' I explain. 'And it technically is. If he wanted to, he could force me to buy him out, which I can't afford to do – he didn't even put any money in, never mind hard work, and I really, really don't want to sell the place, I've just got it perfect.'

'So, it's not his house at all then, is it?'

'Not... I don't know... morally, I guess?' I reply. 'But legally speaking, we bought this house in joint names. It doesn't matter who puts what in. We own this house equally.'

'And you won't let me circle back to killing him becaaause...'

'I just need to think carefully about what the right thing to do is,' I reply with a heavy sigh. 'That's all. Anyway, I think I'll get up, I need coffee. Want one?'

'No thanks, I need sleep,' she replies. 'I haven't had much sleep.'

Grim.

Downstairs, I find my parents where they so often seem to be, together at the kitchen island, my mum preparing food and my dad, in the role of her biggest fan, gleefully eating it all. Their chatter seems to calm down as I join them, which seems a little sus.

'Why is the window open?' I ask. 'It's freezing in here.'

'Oh, because your dad still can't flip a pancake,' Mum says with a laugh. 'There's a burnt one in the bin.'

'I don't know how you do it, Katie,' he gushes. 'You'll make someone a fantastic wife one of these days.'

Oh, my God, what sort of joke is that? I look over at Mum, who gives him a smile, and a look I can't quite figure out – it's like they're communicating right in front of my face, with a secret code I can't decipher, and it's gross.

And speaking of gross, as I close the window, I notice something yucky, and it isn't the discarded pancake in the bin, it's Kenny heading to his car.

I grab a coat as I hurry outside in my slippers. I quickly do up my buttons, to hide my pyjamas, even if they are only plain light grey ones.

'Oi,' I call out, stopping Kenny in his tracks, before he can get into his black BMW.

He's dressed smart, in a suit and tie, with a long black heavy coat over the top. He must be headed to work because he has one of those laptop cases in his hands.

'Good morning,' he says brightly. 'Sleep well? I can't say I got much.'

'I'll sleep much better if you leave my sister alone,' I say sternly, cutting to the chase.

'What?' Kenny replies through a chuckle.

'I'm serious, Kenny, stay hell away from Jess,' I warn him. 'I will ruin your life.'

I'm not exactly sure how I would do that but hopefully it sounds good.

'You already low-key ruin my life,' he points out. 'You're definitely ruining my day, but I don't let it bother me, I'm sure I'll have another good night tonight.'

Kenny gives me a wink before getting into his car.

'I'm serious,' I shout. 'You'll be sorry, if you mess with me.'

Christ, Billie, less is more. With each word that I said, I swear, I sounded less intimidating by the second.

I know that Jess is a grown woman, and that this is technically none of my business, but not only is she my sister, Kenny is my neighbourhood nemesis, and if living next door to him is bad enough now, imagine what it will be like once he's broken my sister's heart. Our usual hurtful sparring over the garden fence will turn into me actually wanting to hurt him.

With Kenny speeding off back down the road, I turn my attention back to myself. I can't worry about that clown now, not when there's a whole circus inside my house. And with the star attraction still fast asleep in my bed, well, I guess it's time I go wake him up.

20

It's a nice idea in theory, making Declan clean up the mess he has made, but in reality, the thought of my bedroom – my carpet, my bed and probably my bathroom too – being covered in take-away and God knows what else at this stage... it's too much to bear.

As much as I don't want to clean up after him (or any drunk person, for that matter), I'm hoping that in doing so I'll be rein-forcing the fact that this isn't Declan's bedroom. If we set aside the fact that Declan and I own this house jointly, this still isn't Declan's bedroom, because until last night, he had never even slept in it. When we first moved in, the master bedroom was in no fit state, so we slept on a mattress in the guest room. Well, Declan did, because he didn't see the point in building up a bed for the sake of a few weeks. My first night in this house was agony. I ended up sleeping on the sofa (downstairs, alone, without blinds, which I hated) until I eventually built the bed up in the guest room myself. Declan was long gone before I even started work on the master bedroom. It's all me, through and through, in every sense. Until last night, I was the only person to have slept in it –

although I probably shouldn't be broadcasting that tragic fact too loudly.

When I walked in here, not too long ago, the only signs of Declan were the remnants of his takeaway, his discarded sweaty-smelling clothes, and the stale smell of booze in the air. Declan himself was already in the shower, so I set about scrubbing the carpet, stripping the bed, and generally cleaning up to try to rid the room of the spirit (or person who had drunk too many spirits, at least) that has been possessing it. First I'm going to get rid of his mess, then I'm going to get rid of him.

As I turn on the electric diffuser, pumping sandalwood into the room in an attempt to get rid of the smell of stale booze and unfinished takeaway, Declan emerges from the bathroom with a towel around his waist. His dark hair, which is just past his shoulders now, is dripping water all over the carpet. I'd tell him to put a towel around it if I weren't worried he would take the one from around his body to do so. From what I can see of his body, it's changed quite drastically. He's lost weight, not that he needed to, and not in a way that looks good. He's skinny, his bony frame almost poking out from under his pale skin, in a way that just makes him look like he hasn't been taking proper care of himself. Not in an unhealthy way or anything, he looks well enough, just sort of scruffy and uncared for.

'Good morning, Billie,' he says brightly.

I wonder if he's been drinking a lot recently because if I got as drunk as he did last night, I would be on my arse today, not emerging cheerily from the shower.

'What the hell are you doing here?' I ask him, cutting to the chase.

'I'm home,' he replies – which is what he said last night but I was hoping that was just drunken garbage. Today he sounds like he means it.

'This isn't your home,' I tell him. 'You left, remember? You didn't want this life.'

'Well, I also don't want to be homeless over Christmas,' he says, pulling a face, a sort of amused grimace, as if to say 'uh-oh'.

'Not my problem,' I point out. 'You chose to leave.'

'Well, now I'm choosing to come back,' he points out with a smile. 'Thanks for cleaning up my bedroom for me.'

'Oh, fuck off,' I can't help but blurt.

'Look, my cheeky, irresistible charm aside, I do remember considering last night that you might not want to share a bed with me, but all the other rooms seemed like they had people in them, and this one was empty, so I got in. I thought you might be in the room we used to sleep in. This one is great, though, I love what you've done with it.'

I don't thank him.

'My parents and Jess are staying here,' I say. 'So all the rooms are spoken for. There's a sofa bed in the office. When Jess is awake, I'll move her out of there, you can put your things and yourself in there, while you work out where you're going to go, because you are not staying here.'

'Well, that's a start,' he replies. 'The office is where we christened the house, do you remember?'

'I don't remember at all,' I reply, which is obviously a lie, but I'm not going to give him the satisfaction. 'I thought it was on the stairs, and that's how we broke the banister, and...'

Declan stares at me blankly.

'Oh, sorry, awkward, that must have been someone else,' I say, which is also a lie.

Declan just laughs, which really winds me up.

'The office it is – for now,' he says. 'We'll see how long you can resist me.'

I look away just in time, as Declan goes to remove his towel. I grab my cleaning products and head back downstairs. I'll do the bathroom later, when Declan is somewhere else. I can shove him in the office for now – just like I did with most of our bags and boxes when we first moved in, while I figured out what to do with them. But there is no way in hell he's going to be here on Christmas Day, not a chance. This house is already at capacity and even if it weren't, he wouldn't be welcome.

I'll let him get his pants on, get his things together, but then he's getting the hell out of here.

I don't know what I've done this year, to secure myself the top spot on Santa Claus's naughty list, but it definitely feels like I'm being punished for something. This house, right now, is like my own personal hell, and after treating it as my sanctuary for the past year, I could panic about my situation. Except I'm not, and I think it's because of Rocco, because I have him to escape to.

Things will be better, once I've got rid of Declan, but I'm starting to get the feeling this ex-orcism is going to take more than diffusing a bit of sandalwood and me asking him nicely to leave, don't you?

21

If you had told me a few weeks ago that I would be sitting down for lunch with my mum, Jess, *my dad* and *bloody Declan*, there's no way in hell I would have believed you. And yet here we are. Mum has made sandwiches, we're all sitting down at the table, it's all awfully civilised, and yet somehow this has to be the most barbaric moment of the holidays yet.

'So, how long have you been back together?' Declan asks my parents. 'That's great news, isn't it?'

Declan gives me a nudge and a smile.

'Oh, we're not back together,' Mum tells him. 'Rowan has actually remarried; his wife is here for Christmas too.'

'Wow, really?' Declan replies through a mouthful of crisps. 'Because I'm getting a serious vibe off the two of you.'

He isn't the only one. Jess and I shoot each other a look.

'I think we've just learned how to be mature, and how to coexist together,' Mum offers.

'We're getting on really well again,' Dad tells him. 'I'm over the moon about it – we all are.'

I notice Jess take her phone from her pocket and tap the

screen a few times before I feel my own phone vibrate in my pocket.

This is weird.

She's not wrong. I type a reply.

Too weird. We should try and talk to them today, try and figure out where their heads are at, and what is going on.

As I wait for Jess's reply to come through, I watch my parents making small talk with my ex.

Definitely. You take Dad, I'll take Mum. And we need to get rid of Declan, this is beyond awkward. He's the last thing we need.

I am distracted from texting Jess when I hear what my mum is saying to Declan.

'Oh, no, Declan, no one should be alone at Christmas,' she replies.

'It's worse than being alone, I'm actually sort of homeless,' he replies.

I shoot him a look. The scumbag is playing my mum for sympathy, and my mum is too nice to resist it.

'Well, I'm sure you can spend Christmas here,' Mum says. 'Until you sort a roof over your head – although this is Billie's house, so only if she's okay with it?'

I appreciate her back-pedalling, but I can't exactly say no now, can I?

'Declan, can I talk to you in the utility room for a moment?' I say.

He follows me.

'Right, cut that out, you can't get around me by tugging on my mum's heartstrings,' I tell him.

'It's not that, Billie, I really am homeless,' he replies. 'I can move in with my folks, when they're back from their holidays, but until then, I'm screwed. Please let me stay here?'

'What, and then you'll just go?' I say. 'Simple as that?'

'If you let me spend Christmas here, yes, I'll go, I'll get out of your hair, I'll leave you in peace again,' he insists.

He seems genuine but he also told me he loved me a bunch of times over the years, so you never really know, do you? Of course, considering this for a second reminds me that I did love him once, or at least I thought I did. If I believe anything it's that he is probably homeless for Christmas. I'm not sure I could leave anyone in that position (and it's not like I don't already have a house full of unwanted guests) so, even if he is a scumbag, I'm not. I'm not as heartless as he is.

'Promise?' I reply.

'I promise,' he says.

Again, he seems sincere, but he did also tell me multiple times that we would be together forever and look how that turned out.

'Okay, fine, so long as you mean it,' I eventually say, 'but only because you're desperate, and I feel sorry for you. That's it.'

'Billie, you're an angel, thank you,' he says, kissing me on the cheek.

'You won't regret this.'

God, I really hope I don't.

22

While I am gutted that today's Mingle All the Way event has been cancelled (it was at an indoor climbing wall place, which has had to close for technical reasons, and thank God because can you imagine me on a climbing wall? I've been known to fall simply running up the stairs), today is the one day I do need to be at home, whether I want to be or not.

Rocco seemed gutted the event was cancelled too. There was talk about maybe trying to arrange a dinner with Leila and Tobias – well, we feel like we owe them something, even if they don't know it – but after Jess and I tried to speak to our parents earlier, we have decided that there is no time like the present to take action.

As the two of us reconvened, after she spoke to Mum, and I spoke to Dad, Jess's conclusion was that Mum was hiding something, and clearly had an extra spring in her step. With Dad, well, all he seemed to talk about was Mum, how well she was doing, how great she looked. I felt like he was getting at something, but I couldn't quite put my finger on it. Either way, something is going on, and with Gail away working again, tonight seemed like the night to act.

You know that scene in *The Parent Trap*, where Annie and Hallie recreate the romantic scene from the night when their parents met, to try to convince them to get back together? Well, tonight Jess and I are going to be, I suppose, reverse Parent Trapping our parents. So, instead of recreating a memorable romantic night, we will be doing the opposite, recreating a bad memory, a night that Jess and I remember being the beginning of the end of our parents' relationship.

Mum and Dad used to throw dinner parties for their friends, with everyone taking it in turns to visit each couple's house, where they would eat, drink and play games. If you were hosting you obviously wouldn't need a babysitter, for what they all called the Saturday Night Club, and that's when Jess and I loved to sneak out of our beds, sit on the stairs, and listen to their conversations.

There are three things Jess and I remember about the Saturday Night Club. The first is that they would drink wine, and lots of it. The second thing is that curry would always be on the menu for the evening. And, finally, the main source of entertainment would come from playing boardgames together.

Given that everyone was in a couple, these games would usually be ones that you played in pairs – even for games like Trivial Pursuit, they would play in their couples. But the night we're recreating, the night they all fell out, the night that signified that beginning of the end for my parents, was the night they played A Matter of Morals, a boardgame from the eighties that my dad had found while clearing out his parents' house and then decided they should all play together, with the whole evening turning out to be a sort of un-PC take on *Jumanji*, and the jungle very much did come to them, because things got wild.

The idea with A Matter of Morals is to read out all these different dilemmas from cards, and not only to answer what you would do in each scenario, but to guess what other people would do too. Naturally, the game always winds up turning into a huge debate on who would do what, and everyone judging everyone else for their different choices.

So, that's what we're going to do tonight, we've both invited Mum and Dad to have dinner with us (saying we'll cook, although we're definitely going to be getting the curries delivered) and we're all going to sit down and play A Matter of Morals together, and as the wine flows and we each answer questions, I'm hoping that the old memories will come flooding back, and Mum and Dad will realise just how awful things were, how wrong they are for each other, and that they should never, ever get back together under any circumstances.

Luckily, when I was helping Mum clear out her house, I happened upon the box of boardgames and I asked if I could bring them to my house, in case we wanted to play one together over Christmas, or for me to play with my friends when they're back from their skiing holiday.

Anyway, in the big box, sure enough, is *the* copy of A Matter of Morals, the one from the night in question. Unfortunately, as Jess and I were going through the cards, rigging the deck so that the questions that came out would be ones that set Mum and Dad at odds, we realised that a lot of them are not only on controversial topics, but they're very much stuck in the seventies, with seriously backward ideas, and some truly despicable questions. By the time we removed all the problematic cards, the deck was significantly shorter, but we've got everything we need, to recreate that night.

'Wow, something smells nice,' Mum says as she enters the room.

Jess is just putting the finishing touches on the table, while I am plating up the last of the food ready to serve.

'You girls have been so vague about dinner tonight, telling me to stay upstairs until it was ready – what are you up to?'

'I was just going to say the same thing,' Dad asks as he appears next to her, right on time. 'Katie, wow, you look amazing.'

We told them both to dress up for dinner – not to make them look as attractive as possible to one another, which seems to be working in my mum's case unfortunately, but to accurately recreate the Saturday Night Club, when everyone would come over dressed in their best. Even Jess and I have made an effort, to try to make this evening as legitimate as possible.

'We thought it would be nice for us all to have dinner together,' Jess says. She's lying but, wow, she's really selling it.

'And then we thought we could play some games together,' I add. 'Maybe open a few bottles of wine, really get into the festive spirit.'

I do feel slightly bad, because both Mum and Dad seem to be delighted at the idea of us all sitting down together, like we're one big happy family.

'The food smells amazing, girls,' Dad says as he approaches the table. 'What are we having?'

With the food served up and the wine flowing, Jess and I join in with the small talk, going through the motions of eating dinner, until it's time to play the game.

It might actually, dare I say it, be sort of nice, were it not for the fact that we simply cannot allow Mum and Dad to get close again, and just having the plan hanging in the balance is making me feel nervous, like I'm standing in the wings, waiting to go up on stage and give a speech. I laugh to myself, when I remember what Jess said to me earlier, about how the best way to tackle not feeling confident in front of people is to imagine them naked, because she clearly didn't properly consider the fact that, with the people in question being my parents, that is a far from ideal solution.

With dinner all done, and at least a couple of glasses of wine in each of us, it's time to pull the pin out of the grenade.

'We were looking through the old games, from when we emptied the house last night, and we found this one,' I say as I set A Matter of Morals down on the table in front of us. 'And we remembered that you never used to let us play it as kids, so we'd love to give it a go now that we're grown-ups.'

I do see the irony in me describing Jess and myself as grown-ups when we're clearly playing a very immature game tonight – a game inspired by a movie we watched when we were kids, no less.

'Oh, I'm not sure that's appropriate,' Mum says, her eyes wide with horror simply laying eyes on the box. The sight of it alone is enough to freak her out. 'This game was famous for ending marriages, back in the day.'

'Good thing none of us are married to each other then,' I point out with a smile.

'Don't worry, we were looking through it earlier, and we took out the dodgy questions,' Jess says. 'Your generation is messed up, by the way.'

'Yeah, the really offensive cards are all out – although lots of them are still quite dated. I guess, when it comes to the questions that mention things like fax machines, we'll just substitute things for a modern equivalent. What do you say?'

'I suppose it could be fun,' Dad says, looking over at Mum. 'It might be good, playing it with the girls, if all the controversial questions are removed. Are you sure there are any cards left?'

'There are,' I say confidently.

The idea is that question one will set them on their way to having clearly very different opinions, Jess and I will have an easy one, to usher us swiftly through our turn, but then the next question for my mum and dad will be the one that implodes the evening, so much so we didn't even bother setting up any more questions after that one, it will most definitely be game over after that.

'Okay, go on then,' Mum says. 'What teams are we going to be on?'

'Billie and I thought we might be on the same team,' Jess says quickly. 'So long as you and Dad don't mind teaming up?'

'Not at all,' Dad says. 'It will be just like old times.'

Hopefully this will be the last time.

'Okay, let's do it,' I say with a nervous excitement.

I set the game up, handing out the little notebooks and pencils that come with it, so we can each write our answers down. I can't help but notice, on my notebook, the imprint of what was previously written, the last time the game was played. As best I can tell, it says 'fake my own death', which is genuinely terrifying. I wonder what was on the card, to make someone say that.

'You guys can go first,' I instruct. 'Dad, why don't you read one for Mum?'

'All right, then,' he says as he draws a card. 'A woman's place is in the kitchen – agree or disagree?'

It's a gentle-ish one to get them started, but Dad always had really traditional ideas about gender roles, whereas Mum is (rightly) the type to think that a woman can do anything that a man can if she wants to, and vice versa. I remember the two of them having a huge argument when we were younger, because Jess wanted to join a football team – one that was only for boys (obviously there wasn't a girls' one, it was the nineties) – but Dad didn't think they should even mention it to the boys' coach, because the team was only for boys and that was that.

Mum jots her answer down on her notebook. Dad writes down what he thinks Mum will say.

'Okay, what are your answers?' I prompt.

'Well, obviously that's a load of rubbish,' Mum says. 'I spend time in the kitchen because I want to, not because I have to. A woman's place is wherever she wants to be.'

'And, Dad, what did you put?' Jess asks.

'Exactly what your mum said,' he replies. 'Your mum has always been a firm believer that you girls could do whatever you wanted.'

'Okay, but what do *you* think?' I ask him, which is the point of the game, but it's also the first step in reminding my mum and dad why they are so wrong for each other.

'Obviously it's in my interest for your mum to be in the kitchen as much as possible, because I do love her cooking,' he jokes. 'But your mum has clearly always been right. Look at the two of you, growing up, doing what you want in life, making your- selves happy. Billie, this house is amazing, and to have done it all yourself just goes to show that women and men *are* equal.'

I narrow my eyes at him. How can I be so mad at him for giving such a good answer? I suppose because that question wasn't the slam-dunk we thought it was going to be.

'Okay, my turn to read one for Billie,' Jess says, moving on. 'You find £1,000 in an envelope in the street. Do you keep it?'

I write down my answer. Jess writes down what she thinks I will say.

'Obviously I wouldn't keep it,' I eventually say. 'I would hand it in to the police.'

'That's what I though you would say,' Jess confirms. 'And that's what I would do too.'

Mum laughs.

'This game wasn't so plain sailing when we used to play it with our friends,' she says through a chuckle.

'You've got that right,' Dad replies, widening his eyes for effect.

'Mum, you're up, read a card for Dad,' I prompt her.

I feel a lump in my throat as I swallow hard. This is the one. The question that's going to solve everything. The game over that we need.

'Okay, here we go,' she starts. 'So... would you remain friends with someone who swapped their partner of many years for someone younger, because they no longer found their partner attractive?'

I don't know why, when we were planning this, having Mum read that question didn't feel as harsh as it does, hearing her read it out loud. Was this a mistake?

She raises her eyebrows at Dad.

'Go on, then, write something down,' she instructs him. She takes her pencil and begins writing straight away, clearly knowing exactly what she's going to say from the get-go. Jess and I exchange a look, while we wait for them to finish.

'Okay,' Jess says. 'Dad?'

'Well, I suppose I would,' Dad says sheepishly. 'Because I would be a hypocrite if I didn't, seeing as I left your mum for someone else.'

My breath catches in my throat. That might be the first time I've heard him say it out loud. I wasn't expecting that at all, neither was Jess.

'And that's what I wrote,' Mum says simply. Then she turns back to Dad. 'And how did that work out for you?'

Right, this is it, it's going to kick off. I brace myself because, even though this is what we wanted to happen, it's still not going to be pleasant to witness.

'It was definitely a mistake,' Dad says seriously, but then his face moves into more of a smile. 'And ironically, somehow, now, you look even younger than you did back then. You look phenomenal, Katie. The last laugh is definitely yours.'

'I think you'll find that's karma,' Mum says through a smile. 'But I'll take "phenomenal" – thank you. You actually don't look so bad either.'

'Give over,' Dad says, blushing slightly.

And just like that, the tension is not only dispelled but Mum and Dad seem to be low-key flirting again. No! That is not what is supposed to happen.

'Your turn,' Dad tells us through a smile as he tops up his wine. 'Wow, this is fun.'

I glance over at Jess. She's cringing. This is not how this was supposed to go.

Unsure what else to do, I pick up a card and read a question to her.

'Would you sleep with someone who your friend or relative warned you against?'

Oh, wow, that's topical.

'Well...' Jess says, holding onto the word, grimacing awkwardly. 'I am sort of dating your neighbour, the one that you hate.'

'Oh, Kenny seems lovely, though,' Mum says, so I take it she already knew about the two of them. 'Do you really hate him, Billie?'

'I do, but wait, you're not actually seeing him again, are you?' I say. 'You said you wouldn't – I warned you off him.'

'Jess, your sister must have good reason,' Dad chimes in. 'You should listen to her, if she knows the bloke is no good.'

'Oh, God, don't you start,' Jess warns him, before turning back to me. 'Obviously I only said that to shut you up. Sorry, sis, but I do really like him.'

'Jess, are you serious?' I say. 'He's not a good guy – just go upstairs and ask Declan, if you don't believe me.'

'Oh, yeah, because Declan is greeeeat, I can totally trust every word that he says,' she replies sarcastically. 'You know what, I think family game night is over. I'm going next door to see Kenny, because – as we all agreed tonight – a woman can do whatever she wants, and whoever she wants, and I make my own decisions. Thank you.'

Jess gets up from the table and walks away.

'I, erm, I think I'm going to go lie down,' I tell Mum and Dad.

'Of course, don't worry, we can clean up,' Mum reassures me.

'And your sister will somehow come to her senses,' Dad chimes in. 'She doesn't have your head on her shoulders, you know how the world is, but she'll work things out for herself sooner or later.'

'Aw, Rowan, that's a lovely thing to say about Billie,' Mum tells him through a smile as she reaches out to squeeze his shoulder.

I head upstairs with my tail between my legs. Not just because the game backfired, and because I've just driven Jess further into Kenny's arms, but because the whole point of this game was to show Mum and Dad how wrong they are together and to drive them further apart.

Somehow, I feel like I've only pushed them further together too. And there's me thinking I was good at creating romance-free zones. Well, I've been doing an excellent job for myself, at least.

Would it be the worst thing in the world if my parents got back together? Yes. Yes, it would. I'm just going to have to come up with something else. But what? I have no idea.

23

I would say you can't beat a bath for trying to de-stress yourself, except my long soak is finally going to have to come to an end, because someone in this house is playing music far too loudly. I can hear the humming through the bathroom door.

I grab my towel and dry off my hair lightly with it, before wrapping it around my body, pulling out the plug, and heading back into the bedroom.

It's only once I'm standing in the en suite doorway, looking into my bedroom, that I realise where the music is coming from. It's coming from inside my room – a room that doesn't look like it did when I closed the door to have my bath, that's for sure.

In a room filled with lit candles and rose petals scattered everywhere, I see Declan lying on the bed, in a pair of black boxer shorts that have seen better days, a pair of odd socks and nothing else apart from a smile. When I enter the room, he cranks up the volume on Another Level's 'Freak Me' – oh, my God, he's trying to seduce me.

'Declan, what are you doing?' I ask him. 'Turn that down.'

'I'm trying to recreate the magic from the first time we had sex,' he tells me.

'Well, you might have considered recreating the alleged magic from the first time you had sex with me,' I point out. 'Candles and Another Level weren't what I got, I got four minutes – that felt like two minutes – after we got in from a night out. And then I watched TV while you snored next to me.'

All true, sadly.

'Turn it down,' I say again, purposefully lowering my voice, so that Declan will have to turn the music down, if he wants to talk.

'Come on, you know you fancy a bit of rumpy pumpy,' he says, thankfully reducing the music slightly, although I would rather not have heard what he just said.

'Hard as it is to resist a man who calls it "rumpy pumpy",' I start sarcastically, 'given the fact that my parents are on the other side of those walls, did you really think I would have gone for this, even if I wanted to?'

'You didn't mind that night in Manchester,' he starts.

'Once again, not me,' I point out.

I really hope none of these mix-ups are from people he slept with behind my back while we were together but, also, I genuinely don't care any more.

'Billie, I've missed you,' he tells me, changing course. 'Leaving you was a mistake. Let me show you just how much I've missed you, and how much I've missed our life together.'

Declan approaches me with puckered lips.

'You've missed having someone pay for everything, so you don't have to work,' I point out. 'You're here because you have nowhere else to go.'

I, unsurprisingly, don't allow Declan to kiss me. Instead, I grab him and frogmarch him to the bedroom door. I'm about to throw him – and his corny, horny music – out when I notice Gail, down the hallway, arriving back from her work thing earlier than I was expecting. She stares at us, so I quickly pull Declan back into the bedroom. I'm grateful for small mercies – at least he had underwear on.

'Listen, go to your room, this isn't going to happen,' I tell him. 'You're here for Christmas and that's it.'

I open the door again. No sign of Gail, so I gesture for Declan to leave.

'We'll see,' he says through a grin.

I close my door behind me. It never occurred to me to put locks on the bedroom doors because I never realised I'd be running a Christmas B&B for so many people so clearly unable to keep it in their pants for a bloody week.

I sigh as I lean back on the door. Fantastic, now I need to blow out all these candles, which is going to make the room absolutely stink, I'm so tired, there are rose petals everywhere – and the fact that he didn't do things like this when we were together makes it all the more annoying.

I am slightly concerned about the look in his eye, when he practically threatened 'we'll see' as he left the room. It makes me worry he might have more tricks up his sleeve. If we can just get through Christmas, and Declan signs the house back over to me, then hopefully all of this will be over. There is a limit to what I'm willing to do to get him out of the house, though, and it absolutely does not involve rose petals and 'Freak Me' while my parents are in the next rooms. Here's hoping he backs down – or God knows what it's going to take to get rid of him.

24

The best thing about the mornings is that, with each one that comes, this whole mess is a day closer to being over.

I open my eyes to see Jess lying in bed next to me.

'Jess, are you awake?' I ask.

'Just about,' she replies through closed eyes.

'I didn't even hear you come in last night,' I tell her. 'I must have been out like a light.'

Thank God it was Jess who got in bed with me and not Declan – although I like to think I would have noticed him being in my bed, although historically he never did make much of an impact when he was.

'I know you're in my bad books, but did you really think rose petals were going to win me over?' she asks through a laugh.

'Oh, they're not for you, don't worry,' I reply. 'Declan put the moves on me last night.'

'Do I need to jump out of this bed screaming?' she asks.

'No, you're okay,' I reply. 'Hopefully he's got the message that I'm not interested but somehow, I doubt it. I am sorry, though. Last night super backfired.'

'I'm sorry too,' Jess replies. 'You've got to laugh at how it blew up in our faces, though, haven't you?'

'You do,' I reply. 'Although Mum and Dad seemed to be getting on better than ever when I came up to bed.'

'You left them unattended?' she replies, rolling onto her side to face me.

'Gail got back from her work thing last night, so they weren't alone for long,' I reply. 'They're not horny teenagers that we need to keep separate – even if it feels like they are. I think we might need to just accept that things are what they are, and let them make their own mistakes.'

'I don't know, parents, who'd have them?' Jess jokes.

'Sharing a room together like this reminds me of old times, when we shared a room together growing up – even after Mum gave us separate rooms, we would still go in each other's rooms and chat like this,' I remind her.

'I know, it's kind of nice,' she replies as she closes her eyes again. 'Oh, by the way, not to ruin a beautiful moment, but I figured you need to make it up to me after last night, so I've invited Kenny to have Christmas dinner with us. I hope you don't mind.'

'Of course I mind,' I reply. 'I hate the guy.'

'Well, I like him,' she says firmly, as though I have no say in the matter.

I don't have the energy for a fight right now. I also don't think I'd win, regardless.

Well, there's already going to be enough people at the Christmas dinner table who I don't like, will one more really make a difference? Probably, but I'll figure out how to deal with this one later.

25

There's nothing like spending time away from someone to make you realise how much you like being around them. I don't know if it's because I had the day from hell yesterday, or if it's because the feelings I'm developing for Rocco are much stronger than I'm daring to admit, but absence really does make the heart grow fonder.

Either way, as Rocco pulls up to pick me up in his car, I can't contain my excitement.

'Good afternoon,' I say brightly as I climb in and put my seat-belt on.

'Hello, stranger,' he replies. 'Someone is excited for where we're going today. And you're looking great – again.'

'I really am excited,' I reply. I don't mention that it's because I've missed him. Inspired by the response to my last attempt at a sexier look, today I've opted for another sexy-ish dress – a black one that is lower and also higher (in different parts, obviously) than anything he's seen me in before. I know, I know, I said that sex with Rocco was the last thing on my mind, I don't know why

I'm trying to edge myself in that direction when I know it's really not a good idea.

'Me too,' he says. 'I've been looking forward to this one for a while.'

A quick glance over the event attendees earlier confirmed that it's a completely different crowd, none of the usual suspects apart from me and Rocco. Perhaps the idea of an Eiffel Tower party doesn't appeal – well, it makes sense that a French-themed gathering might sound a bit boring, when your usual idea of fun is boozy bingo and disco bowling.

Oh, it's at a house, I wasn't expecting that. A detached property behind a big wooden gate. I wish I'd known it was a party someone was throwing at their home; I would have picked up a bottle of wine or something.

The electric gate opens for us. Ooh, we must be somewhere fancy. Now I really am excited. It will be nice to do something classy – not that I think I'm classy, but it's nice to pretend, isn't it?

'Right, let's do this,' I say excitedly.

'After you,' Rocco replies.

I head up the pathway, to the front door, before knocking the large golden pineapple doorknocker. There's a sign on the wall that says Pampas House, what a beautiful name.

'Hello, hello,' a woman in a silky red wraparound dress says as she greets us. She has a half-empty glass of champagne in one hand, extended out by her side. Her eyes light up at the sight of new guests. 'Are you from the app?'

'We are,' Rocco replies.

'Fabulous,' she says. 'We're always keen to make younger friends.'

I'd guess the woman is in her forties. She looks great with her hair tied up in a bun on the back of her head. Classy is, again, the word that springs to mind.

'Come through to the kitchen, let's get you some drinks,' she insists. 'I'm Lu, my husband is Nigel, if I can grab him while he isn't busy, I'll introduce you properly.'

The kitchen is huge, but there isn't a soul in there apart from us.

'Champagne?' Lu asks us.

'Yes, please,' I reply.

'I'm driving,' Rocco tells her. 'Anything soft.'

'You won't find anything soft in this house,' Lu practically cackles. 'Here, have a champers. You'll just have to stay a while, and work it off before you drive. We'll be putting out the food later too. Back in a mo, need to grab another bottle.'

God, work it off? Nothing will ruin a party like my dancing. I can clear a room.

'No worries,' I reply.

I'm sure, if we stay a while and have something to eat, that Rocco will be fine with one glass, he's a big guy. I never had him down as a dancer at parties, though. I wonder what makes Lu thinks he's the type.

'Are you much of a mover?' I ask him.

'I can be when I get going,' Rocco replies. 'Ironically, the drink helps, so I should level out in the middle.'

'Right, here we go,' Lu says. She hands me a glass. 'So, head down the hallway, everyone is scattered around the rooms, feel free to go where you please. And I will see you both later. Just waiting on a few more guests.'

'Okay, brilliant,' I reply.

Now that we're out of the car, I can see Rocco's outfit. He's always such a sharp dresser (even when he's shirtless and wearing his coat, he looks great, although we all know why I think that) and today is no exception. I feel like he's put the extra effort in too, in a pair of black trousers and crisp white shirt. I don't know what his aftershave is, but it always leaves me feeling a little drunk. It isn't strong at all, but it smells delicious. I get these little bursts of it when I'm around him and it never quite seems to wear off, whereas my own perfume always seems to have evaporated into thin air before I've even left the house.

'This is a gorgeous house,' Rocco says as we head back into the hallway. 'It's got so many of its original features. I love how true to its origins they've kept the décor.'

'It's beautiful,' I echo. 'I think th— ow!'

I, being my clumsy self, clip my legs on one of the suitcases lined up in the hallway.

'Are you okay?' Rocco asks.

'I'm fine,' I reply. 'Just always looking for new and interesting ways to embarrass myself.'

I think a nice, civilised party will be the perfect way to take my mind off getting my hands on Rocco. Just drinking lovely drinks, eating good food and mixing with interesting people. No taking clothes off, no getting up close and personal for any sports, and not being at an event designed to match people up has to help. If that doesn't do the trick, I'm sure my generally clumsy demeanour and the ease with which I embarrass myself will work in my favour. Either way, I think sex is going to be the furthest things from our minds tonight.

As I regain my composure, after tripping and almost majorly embarrassing myself, I can't help but glance into the open doorway next to me. My eye is caught by a man in a pig mask sitting on a sofa. A woman in a pair of bunny ears is kneeling on the floor in front of him and she's... she's... No! You know that scene in *The Shining*, with the two people in the room, one in a tux and the other in some sort of dog costume? What the hell is in this champagne? I've got to be seeing things.

I quickly carry on walking. Rocco had to have seen that too, right? He didn't say anything, though.

I'm hesitant to walk past another doorway but I'm being silly. There's lots of chatter coming from this room, this must be where the real party is.

Rocco and I hover in the doorway. There are a group of people, dispersed around the room, on various bits of furniture. Pretty much everyone is naked, or at least down to their underwear. In the middle of the room, two completely naked men stand opposite each other. It baffles me that they're having a casual chat and a laugh with each other, given that there's a naked woman bent over between them. You would think seeing something so shocking would cause me to spring to action – fight or flight, right? – but it doesn't. it stuns me into a silent stillness for a few seconds. Oh, my God, it's going to look like I'm watching. I quickly look to Rocco. His face doesn't give anything away. He knew we were coming here today, right? My attendance is a last-minute, misguided push of a button that made me RSVP to everything in the calendar, but is this what Rocco is into?

He opens his mouth to say something, but I don't give him chance to get his words out – mostly because (even though I don't know what he's going to say) I have no idea how I'll reply.

'I'm just going to find the loo,' I tell him, making an excuse to leave the room.

'I'll come with you,' he replies.

Oh, my God, it's starting.

The next room, a living room, has more of a relaxed vibe. Relaxed in that the people seem relaxed, at least. I'm anything but relaxed. I am a firm believer in each to their own. Personally, I can only handle sexually underwhelming one person at a time, but I think the biggest shock of all is that I just was not expecting this to be the kind of party I was attending.

It's dressing gowns or less in this room. Actually, now that I think about it, I think Lu might have been wearing a silk robe, and not a wraparound dress. Oh, God, and all that stuff she was saying about Rocco burning off his alcohol, and what did I ask him? If he was a mover or something like that? I obviously meant dancing – why didn't I say dancing? Oh, and then there's my attempt to dress a little sexier than I usually do, which was just me making an effort for a change, but now it's going to seem like I'm dressing for whatever this is. I seem like I'm in my sex attire. Rocco is going to think I want to participate!

'New blood,' a large man in pair of black silk boxers announces as we walk into the room. 'I'm Nigel. Who have we got here?'

'I'm Anita,' I lie.

'John,' Rocco adds.

Wait, is this what you're supposed to do? Now he really will think I'm participating.

Nigel offers me his right hand to shake. Just before it reaches me, he examines his palm and quickly swaps hands. I hold up my drink in one hand and my bag in another, as if to say my hands are tied, but not like the woman I saw in the second room.

'Where's your loo, please?' I ask him.

'Just upstairs, on the left,' he replies.

'Great, back in a sex,' I reply. No, wait. '*Sec*. Back in a *sec*.'

'You can go in there alone together because you're new, but typically we all do this stuff as a group,' he calls after us. 'You can shag in private at home.'

A few people laugh. My God, who even are these people? I don't recognise anyone from any of the other events. I guess it's a different crowd, who come to these sorts of things.

I glance back and see that Rocco is following me. By the time I get to the bathroom, he moves closer.

'Can I come in with you?' he asks. 'Just for a moment.'

'Erm, okay,' I reply – because what else do I say?

Once the bathroom door is closed behind us, we both wind up speaking at the exact same time.

'I didn't know this was what this is,' I blurt.

'I'm not a swinger,' Rocco insists.

We both laugh. Okay, so it seems like we both might actually be on the same page. Still, I need to make things crystal clear.

'I need to be honest with you,' I start. I take a deep breath. 'I had no idea where we were going today, I've had no idea what I was doing on any day. Basically, I couldn't stand the idea of spending every second of Christmas around my over-extended family, so I lied about having all these plans, but my friends are all on holiday, so I had to pull *something* out of the bag. I hit the button on Matcher, the "feeling brave" one that RSVP'd yes to all the events. There weren't that many, but I never thought any of them would be sex parties.'

Rocco laughs but he can't hide his genuine relief.

'I did exactly the same thing,' he admits. 'I hit the button too. The only difference is that I was hoping to spend time with my family but they're all too busy. I've been at a loose end, in that hotel on my own, it felt like a good way to meet people.'

Rocco looks as relieved as I feel to be telling me this.

'See, I just thought this was your scene,' I tell him. I'm smiling really widely considering I'm hiding in the bathroom at a swingers' party.

'And I thought *you* wanted to be here,' he replies. 'My red flag went up when you didn't bat an eye at the man in the pig mask.'

I just laugh and shake my head.

'Honestly, I had no idea what was going on,' I confess. 'Why do they call it an Eiffel Tower party? What's an Eiffel Tower in this context?'

'You know the thing we saw in the second room?' Rocco replies.

'Yeah...'

'That.'

'Oh. Wow, I've lived such a sheltered life,' I admit. 'But I think we can both agree that we should probably get out of here?'

'We really should,' he replies. 'I know this is weird, because we're standing either side of a toilet at a sex party, but while we're getting it all out there, so to speak, I was wondering... would you like to have dinner with me? I know we've got the bar opening with Leila and Tobias tonight – so relieved they aren't here right now, by the way, but perhaps tomorrow night?'

I wasn't expecting him to say that – here or otherwise.

'Just us?' I ask.

'We can order enough food for multiple people but, yes, I'm thinking just the two of us,' he says with a smile. 'I think now that we know we're in the same boat, we're probably fine to hang out like normal friends, no app events required.'

'Normal friends,' I repeat back to him.

'Oh, not that I'm saying this isn't normal,' he quickly adds. 'I mean normal friends, not Matcher event buddies.'

It's not that I think he's judging the swingers, more that he seems to be firmly assigning me to the friendzone, but that's okay.

'I'd like that very much,' I reply.

'Tomorrow night?' he says. 'I'll book somewhere. The day after tomorrow is Christmas Eve, so it might be our last chance before Christmas.'

'Tomorrow works for me,' I say. God, it's weird to be making dinner plans in a bathroom at a swingers' party. Weird but great.

'Now, how do we get out of here?' I ask.

'You can get downstairs without going near the living room

where Nigel is, and the front door is closer than the kitchen, we can just leave, run for the car, make a break for it?'

'Sounds fun,' I reply. 'I wish I'd told you what was going on with me sooner.'

'Me too,' he replies. 'But I have had more fun than I expected to at these events – this one excluded – and now the fun can really start.'

'I can't wait,' I reply.

Things might be a mess at home, but suddenly it feels like things might be going right for me. I'll worry about everything else tomorrow.

26

With everything that's been going on these past few days, it's reminded me of something: you can't beat just a regular old night out, sitting in a bar, having a drink and talking. No gimmicks, no way to get myself in trouble, nothing to be bad at. Simply a normal night out with friends.

Well, I say normal, but there's nothing normal about this situation, and calling this lot my friends may not be exactly the right term, given that I didn't even know them over a week ago, but it feels like it's been so much longer. From Sconegate to our speed dates – not to mention our brief love square kind of thing – it feels like we've been through so much together.

This evening we're at the opening of the Candy Club, a new bar in town. Everywhere I've been this month – and I mean everywhere, even the dentist – has been thoroughly festive. From the decorations to the Christmas cheer, it's been all around me. Until tonight, that is.

With this being the Candy Club's opening night, keen to establish their theme, there isn't so much as a bauble or a glass of mulled wine in sight. It's actually quite nice, not because I don't love Christmas, I absolutely adore it, but I think it's more to do with the festive state of mind. At Christmas, everything is sparkly, everyone is cheery. There's presents, delicious things to eat and drink that you only really get at this time of year, and (okay, admittedly this year I personally am not exactly vibing with it, but) there's so much to do, so many events, time to spend with family and friends, everyone getting together to have a wonderful time... but we all know that Christmas is a temporary state. After Christmas Day, and that weird no man's week in the run-up to New Year's Eve, January suddenly hits and that's that. The decorations come down. The picture-perfect weather that you want to see around the big day is suddenly a cold, slushy inconvenience. Family members go home, we all go back to work, and that's it. It's over.

I suppose I feel a little strange this year because the Christmas period represents more to me than a week off from real life. On the one hand, it isn't only my Christmas decorations that will be gone from my house come January, all my house guests will go with it, and my home will be mine again, quiet, calm and free from people I don't enjoy spending time with. Of course, on the other hand, the time I'm spending with Rocco is temporary too. These events are just for the holidays. Our relationship, for lack of a clearer term for it, is just for Christmas. When it's all over, and life goes back to normal, Rocco will be gone too. It will be like none of this ever happened so, needless to say, I have very mixed emotions at the moment.

I did wonder, on my way here, whether or not I was being a bit of a dick, not spending much time with my family over the holidays, but being at home at the moment is just too much. I wouldn't usually be spending Christmas with my dad at all, so I don't feel guilty about not being around him and Gail, and Declan took off before last Christmas, so I don't think anyone (other than him, the deluded moron) has any expectations of me spending time with him. That just leaves my mum and Jess, and Mum seems to be spending all her time with Dad (which I'm still majorly unhappy with) and Jess is spending all her time with Kenny, so it's not like either of them is sitting around waiting for me, but Mum is only going to be living down the road, and it doesn't sound like Jess is going to be going anywhere – not until she figures out her next move – so it's not like I can't spend time with them in the new year.

I suppose I just feel a bit bad this evening specifically because Dad and Gail were going out to visit Gail's family members, and it seemed like Mum and Jess were both actually home. But Declan was still there, and avoiding him is still a top priority – he actually invited me out for a drink with him this evening, he must be crazy – and if I had stayed home, it would have been a missed opportunity to spend time with Rocco and... wow, my head is a mess.

So I'm glad to be here, at the Candy Club, a festive-free zone, with Rocco – the person who seems to be dominating my thoughts at the moment – and our new friends, Leila and Tobias.

The Candy Club has a fairground theme and they've really gone all out with it. The bar itself is inside what looks like a carousel at the back of the room, the rest of which is divided into different zones, each representing different rides. This evening we're sitting in the waltzer section, which looks exactly as you would expect it to, with booths made to look like waltzer cars.

'These are pretty cute,' Leila says, brandishing a hot pink Candy Club-branded poker chip. We all got one, on the way in, entitling us to one free drink. Leila hasn't cashed hers yet. 'I'm trying to work out if I'd rather have the free drink or keep this as a souvenir.'

'The free drink every time, surely?' Tobias replies.

'I don't know, I think I'll hang onto it,' Leila says. 'Do you think you can only cash it tonight, or do you reckon I can turn up weeks later and trade it for a drink?'

'What, like in an emergency?' Tobias asks.

'It's hard to imagine an emergency where you need a toffee apple martini, stat,' Rocco jokes.

I pick up my glass and hand it to him.

'Try it and tell me it's not the best drink you've ever had,' I insist.

He looks at me for a second. God, it feels good, when his eyes are on you. There's something about being seen by him that I really like.

Rocco does as he's told, raising my glass to his lips before taking a sip. His eyes almost roll into the back of his head.

'Okay, fair enough,' he says through a grin. 'That's probably the nicest cocktail I've ever had.'

'Well, how about I buy a round of them?' I suggest. 'What do you say?'

I'm in such a good mood this evening. I can't hide it. As messy as things are, and as up in the air as relationships seem, the thought of going for dinner tomorrow night, just me and Rocco, is a thought that is keeping me going. I'm focusing on that, wondering what he's got planned, where we might be going. He's keeping pretty tight-lipped about it, which is exciting.

'Do you need a hand?' Rocco asks, once everyone accepts my offer.

'No, no, you stay there,' I insist. 'I'll be back in a minute.'

I'm going to nip to the loos too, while I'm up, and I'd rather Rocco wasn't waiting outside for me. I don't know why, it just doesn't feel cool or sexy, to use the loo – yes, I realise how ridiculous that sounds, and yes, I am overthinking everything now. I'm just so looking forward to tomorrow night and I don't want to ruin it. Obviously I don't think Rocco will run scared, if he realises I have a bladder like all the other girls, but I am constantly embarrassing myself, so there's that.

This place really is like a fairground, not just because they've worked really hard to make it look that way, but because the décor and the layout – along with the size of the place – gives it that sort of chaotic, maze-like vibe you often find at fairgrounds and theme parks. The bar is an easy spot, given that it's so big, and in the middle, covered in large colourful lightbulbs, but I have no idea where the toilets are, so I catch the attention of one of the jugglers before asking him. He kindly points them out to me.

I smile to myself as I make my way through the funhouse section, past the large painting of a clown, past the large slide that leads down into a ball pool – which cannot possibly be a sensible thing for drunk people to have access to. I'm just so (admittedly briefly, at the moment) happy to be here tonight. Away from home, away from...

'Declan!'

'Billie, hello,' he says brightly. 'What are you doing here?'

'What are *you* doing here?' I ask him.

Declan places a hand on my back and ushers me to one side. I move with him, eager to stay in the fun house section because it's where my friends aren't. If there's one thing I don't need right now – one thing that could ruin everything – it's having to introduce Rocco to my ex. I can't think of anything worse.

Declan gestures to a table covered in free drink poker chips. As I look up from the table, I realise my mum and Jess are sitting with him. Okay, scratch what I just said, there is something worse than introducing Rocco to my ex, it's introducing him to my mum too. Not that there's anything wrong with my mum. Of all the people in my life, she's the easiest one for new people to meet, for sure, but there's something intense about introducing a guy to your mum, especially when he isn't expecting it – even more so when said mum is out for drinks with your ex. What?!

'What are you guys doing here?' I ask as I take a seat at the table with them.

'Billie, darling, what a wonderful surprise,' Mum says through a beaming smile. 'Declan invited us to the big opening. He said he'd buy us drinks.'

'I thought you were skint,' I point out accusingly.

'I am,' he replies, in as hushed tones as possible. 'Did you see the gigantic clown face on the wall over there? I painted it for them. My choices were money or they offered me more bang for my buck if I took part of my payment in free drink tokens. So I figured I'd take more tokens than money, so that it would be a long time before I needed to buy drinks on a night out. That way, I can spend money on things that matter, and not waste it on drinks, because the drinks are free.'

Oh lord, have mercy, he thinks he's a genius. He has no idea how stupid that sounds. I'm so glad I don't have to worry about *this* clown any more.

'So, where's Fee?' Mum asks. 'I have to admit, I was surprised, when you said you were meeting her for a drink tonight, given how you usually describe her. I'd be interested to meet her.'

So obviously, when people were asking me what I was doing tonight, and Declan invited me out drinking with him, I made up something about going to a pre-Christmas drink with Fee from work, even thought I'd rather drink from the toilet than socialise with her out of hours.

'She's gone home,' I reply quickly. 'You just missed her. Her daughter has just had a baby so she's spending the holidays with them. She needed to get home, to bed, she's got an early start tomorrow.'

It always helps to legitimise a lie, by throwing something true in there with it, blurring the line between what's true and what's false.

'Were you on your way home then?' Jess asks, sort of suspiciously, but a long way away from accusing me of anything.

'I was,' I reply.

'Well, now you're not,' Declan insists. 'The drinks are on me. I'll go grab a round.'

'Are you okay?' Mum asks me. Obviously I'm not, I'm in a real pickle, but I can't admit that, not without telling them who I'm really here with, and there's no way Mum and Jess wouldn't be bursting to meet Rocco, once they found out I was here with a boy. 'You're not upset that we're here with Declan, are you?'

'We're only here for the free drinks,' Jess points out, although I'd already guessed as much. 'We might as well get something out of him.'

'Oh, no, it's fine,' I insist. 'I'm just tired.'

'A few cocktails will change that,' Jess insists.

I shift uncomfortably in my seat. How the hell am I going to get myself out of this one?

'I'll say this quickly, before Declan gets back.' Mum starts leaning closer for a moment. 'I thought you were meeting a boy. I was even more convinced, when I saw how panicked you were about bumping into Declan. Of course, now I realise that your reaction was probably just appropriate, given that he's your ex. It's a shame Fee had to go home so early, but what a lovely coincidence, that we're here together.'

'See, that's a normal reaction to seeing a no-good ex,' Jess points out. 'You don't laugh at their jokes and make French toast together.'

'Jessica May, we're all under one roof for Christmas, are you honestly saying you would prefer it if your dad and I were not civil with one another?' Mum asks, full-naming her.

'Erm, there's being civil, and then there's him bending you over the kitchen island.'

'Not my kitchen island?' I blurt stupidly. First of all, because my worktops are not the things that need to be worried about the most in this scenario. Also, because who else's kitchen island is it going to be? Everyone lives with me at the moment.

Mum laughs and rolls her eyes.

'He was showing me how to knead,' she insists.

'He was showing you how to need *something*,' Jess says in disgust. 'Honestly, it was like a really gross remake of *Ghost*. One where I wished I was the dead one.'

'He was just showing me his new technique,' Mum tells me.

That's what I'm afraid of.

'Okay, ladies, here we go,' Declan announces as he places a tray of three bright pink drinks garnished with candy floss down on the table in front of us.

'These look great,' Jess says, her smile the only thing wider than her eyes. But then she notices me noticing how delighted she looks. 'But none of this means we forgive you. You're still in the family bad books – forever.'

'I know, I know,' he replies. 'I'm trying to do better. I'm going to make things right, though, just you watch.'

I roll my eyes. If he thinks a few cocktails will make up for him abandoning me then he can think again, it doesn't even come close. Unless, of course, he thinks it makes up for him putting the moves on me last night – it doesn't even do that. Anyway, I don't care about that right now, it isn't exactly a priority, when I have more pressing dramas threatening to ruin everything. I need to get back to my friends – back to Rocco – but now this lot are here, and I can't risk them all meeting. What the hell do I do?

'Wow, this drink is amazing,' Mum groans as she takes a sip.

Drinks! I'm supposed to be getting drinks. Everyone is going to wonder where I am.

'I was actually just on my way to the loos when I bumped into you,' I announces – which is true. 'I'll be right back.'

I spring to my feet – the two cocktails I've had already cause me to wobble slightly, but I'm okay – and head over to the bar, to get the drinks for my friends. I'll just have to go to the loo later. I wait patiently at the busy bar, order four toffee apple martinis, carefully load a tray with them and then set off weaving my way through the partygoers, trying to navigate my way back to the table without accident or incident – both of which I'm usually prone to.

I've no sooner noticed the large painting of the clown when I realise I'm back in front of the table with Mum, Jess and Declan sitting at it. They all stare at me for a second.

'More drinks?' Jess says through a puzzled look.

'Yes,' I reply, owning it. 'These, er, these ones are better. I had one earlier, I thought you guys might like to try one.'

'Did you pay for them?' Declan asks me. 'You should have taken some tokens and got them for free.'

'Yeah, I forgot all about them,' I reply. 'But also, I wanted to pay for them, it wouldn't be a gift from me if I didn't.'

Shit, I should have just given the second excuse from the get-go, because as lame as it sounds, it's more believable than me forgetting the fact that my ex got paid for his labour in free drink tokens – a fact I only learned minutes ago.

Jess sips the drink suspiciously.

'Okay, wow, they are good,' she reasons.

This instantly gets me off the hook. My story checks out.

'To trying the whole menu,' Mum says, raising a glass.

We all clink our glasses before taking a drink. I need to go easy on these cocktails. They're so strong and I currently have two in front of me.

'Oh, wow, they're even better combined,' Jess insists. 'Billie, sip one then the other.'

'Nah,' I insist. 'I don't fancy it.'

'Trust me,' she insists. 'Try it.'

The best way to avoid raising the alarm is to just go for it. She's right, it's gorgeous – gorgeous but super strong.

'What are the toilets like?' Mum asks curiously. Such a mum question. She probably doesn't even need to go, she's either wondering for later, or she's going to be eyeing up fancy taps for her new house. She's made countless notes, and asked a bunch of questions, about my place. I won't be surprised if when I visit her new place, I see a lot of my own house in there.

'Oh, I didn't go,' I say, almost excitedly, relieved to have a reason to leave the table. 'Back in a sec.'

I jump up, hurry back towards the bar, order another four cocktails – this is turning out to be one hell of an expensive round – and carefully head back to my friends' table, no getting lost this time.

'There you are,' Leila says as I approach the table. 'We were worried about you.'

'Sorry, the bar is so busy,' I reply as I set the drinks down. 'Here we are.'

'I came looking for you, to give you a hand at the bar, but you weren't there,' Tobias says. He sounds innocent enough, not like he's interrogating me, I think he's just curious. Still, it means I have to offer up an explanation.

'Oh, I went to the loo as well,' I reply. 'You must have just missed me.'

I do still really, really need to pee. Every time I have to mention it, the feeling only intensifies.

'Thanks for the drink,' Leila says. 'Shall we toast?'

No, please, God, not more drinking.

'Yes, okay,' I say with a forced smile.

'To the friends we make through dating apps,' she says. 'There are no people I would rather be friendzoned by.'

'To the friendzone,' Tobias laughs.

We all clink our glasses. I take the smallest sip I can get away with.

'I was just telling the boys about the summer I spent in Kerala,' Leila continues. 'I was picking tea when...'

I try my best to listen. I wriggle in my seat. I start bouncing one of my legs lightly on the floor, to try to distract from my aggressively full bladder.

'Billie, are you okay?' Rocco asks me, concerned, noticing my leg.

'Yes, yes,' I quickly insist. 'Actually, I'm just going to nip to the loo again.'

Amazing. I didn't want him thinking I used the toilet at all – now I'm making myself seem like I have some sort of problem.

'Are you okay?' Leila asks.

'Oh, yeah, I'm fine, I won't be long,' I reply as I hurry off.

This time, I'm careful to make my way to the toilets without passing Mum, Jess and Declan, which I do succeed in doing. The problem is that, as I walk out of the cubicle, and over to the sinks to wash my hands, I pull up next to my mum as she washes hers.

'There you are, darling,' she replies. 'I was worried you'd got lost. Have you seen these taps? I've taken a photo of them. I'm thinking they would look good in the downstairs WC. Is everything okay?'

Her tone quickly changes as she sees the look on my face.

'Yeah, I'm fine,' I reply with a smile.

Well, I'm not fine, but I'm better now I'm empty.

Mum waits for me to wash my hands before hooking her arm through mine.

'Come on, let's go enjoy our drinks,' she says. 'It's nice, to finally be on a night out together.'

'It really is,' I reply. I can't help but cock my head as something occurs to me. This is my opportunity to do some digging. 'We can finally be one another's wingwoman, help each other find a man, what do you say?'

'Oh, I don't know about that,' she replies with a laugh. 'I'm more than happy to help you find a nice young man but, as for me, I'm content as things are at the moment.'

'I thought you were on the look-out for someone,' I say, a little too quickly.

'I'm happy, darling,' she insists. 'Don't worry about me.'

Words echo in my head as we head back to our table. She's happy. She isn't looking for anyone. Is that because she's found someone? Is that someone my dad? I really, really hope it isn't, for everyone's sake.

We arrive back at the table to find another man standing there with Jess and Declan. As I take my seat, I realise who he is – or what he is, at least. He's a magician, working the room, doing tricks for the customers. He's a twenty-something who looks the part – think more David Blaine than Paul Daniels, though. We pull up alongside him as he's performing a trick where he places his thumb between his teeth and then pulls down, creating the illusion that he is stretching his thumb, of course being alongside him gives us a peek behind the curtain, revealing that he switches from one thumb to the other, to make the first thumb look twice as long.

Declan pulls a face at him, suggesting that the trick looked rubbish head-on too.

'Okay, how about this one,' the magician says, pulling a

playing card from his pocket. One of the corners is missing – he shows us the missing piece in his other hand.

Mum and I take our seats again. I sigh as I grab one of my cocktails. I'm not really a magician kind of girl. In fact, no one at this table seems to be enjoying it all that much.

The magician places the two pieces of card together and then, with a few speedy hand movements, reveals that the card is whole again.

He looks at me, his eyes wide with optimism, to see if I'm impressed. Not only can I see the fold in the card, where he was pretending it was torn, but he's also dropped the smaller piece of card, the one he was pretending to stick back together on the floor.

'Erm...'

I nod towards the floor. The magician quickly bends to pick it up.

'You're rubbish, mate,' Declan tells him.

'You guys just aren't a very good audience,' the magician claps back. 'You're too grumpy, too cynical. You need to be open-minded for magic to work, not old and jaded.'

'Okay, why don't you make yourself disappear,' Jess tells him. 'Before one of us rips you in half.'

The magician skulks off.

'Old and jaded,' I can't help but repeat.

'He's just having a bad day,' Mum offers up in his defence. 'I'm sure everyone is giving him a hard time.'

'He shouldn't be so rude,' Jess says.

'It's nearly Christmas,' Mum reminds her. 'Let's give the guy a break.'

'Just please, God, no one invite him for Christmas dinner,' I quickly insist. 'We've got a house full already.'

'Jess said we might be having one more,' Mum says tactfully. 'Is that right?'

I glance at Jess, who is half-grinning, half-gurning, as she optimistically waits for my blessing to officially invite Kenny for Christmas dinner.

'Jess was saying Kenny would be alone otherwise,' Mum continues.

I feel like they're playing me. Well, I know they are, trying to tug at my heartstrings, to get me to feel sorry for the guy.

'Yeah, okay, sure, fine, whatever,' I babble. 'What's one more, right?'

'Sis, you are not going to regret this,' Jess says excitedly. She grabs my face and gives me a big kiss on the cheek. 'The next round of free drinks is definitely on me.'

I laugh, but then I remember my situation, the friends that are waiting for me at another table. Shit.

I look down at my drinks. Both glasses are near enough full. I doubt I can still pull off another trip to the bathroom, though, so I don't know how many other options I have. I pick up one cocktail and knock it back like a shot – except of course it's too big, so I have to chug it like a bottle of water on a hot day. Then I make the second one disappear. The magician could certainly learn a thing or two from me.

'Bloody hell,' Jess says.

'What?' I reply as casually as I can, of course my voice comes out like a robot's, because I'm not a hardened drinker, and I just put away at least four measures of alcohol. 'We're celebrating, I'm off to get another. Back in minute.'

I really am starting to feel quite tipsy now. I keep my eyes on the floor (the one in the middle) as I make my way back to my table – my first table.

I plonk myself down inside the waltzer car.

'Whew, the queues for the loos are crazy,' I announce. 'So, where were we?'

'Where were we?' Leila relates back to me. 'Where were you? You've been ages.'

'Just to the toilets,' I say again. 'I'm here now.'

I pick up my drink. I want to take a sip, to try and seem normal, but the sight of it makes me throw up in my mouth a little.

'Is that lipstick?' Rocco asks me.

I raise my fingers to my lips – as though I could even feel what was on them. My lipstick will be long faded by now. If it's anything, it's probably pink staining for the cocktail I just necked.

'No, on your cheek,' he says, pointing.

It only takes me a second to realise what has happened. It's from Jess kissing me on the cheek.

'It must be a bit of my own,' I say as I wipe at my face, guessing where it is.

'It's lip print-shaped,' Tobias says through a laugh. 'I'd spend all my time in the toilets too, if I came out covered in lipstick. Do you have a gang of friends somewhere else you're not telling us about?'

I'm sure he's joking but it rattles me.

'No, no. Maybe it's transferred from my glass or something,' I reply. 'Or maybe it's magic, I don't know.'

'Did I hear someone say magic?' a voice chimes in.

I glance to my right to see a very smug-looking familiar face.

'Now, you look like a girl who enjoys magic tricks,' he says to me.

There's a knowing look in his eye, one that suggests he over-heard our conversation just now, and that he knows I'm up to something – something I would rather my friends didn't know about.

'You got me,' I say, faking a smile. 'I'm a sucker for magic.'

'Really?' Leila says, pulling a face.

'Yep,' I continue.

'Well, allow me to show you some tricks,' the magician beams.

He takes out the card with the corner 'missing' and repeats the trick. This time, he allows the fake corner to simply fall to the floor, in a spot where only I would see it.

'Oh, my God, amazing,' I say with an entirely put on enthusiasm.

'Yeah?' he replies.

'Yeah!' I echo. 'I don't know how you do it but, just, wow.'

The others give me a few funny looks here, a few laughs there, but they don't suspect a thing, they just think I'm being a bit goofy. The alcohol in my system is certainly helping.

I continue to fake my way through the rest of his act. It's rubbish, but I'm the perfect plant.

'What about a tip?' he asks me, as he prepares to move onto another table.

'Here's a tip, don't push your luck,' I say, slurring slightly.

'Are you okay?' Leila asks.

How long have I been here? Is it time to go back to the other table for a while? My head feels so fuzzy.

'Yeah, I just need another drink,' I say, standing up.

'You've hardly touched your drink,' Leila points. She cocks her head. 'And yet somehow you seem like you've had way too much.'

'Then I guess I need the loo again,' I say with a shrug. 'Back in a minute.'

Christ, this is exhausting. Morally I could never cheat on anyone but after this evening, I think I can rule it out on logistical grounds too.

I feel seriously wobbly on my feet, as I head back to the other table. I'm just approaching the clown painting when Rocco catches up with me.

'Billie, is everything okay?' he asks me, taking me by the hand. 'You seem a bit... I don't know.'

'I'm fine, I'm fine,' I insist. I can just about make out my mum and Jess from where we're standing. If they looked over here, they would see us for sure.

I notice the slide next to me, the one that goes into the ball pool, and before I've really thought about what I'm doing, I'm sliding down it.

'Follow me,' I just about manage to call out before I disappear.

I cackle like a child as I disappear under the balls at the bottom. Eventually, Rocco joins me.

'Isn't this better?' I say through a smile. 'Just me and you, away from everyone.'

Rocco laughs.

'Are you drunk?' he asks. 'Is that why you're being so... so whatever this is?'

'Maybe,' I reply. I purse my lips to hide my smile. 'Okay, yes.'

'I knew it,' he says with a laugh. 'Well, that's a relief, I thought maybe me inviting you to dinner, without the others, was making you feel uncomfortable or something.'

'No, no,' I quickly insist, as I hook my arms around his neck. 'I was the first one here, and it turns out I know the guy who painted the clown, and he gave me free drinks, and then whenever I passed the bar, they gave me another one and I suppose I just lost count.'

'Is it weird that I find that cute?' he replies.

'Who am I to say what's weird?' I say. 'I'm a thirtysomething-year-old in a ball pool.'

I fling myself backwards and let the balls cover me again. Rocco quickly scoops me back out.

'This thing is a terrible idea for a bar,' he muses. 'Someone is going to suffocate.'

'Not me,' I point out smugly. 'Because I've got you.'

'Yes, you do,' he replies through a smile.

For a moment, we fall silent, neither of us moving a muscle. I feel my heartbeat quicken, as Rocco holds me in his arms. This would be a really good time to kiss, if it weren't also somehow the worst time, place and scenario to do it. Still, I'm sure I could live with it.

'I think your phone is ringing,' Rocco says.

'What?' I reply.

'Yeah, I can feel your watch vibrating against my neck,' he replies, loosening his grip on me.

I rummage through my bag until I find my phone. I have three missed calls from my dad. Shit. There's a message too.

House is flooding! Pick up! Hurry home! Where's the stop tap?

'Oh, my God, it's my dad, I've got to go,' I tell him, sobering up suddenly as I try to find my feet. 'He says my house is flooding.'

'Shit,' Rocco replies. 'Do you want me to help you to get home, or to come and help?'

'No, no,' I insist, perhaps a little too firmly. 'I'll be fine. I'll grab a taxi. You stay here, have fun, explain to Leila and Tobias that I'm okay.'

'Then I guess I'll see you tomorrow,' he says. 'At our dinner date.'

'Absolutely, I can't wait,' I tell him honestly, in a way that is far more enthusiastic than we're encouraged to be around men after knowing them for so little time, but I don't have time to be cool, I need to grab my family and head home ASAP. I just hope there isn't too much damage. I just spent the last year fixing it up, for crying out loud. I can't face doing more repairs, more decorating – and just a few days before Christmas too. My house is the only one we have between us, without it, God knows where we'll be eating Christmas dinner.

I just need to hurry home and assess the damage. Perhaps it's not as bad as it seems?

27

After I set my curls with a generous blast of hairspray, and touch up my lipstick, I check myself out in the mirror. Against all odds, I am date ready.

I woke up this morning seriously hungover, and as I attempted to brush my teeth with bottled water, I honestly though there was no way I was going to be able to have a shower before my date tonight, but here I am, fresh and clean, and good to go.

I leave my bedroom and find the plumber, just finishing up at the top of the stairs, as Declan watches over him.

'That's me pretty much done,' the plumber announces as he lays the carpet back down.

'Perfect timing,' I reply. 'I was just about to head out.'

The plumber has been here for a couple of hours now but the second he said we were able to switch the water back on, I made a dash for the shower, not wanting to be late, but so desperately wanting to be clean.

When I arrived home last night, the house was such a mess. There were buckets in the hallway, wet towels all over the floor, and a big pile of floorboards next to the front door – and this was all before the plumber got here.

When Dad and Gail got in last night, all seemed fine – until shortly after he closed the door behind him, when he said water starting pouring out of the wooden archway that separates the hallway from the living room. He said it was like a waterfall, flowing down, but even though it was thankfully clean water, he couldn't find the stop tap. The pile of floorboards was from him ripping it up, out of the cupboard where all the bits for the heating are, to try to find it – except it wasn't there, but he did eventually find it and stop the water.

I should be grateful that we were able to get an emergency plumber today, the day before Christmas Eve, but I spent last night and this morning not only without running water, but terrified of what the problem was going to be. That much water raining down into your hallway has to be something expensive, right?

'Is it all fixed?' I ask optimistically.

'All fixed,' the plumber announces proudly. 'These floorboards were screwed down tight.'

'That was me,' Declan says proudly. 'It was the last job I did, before I, erm, left.'

'It was the only job you did, before you, erm, left,' I remind him.

'I hate to break it to you, buddy, but that's what caused the problem,' the plumber tells him. 'You screwed a floorboard into a waterpipe, see.'

The plumber holds up a copper-coloured piece of skinny pipe with a hole in it.

'The screw was keeping the water in, but this was a time bomb, see the rust? The screw had to come back out sooner or later. Something as simple as walking over the floorboards could have been the final nail in the coffin, no pun intended. You've been really lucky, though. The floor will dry out, and as for the water that leaked downstairs, it went into your cavity wall, and out through the wooden archway, so your plasterboard and your ceilings are still perfect. Once you move those buckets, it will be like it never happened, aside from maybe repainting the arch. It's not worth thinking about what would have happened if it had been even a metre to the left or right.'

'I can't thank you enough,' I tell him as he gathers up his things and heads for the door, leaving me alone with Declan, who continues to find new and interesting ways to screw up my life.

'Fuck, Billie, I'm so sorry,' he says. 'Was it expensive?'

'Let's just forget about it,' I tell him. 'We got off really lucky, and it didn't cost a thing.'

'An emergency plumber a couple of days before Christmas?' he replies in disbelief.

'Well, it cost £30, I think,' I tell him. 'Just the excess payment for an emergency call out.'

Declan just stares at me.

'From the house insurance,' I continue.

'You called the insurance company?' he replies. 'I didn't realise you could do that, for emergencies, I thought it was just for repairs, after the fact.'

'Nope, that's what we pay for,' I reply. I roll my eyes. 'We. Ha! That's what *I* pay for.'

'And I'm really sorry about that, about this, about everything,' he babbles. 'But I have a surprise for you, and I think it's going to make it all better. Follow me into the office.'

I narrow my eyes at him for a moment, before following his lead.

I don't know what I was expecting to find, given that set-up. To be honest, my best guess was another ill-advised attempt at seducing me, but what I'm looking at is so, *so* much worse.

'What is this?' I ask him, my eyes so wide I'm probably putting creases in my make-up. 'What the hell have you done?'

An entire previously light pink wall in the office is now completely covered with a graffiti-style mural, with so much going on it's hard to know where to look first. I want to look away, but I can't.

There are love hearts, doves, words in big black letters like 'forever', 'amour' and 'sex', weirdly – not that it would have been okay without that final detail. It doesn't exactly ruin the mural, although the mural does completely ruin the wall.

The worst part of all are the caricatures of the two of us, right in the middle, both naked and entwined with one another. It's as gross as it is offensive, and that's without getting into that fact that while my likeness looks absolutely monstrous, he's made improvements to me too, like changing the proportions of my body, and making my boobs enormous.

'It's a mural, a declaration of our love and, not only that, but you were right, this house is all you, I haven't been here, I haven't done anything – apart from those floorboards, and I royally fucked those up. So this is my contribution, to make this place mine too, to show you that I'm in it for keeps this time, and that I want to contribute, I want to make my mark, to see my own improvements and changes.'

'You're out of your mind,' I tell him. 'The first improvement you can make is changing that wall back to being pink. There's some paint left, in the shed I think, I'll get it for you before I go.'

'Billie, no, you don't understand, it's to show you that I love you,' he insists. 'I had such a wonderful time last night with you, your mum, and Jess – I'm even getting on with your dad. I want to be a part of this family again.'

'Fine, leave it there, you're the one who has to sleep next to it, but make the most of the image because it's the closest thing you're going to get to the two of us ever getting back together.'

'Can we just talk about this, please?' he asks.

'No, I've got a date,' I inform him. 'And I'm not going to let this ruin it.'

I try to keep my cool as I leave the room. I can paint over this myself, later – I'm not the one who is going to have to look at it in the meantime.

The problem isn't the paintwork, that can be fixed, I'm good at fixing things like that. The problem is Declan, and his claim on this house, and his desire to suddenly become a part of everything. I wanted that a year ago, but he wasn't interested. Now, when I want him to piss off, he's working overtime to reassert himself as man of the house.

What I refuse to do right now is worry about it, I'll do that later, because I'll be damned if I'm going to let him ruin my date with Rocco for me, even if he is trying to ruin my life.

28

When Rocco said he was arranging a dinner date for the two of us, I figured he would book somewhere impressive, maybe somewhere expensive, or pull some strings to get us in somewhere exclusive. He had been messaging all day, talking such a big game, that I dared to look forward to something wonderful. What Rocco has delivered is beyond my wildest dreams.

Rocco was waiting for me outside his hotel, on the bank of the Great Stour, at the side of a boat. I just laughed when I saw him. I couldn't even begin to imagine how a small boat factored into our dinner plans.

'And which restaurant is this boat taking us to?' I asked through a smile. 'Surely it's too small to be eating on.'

'It is taking us to several restaurants,' he replied. 'Tonight, I want you to have nothing but the best, so we'll be heading to one restaurant for the starter, another for the main course, and then one final location for dessert. And they're all along the river so I thought, why not? Let's take a boat. We even have our own personal boat chauffer, so you don't have to worry about me sinking us.'

Romantic and funny. You just don't see creativity like that when it comes to first dates any more – well, not that this is a first date in the traditional sense, but you know what I mean.

Our starter, at Fred's Fish Bar, our first location, was salmon, lightly coated in lemon and black pepper breadcrumbs, served with a sweet chilli salad. Fred's was a place I'd never eaten before – it's decidedly more boujee than its name suggests, and of course Declan would always refuse to go anywhere that specialised in fish.

Next up it was back on the boat, to the White Rabbit, where we're currently enjoying our main courses: barbecue chicken with pineapple in a brioche roll, with sweet potato fries and pineapple fritter on the side.

I love that Rocco took the time to find out what the most praised dish from each eatery was, and while he did give me the option to have whatever I wanted, I was excited to go with his recommendations. So far, both have been absolutely fantastic.

'Pineapple fritters are my new favourite thing,' I announce, practically groaning, and speaking with my mouth full, which I know you're not supposed to do but I don't want to break from eating, not even to speak. 'I don't know where they've been all my life.'

'I'll never understand why pineapple is so divisive in savoury food,' Rocco replies. 'Or why people get so upset.'

'Have I just passed a test?' I ask through a smile.

'You've passed two,' he replies. 'Seafood and pineapple. To be honest, it's not really something that bothers me, but it's no fun going for food with someone who doesn't like to eat anything.'

'Things I don't like to eat...' I say thoughtfully. 'Too much coriander can ruin a dish for me. I can take or leave green beans. I don't like duck, that's a firm no.'

'That's an okay list,' he replies. 'It doesn't rule out any cuisines. There are only two foods I absolutely cannot stand. Kiwis and cauliflower cheese.'

'Oh, I love cauliflower cheese,' I reply.

'Have I just failed a test?' he asks.

'I'll let you off,' I say seriously. 'This time. Cauliflower cheese is one of my mum's specialities – it's genuinely one of the highlights of Christmas dinner, I can't wait.'

'For me, it's my mum's parsnips or – hear me out – my dad's sprouts.'

'Sprouts?' I squeak.

'He cooks them in honey and bacon,' he explains. 'So they're sort of sweet and, well, bacon-y.'

'It's like eating opposite a male Nigella Lawson,' I tease him.

'My dad's so busy this Christmas,' he tells me. 'So I might not get any.'

'What do your parents do?' I ask curiously.

'My dad is a surgeon and my mum is a therapist,' he replies, raising an eyebrow, acknowledging that it can't have been an easy childhood. 'So, between them, they always thought they could fix everything. They're both working so much at the moment, hardly home, hence me staying in a hotel.'

'You sound like you're close,' I say with a smile.

'Yeah, even though I've been working away, we all make the effort,' he says. 'I've been offered a job, working on a new project in the city, I can't say too much because I've had to sign an NDA. So I'll swiftly change the subject. You said you're close with your mum?'

'Yeah, with my mum, not really with my dad, though,' I reply. I humour him, getting the conversation back on track, but I can't stop wondering about what could happen if Rocco did take on a local project. I need to focus on the conversation at hand, not let my mind race away with me.

'My parents are separated, I'm not close with my dad at all, and his new wife isn't ideal so I don't spend any time with them, if I can help it.'

'I'm sorry,' Rocco replies. 'That's rough. But you sound like you get everything you need from your mum.'

I smile.

'Okay, not that I'm trying to blast through the motions or anything, but my plate is clear, you've knocked it out of the park with the first two courses, I'm excited to see what this dessert is.'

'No more wicked step-mothers, no more cauliflower cheese, let's focus on the food things, and I think dessert might be your favourite course yet,' he says. 'To the boat!'

After grabbing our coats and making our way back out to the boat, where our driver is dutifully waiting for us, we get inside to make the short journey back to the hotel – so I will be getting to eat something in the Michelin-starred restaurant there after all.

There's a small cabin in the boat but, despite it being cold out, it's so nice sitting outside, looking out over the water, and at the city around us. I've lived here all my life, and been to the city centre hundreds of times, but there's nothing like seeing things from a different perspective, to view things in a whole new light.

The pretty lights all around us, the gentle bob of the boat on the water, sitting on this small seat alongside Rocco, it's... dare I say it? Romantic.

I don't think I could be any closer to him right now, but I try anyway. I hook my arm round his and rest my head on his shoulder.

'I'm having such a wonderful night,' I tell him sincerely. 'Honestly, just the best I've had in ages.'

It's not the most eloquent declaration but I'm kind of stunned. I never expected such a truly perfect evening.

'Are you wet?' Rocco asks me.

I quickly lift my head up again to look at him. Did he just ask me what I think he asked me?

'What?'

'Are you wet?' he asks again. 'Buddy, are we sinking?'

Rocco's question to our driver makes me panic for a second. Now that he's mentioned it, my seat does feel a bit wet.

'Nothing to worry about,' he replies in his West Country accent. 'It'll be a bit of built-up rainwater, trapped in the seat. These things happen at sea.'

We're less than a minute away from the hotel but by the time we're safe on dry land, the damage is done.

'My bum is soaking,' I whisper to Rocco as we walk into the lobby. 'Can you tell?'

I twist around, to show Rocco my bum. I wore a red dress tonight, and cropped leather jacket, so if you can see, you can really see.

'Yep, it looks like you've been sitting in a puddle,' he replies quietly. 'To put it politely.'

'I can't go into a restaurant like this,' I reply. 'Your trousers look fine. Obviously I chose tonight not to wear black.'

Rocco laughs.

'You might not be able to see, but I'm not very comfortable,' he admits.

'Gutted,' I say with a sigh.

'We could eat it in my room?' he suggests. 'At the table, sitting on towels.'

I snort.

'The perfect end to a perfect night,' I tease. 'Let's do it.'

I stand with my back against the wall, near the lifts, while

Rocco goes to order our desserts. I've no idea what it's going to be, but I feel like I've had to battle for it.

'Right, they're going to bring them up,' he says. 'Let's go.'

We step into the lift together, just the two of us, and make our way to the floor where Rocco's room is. I have to confess, I don't really remember doing this the first time, but this time you could cut the tension with a knife. Perhaps it's just me but suddenly the gravity of what we're doing sinks in. We're going to his hotel room, after an absolute dream of a dinner date, and Rocco is charming, funny, and unbelievably handsome.

'Floor sex,' he announces as the doors open.

Did he just say... I notice the number on the number panel. Six. He said floor six. What is wrong with me?

We head inside Rocco's room and close the door behind us. Hovering in the doorway, something occurs to him.

'Oh, there's a hairdryer in here,' he says. 'And robes. I could give you one, a, erm, a robe.'

Rocco briefly shapeshifting into Hugh Grant puts me a little more at ease.

'Much better than sitting on a towel,' I say with a smile. 'Thank you.'

I remember what Jess told me, about how when you're feeling nervous in front of someone, you should just imagine them naked. Bloody hell, that's the last thing I should be doing right now, that's not going to help this situation *at all*.

Rocco leans past me, to take a robe from the wardrobe behind me. As his arm brushes against mine, I feel that feeling again, that indescribable feeling, almost like static.

'Here you go,' he says as he hands it to me. 'Can I get you anything else?'

'Nope, all good,' I reply. 'Oh, actually, can you unzip my dress for me, please? I had to have my sister zip me into it, I can't get out of it on my own.'

'That old one,' he jokes. 'Of course I can.'

I slip off my jacket and turn around so that Rocco can get to my zip. It's a long one that runs from the bottom of my neck to the small of my back – not even the coat hanger trick can get me in and out of this one without assistance.

Rocco places his left hand on my shoulder as he uses his right to slowly undo my zip. As his hand nears the bottom, I feel his knuckles graze the bare skin on my back. I can't help but let out sound, something between a sigh and a gasp.

'Sorry, ticklish,' I practically whisper.

'That's okay,' Rocco replies.

He fidgets with the bottom of the zip – in a way that has to be unnecessary – until his fingers graze the small of my back. I squirm with delight. Is he teasing me?

I've tried so hard to keep the idea of sex with Rocco far, far from my mind. I've also been to a sex party with him. Something in the middle would be great.

I back my body right into his, the clearest message I can send without coming out and saying it: I want him.

Rocco wraps his arms around my waist and kisses my neck. I lean to one side, eager to feel his lips on every part of me. Eventually he spins me around and our lips meet for the first time. Static again, this time in my lips, then surging through my entire body. I've thought about kissing Rocco so many times, but I had no idea it was going to feel like this. I think it's me who instigates kicking things up a gear – I'm not usually an instigator, I swear – but the hungrier I get for him, the more passionate the kissing becomes. As Rocco picks me up, I wrap my legs around his waist, and as he pushes me back against the door with a loud bang, the door appears to knock back. It stops us in our tracks for a second.

'Room service,' a voice eventually calls out.

Rocco laughs.

'Can you leave it outside the door?' Rocco calls back. Now I'm kissing his neck.

'Okay,' the voice calls back.

'So, what is this amazing dessert?' I whisper into his ear.

'You can find out in the morning,' he replies.

29

Sleeping in the bed in Rocco's hotel room is much better than sleeping on the sofa. I don't know what kind of mattress it is, but it seems to shape around your body. The sheets do an excellent job of keeping you warm, but somehow nice and cool at the same time, oh, and Rocco is here too, which is nice.

'How did you sleep?' he asks me.

'For about an hour,' I reply. 'Same as you.'

Right on cue, he yawns.

'It was worth it, though,' he says. 'Happy Christmas Eve.'

'I can't believe it's Christmas Eve already,' I reply.

'Not much longer to go,' he says. 'Then you won't have to avoid your family much longer. It will be back to work, back to real life.'

He laughs as he says this, but something hits me.

'You know what, taking a step back from them, spending time with you, being happy... I suddenly don't care all that much about it and, to be honest, I'm weirdly looking forward to Christmas.'

'That's a good attitude to have,' he replies, giving me a squeeze. 'I think perhaps I should take a little of your advice too.'

I cuddle up closer to him, resting my head on his chest.

'I don't want to be *that* girl, but can I be *that girl* for a moment?' I ask him.

'Uh-oh,' he jokes. 'Go on, go for it.'

'This project you've been offered, the local one,' I start. 'Do you think you'll take it?'

'I'd been on the fence about it,' he replies. 'I wasn't sure whether or not a move back here was the right choice for me, but what you said may have just swayed me. A bit of time back home with the family might do me some good.'

I can't control my grin.

'I only ask because I was pretty upset last night to not get the marvellous, magical, best dessert ever that you promised me,' I reply.

'It might still be on the floor, outside the door,' he replies. I can't see his face, but I can hear his smile.

'I think I've earned a fresh one,' I inform him. 'Would it work for breakfast?'

'Well, it's Christmas Eve, we've both got places to be,' he starts. 'So you've got two choices. We can get up and have dessert for breakfast or we spend all the time we've got this morning here, in bed. But then of course you'll have to come back here another day for the dessert. My vote is for bed, but do you mind coming back?'

'Oh, I'll definitely come back,' I reply. 'Bed it is.'

30

I think I've made a decent effort at filling my pre-Christmas free time with so many things, given that my friends are on holiday and I didn't have much notice. If I haven't been at the events, I'd have been hiding in my bedroom, spending minimal time with the others in the house. But it is Christmas Eve, and there is no one I'd rather spend Christmas Eve with than my mum and Jess, it's a May family tradition. We might have some extra guests this year, but I'm not about to let that ruin tradition.

We're all in the living room. After spending time apart to wrap presents, Mum, Jess and I are gathered around the island making gingerbread men. Dad and Gail are at the dining room table, setting up a board game, and Declan is on the sofa watching TV. I glance over at him right as he reaches down into his trackies and gives himself a good scratch. I don't think he quite knows what to do with himself, since I spelled things out to him yesterday. I don't know why I feel bad, because he is the one who walked out on me last Christmas, but of course I do. It's strange, looking at him, comparing him to Rocco, and how Rocco makes me feel. I know it sounds corny, but I felt more in one night with Rocco than I ever did with Declan. I suppose I'd been with him so long that I'd forgotten what it felt like to be with someone who set you alight. Rocco hasn't just made me feel good, he's made me feel better. That's why, this morning, I poked my head inside the room Declan is sleeping in to tell him that he's still welcome to spend Christmas with us. I don't think I could kick anyone out with nowhere to go on Christmas Eve, and I know it might seem like I'm soft, but to me, I think it shows that I'm over him, and that can only be a good thing.

I'm a little apprehensive about sitting down to play board games with Dad and Gail – especially Gail. Between my avoidance techniques, and her spending a lot of time at work, or hiding in their room here, Gail and I haven't clocked that much interaction. I gave it my best shot with her when she arrived – at least, I think I did. I let them stay here, when they needed help, but I didn't feel much warmth or appreciation from her when she arrived. I'm sure Dad has convinced her to play Cluedo with us, just like Mum has convinced me to play with them. I'm just relieved that Jess is here too. I thought she might be out, or over at Kenny's – which reminds me that he's coming for Christmas dinner. But, again, why not? When you've got enough people around that you struggle to get on with, what's a few more? Unless they incite each other against me, for some kind of 'my enemy's enemy is my friend' kind of deal.

'Right, the biscuits are in the oven,' Mum announces. 'Let's play.'

'Can I just borrow Billie for a moment?' Gail asks. 'Just... something upstairs.'

Oh, God, what is she going to do? I think I might have seen Black Christmas too many times, my imagination is running away with me.

'Yeah, okay,' I reply anyway.

I follow Gail upstairs to the guest room she and Dad are staying in. Gail rummaged around in a bag, eventually pulling out a small blue box with a gold edge.

'I owe you an apology,' she starts.

I feel my eyebrows shoot up. I wasn't expecting her to say that.

'You've extended us this huge courtesy, by letting us stay here, in your home, at a special time of year,' she continues. 'But I must admit, knowing that your dad's whole old family – no, just family – was going to be here, it did make me feel slightly defensive, and that may have come across as hostility on my part. But you've been a gracious host, we've had everything we needed, and I just want us all to have a nice Christmas tomorrow.'

Who can blame Gail, being a bit freaked out to be moving in with the step-kids she's never met and her husband's ex-wife? That takes one hell of an understanding person. I wasn't in anywhere near as awkward a position, and I went so nuclear to avoid it I ended up at a sex party.

'I'm sorry too,' I reply. 'I could have been more welcoming; I could have cancelled some of my plans. I'm sorry you've felt like you couldn't mix with us.'

Gail smiles. I see a visible wave of relief wash over her and I feel it myself too. Any issues I have with my dad are not ones I have with Gail. Perhaps we can establish some sort of relation-ship. That would actually be really nice.

I really, really, sincerely hope my dad isn't messing her around – because of my mum, or anyone else, really. He's already ruined one family with his antics. I would hate to see him do it to another.

'Anyway, to show you that I want to make an effort, and to thank you for letting us stay here, I wanted to give you this,' she says as she hands me the blue box. 'I was going to wait until morning, but I thought having this conversation tonight might make the next few hours easier.'

I laugh.

'Oh, yeah, imagine playing Monopoly for eight hours in awkward silence,' I reply.

I carefully open the box. Inside there's a delicate gold locket on a chain. It doesn't look like something new; it looks like something she's had for years.

'Oh, wow, it's gorgeous,' I say.

'It was my mum's,' she replies. 'And her mum's before that. The idea was always that I pass it down to my daughter, but then I had horrible boys.'

Gail smiles and laughs and it's like I'm in a room with a whole new person. A person I could really like.

'You can't give this to me,' I insist.

'You are my daughter now,' she points out. 'I know Jess is too, but you've put a roof over our heads, so... 1-0.'

'I will treasure this,' I tell her sincerely. 'Thank you so much.'

Moved by such a sweet gesture, I close the box, reach out and throw my arms around her. I release her just as Dad joins us.

'Are you two doing okay?' he asks.

'We couldn't be better,' Gail replies. 'Now, come on, let's play games before you dad and Declan fall asleep together watching TV.'

I get the sense that Gail thinks Declan and I might still be together, or that we might be heading that way, which isn't surprising, given that he's here for Christmas. Now doesn't seem like the time to set her right. It's Christmas, and Christmas really is a time for peace and good will to all men – yes, all men. I might not be spending it with the one I want to, although I have been messaging him all day. I'm trying not to let my imagination run away with me, but the idea of him taking on a job gives me this twisted feeling in my stomach. Imagine if he lives locally, even if it's just for one project, it would give us the chance to see if what we have between us is real, or just for Christmas. If Santa Claus could pull some serious strings, that would be great. In fact, it's all I want for Christmas.

31

'Good morning, girls,' Mum sings loudly. 'Alexa, play "It's Beginning to Look a Lot Like Christmas" by Michael Bublé.'

'It's not an Alexa,' Jess and I say in unison, both still face down in our pillows.

'Okay, Google.'

'It's not a Google,' Dad calls from the other room.

'I'm going to write it on your hand,' I joke as I roll over and sit up on my elbows.

'Oh, I don't know, Tom, Dick, Harry – stop being a smart-arse and play Michael Bublé – a Christmas album.'

'Playing Michael Bublé, Christmas, Deluxe Holiday Edition,' the Smarty announces.

'Oh, there we go,' Mum says victoriously. 'Okay, out of bed, come downstairs, I've got a surprise for everyone.'

'What time is it?' Jess asks.

'Quarter to eleven,' Mum replies. 'I let you sleep in.'

Jess has been almost exclusively getting up in the afternoon every day she has been here. This is not a lie-in for her, this is an early start.

'Come on,' Mum sings as she heads down the hallway. 'You too, Declan, you're not off the hook.'

'Right, well, I suppose we'd better get up then,' I tell Jess.

'I suppose so,' she replies. 'You make the coffee, I'll... drink it and try to be nice.'

'That seems fair,' I say sarcastically.

'Can I request a Christmas present from you please?' Jess asks as she rolls over to face me.

'I've already got you a present,' I reply. 'A good one. You'll love it.'

'Well, this can be an extra present, for being so good,' she insists.

'Erm, I'm no expert on the naughty/nice list but I'm pretty sure Santa Claus would take a hard stance on you shagging the neighbour.'

I'm joking. Well, maybe half joking.

'That's actually what it's about,' Jess starts, suddenly serious. 'Can you be nice to Kenny?'

'Not usually,' I reply.

'I mean today, obviously,' she adds. 'He's not the guy you think he is. Please? It's my one Christmas wish.'

'I'll do my best,' I tell her as I take my phone from the bedside table.

I've got a cute good morning/merry Christmas message from Rocco.

Good morning, gorgeous. Thanks for making a dull week such a memorable one, and for encouraging me to do Christmas right. Can't wait to see you in a couple of days – merry Christmas. x

'Okay, what is going on?' Jess asks.

'What?' I reply innocently.

'You're doing the face,' she replies. 'The phone face. The one when... oh, my God, Billie, have you met a boy too?'

I blush as I grin like an idiot.

'Maybe,' I reply. 'If you come downstairs now, and make Mum happy, then I'll tell you after breakfast and presents, deal?'

'Deal,' she replies.

'Can I use the bathroom first?' I ask.

'Yeah, I'm not getting dressed,' she says through a yawn. 'It's tradition.'

It is tradition, for me, my mum and Jess, to spend the best part of Christmas Day in our pyjamas, only changing into our festive best for dinner, before swiftly changing back into our pyjamas sometimes before dessert. Well, after eating too much for dinner, if you don't take your tights off willingly, your body will slowly reject them anyway.

After nipping into the bathroom, I pull up in front of my dressing table mirror to moisturise and put on a little bit of make-up. Just a bit of concealer and a little something brushed through my eyebrows. The kind of make-up that you can't really see, but you look generally better for wearing it. I don't do this any other morning apart from Christmas morning. Perhaps it comes from growing up in a generation that, even before phones had cameras, would usually see the family with some kind of new camera every year. Whether it was Dad's old film one, the gigantic camcorder he used to take everywhere, my first digital camera, or the Polaroid Jess got for fun one year. It's good to be camera-ready on Christmas morning.

'I couldn't be arsed putting make-up on,' Jess says as she emerges from the bathroom. 'I've got a bit of eyeliner still on from last night. We'll style that out as a festive smoky eye.'

'Classy,' I tease her.

Jess and I are the last people to make it downstairs, heading down together when we're both as ready as we are willing to be.

Mum is buzzing around the kitchen, doing bits to put the finishing touches on the breakfast table.

'Oh, my God, Mum, this looks great!' I blurt excitedly.

You know in American movies, where the mum lays out the absolute works for breakfast, and yet her kids still just sip some orange juice and grab a dry piece of toast as they run for the bus? That's the kind of breakfast spread we're working with today. The main difference being that, at the very least, Jess and I will graze indiscriminately, without giving a second thought to the big meal that we know is coming later in the day.

Dad reaches out to take a strawberry.

'Oi,' Mum ticks him off. 'There's one condition, before anyone can eat. Family tradition.'

As I look closer, I realise there is a wrapped present on the dining chairs, one for each of us.

'What's this?' Gail asks enthusiastically.

Mum removes her dressing gown to reveal the dorkiest pair of festive pyjamas I've ever seen. They're bright red with various Christmas items and slogans all over them. They're loud and busy – a real festive overload. She looks adorable in them.

'It's our family's tradition, to wear our Christmas pyjamas on Christmas Day,' Mum points out. 'So I got matching sets for the whole family.'

'Even me?' Declan asks in disbelief.

'Even you,' Mum replies through a laugh. 'So, if anyone wants to eat breakfast and open presents, best change into your uniform.'

Gail takes hers excitedly and hurries upstairs. My dad takes his but, before he joins Gail, I watch him approach my mum in the kitchen and whisper something into her ear before kissing her on the cheek.

I look over at Jess, who has taken this opportunity to sneak a pastry. As she crams a whole vanilla crown (a mini one, thankfully) into her mouth, we exchange a look. Something is going on with those two. Perhaps if I keep a close eye on them today, I can figure it out.

Jess and I grab our pyjamas and head upstairs together.

'What do you think they're doing?' Jess asks me once we're in the sanctuary of our bedroom. It feels like being kids again, hiding in our room, wondering what was going on with Mum and Dad. 'You don't really think they're having an affair, do you?'

'Without any of the evidence, I would have bet my life that Mum would never do to anyone what Dad did to her,' I say as I swap the pyjamas I slept in for my new festive ones.

'Maybe she feels like it's different, because Dad was hers first?' Jess suggests.

'I don't know, it must be something more? But the only things I can think of are much worse. Like maybe one of them is ill?'

The thought makes me go cold. You've got to wonder what sort of thing could be going on that would reunite our parents, though.

'It makes me think that maybe it's something that relates to us,' I offer up. 'Something they're dealing with together.'

'Yeah, like the two of them getting back together,' Jess replies. 'You've seen what Dad's like around Mum now, which is gross, because it's all down to her new look, she's still the same person on the inside, the same one he left.'

I shudder.

'Right, how do we look?' I ask as I do up my last button.

Jess and I stand in front of the full-length mirror in my bedroom, taking in our pyjamas. Jess hooks an arm around my neck and hangs off me as she takes a photo of us together in the mirror.

'We look like absolute losers,' she says. 'But cute ones, at least. You know, with the family freak show we've got going on, I'm pretty sure we could go viral on TikTok, if we all did a video in our matching pyjamas, showing how cute our disturbing family unit is. Our divorced parents, Dad's new wife, us and your ex, all in our matching jammies.'

I laugh.

'I think you're going to have to wait until everyone is up to their necks in Bailey's for that,' I reply. 'Come on, let's go take down that breakfast table.'

I open the bedroom door to find Declan lingering behind it. He looks so funny in his Christmas pyjamas; I can't help but laugh at him.

'Can I have a quick word?' he asks.

'I'll be heading down,' Jess says as she scarpers.

'Don't eat all the pastries,' I call after her.

Declan steps into the bedroom and closes the door behind him.

'I really do love what you've done with the place,' he says. 'Not just this room, but the whole house. You've really made it your own.'

'Thanks,' I reply. 'I really threw myself into it, after you left. It gave me the push I needed.'

'I'm proud of you,' he replies. 'If I were still here, we would probably be eating a takeaway for Christmas dinner, in a room that looked like a bomb had hit it.'

I smile. I do feel sorry for him.

'Look, I'm not going to bang on about how I feel, what I should or shouldn't have done, because what does it all matter now?' he says. Then he sighs. 'Let's just say I've been talking to someone who has really made me stop and take a look at the situation. I'm going to do the right thing. This house is yours in all the ways that count. I'm going to sign my half over to you.'

'Really?' I reply, sceptical at first. 'No tricks? No angle?

'Consider it your weird Christmas present,' he replies. 'Because I haven't actually got you anything else.'

I don't know who spoke to him, I'd guess it was my mum or even my dad, but I'm so pleased he's doing the right thing. I couldn't stand the thought of selling this place.

As we head downstairs together, it finally feels like everything is falling into place.

'Hey, we were friends before we were a couple,' Declan reminds me. 'It wouldn't be so hard to get back to that, would it?'

As we turn the corner into the living room, I laugh and give him a playful shove.

'You always were the optimist in the relationship,' I remind him.

'One more for Christmas dinner,' Mum calls out.

'Oh, yeah?' I reply. I shift my gaze from Declan, into the living room, I see our extra guest standing in front of me, and I have the biggest smile on my face for about half a second.

Gail rushes over to me.

'I hope you don't mind, Billie, it was such a lovely surprise,' she says, hooking an arm around the waist of our extra guest. 'Billie, this is my son, Rocco. Rocco, this is Rowan's daughter, Billie. Well, my daughter too. Stepdaughter, but I think we're over the stigma around step-relations, aren't we?'

I feel frozen on the spot. Rocco is too. We just stare at each other for what feels like a lifetime.

Obviously the mega cringe of the man I just slept with little more than a day ago turning out to be my stepbrother has practically sent my entire body into cramp but, worse than that, and the main reason my smile fell so quickly was my other realisation: that both Gail's sons are married. Rocco is married.

Rocco doesn't look happy to see me either. I imagine he's livid with himself, to be rumbled. I don't know what to say or what to do.

'Oh, and that's Declan behind her,' Gail adds.

Glancing back at Declan for a second reminds me of the fact that we're all wearing these dorky matching pyjamas. Oh, for God's sake, why did I have to be wearing these? Hardly my biggest problem but it's definitely made everything worse.

'It's nice to meet you both,' Rocco says.

Wow, okay, we're playing it like that, are we? Fine.

'Cuppa tea?' Mum asks, interrupting our stand-off.

I glance over Rocco's shoulder at Jess.

'Can I borrow you, sis?' I ask.

'Erm, yeah,' she replies.

Declan, more like his old self now that we've figured things out, snaps into friendly mode.

'Come with me, pal,' he tells Rocco. 'Let's get you a drink.'

I hurry up the stairs, into my bedroom, and close the door behind us.

'So, that's our brother,' Jess says. 'Christmas just keeps getting bigger and bigger.'

'You know this morning, when you asked me about who I was messaging, and you thought it was a boy?' I say, cutting to the chase.

'Yeah,' she replies. 'Ooh, am I finally getting all the details?'

'It's Rocco,' I say, giving her the only detail she needs.

'Our brother?' she squeaks loudly.

'Stop calling him that,' I quickly insist. 'He isn't actually our brother, is he? Not really.'

'It's still a bit awkward, isn't it?' she replies. 'He's hot, though. If you've got a hot stepbrother, what are you going to do?'

Jess is trying to lighten the mood but she's missing an obvious detail.

'So why didn't you tell everyone?' she asks. 'I know it's a bit weird, but only for a few seconds, he's not actually related to us, and it's not even like you grew up as siblings, is it? I'm teasing you – because I *am* your sibling – but there's absolutely nothing wrong with it.'

'Except...' I start, pausing to see if she realises. She doesn't. 'The only detail we've ever know about Gail's sons is that they live away from home and...'

'...and they're both married,' Jess says, somehow managing to finish my sentence with her jaw dropped. 'Don't they have kids too? Gail has mentioned her grandkids, I'm sure of it.'

'I don't know,' I reply. 'I remember some grandkids being mentioned, but I absolutely, without a doubt, remember that both her sons are married.'

'Ugh, what a pig,' Jess says. 'It's always the ones closest to you who hurt you.'

I shoot her a look.

'Jokes aside, he might be hot, but he's definitely a creep,' she says. 'What are you going to do?'

'I feel like I've been working my arse off to make sure that this Christmas was a happy, normal one,' I reply. 'So I'll be damned if I'm going to let him ruin it.'

'Brave faces and no one mentioning the elephant in the room then?' she says.

'It will be just like the good old days,' I reply. 'I'll be damned if he's going to ruin my breakfast for me either. Come on.'

Back downstairs, everyone has finally gathered around the breakfast table. As Jess and I join them, it becomes apparent that there are two seats available to us: one next to Rocco, and one opposite him. Jess hangs back, giving me my first choice of where I want to sit, which I appreciate, although both sound awful. In the end, I choose to sit opposite him, next to Gail.

'Our family just keeps getting bigger and bigger,' Mum points out. 'I'm going to have to start buying extra pyjamas, just in case.'

'Did you get Kenny some?' Jess asks.

Oh, God, I'd forgotten about Kenny for a moment. I need to make a point of telling Jess not to say anything to him about Rocco because he will terrorise me if he has dirt on me like that. I really would have to move.

'I didn't,' Mum replies. 'But I thought with him only being here for dinner, he wouldn't need any.'

'Kenny is the next-door neighbour,' Gail tells Rocco. 'And Jess's, erm, friend.'

Jess chuckles.

'It's lovely to have you here, Rocco,' Mum tells him. 'At least later, when we're all playing games, we'll have an even number. You can be in a couple with me – so to speak.'

As Jess starts sniggering, I go to kick her under the table. Of course, I miss, hitting nothing, which just causes my silky pyjama-covered bum to slide on the leather dining chair. I quickly sit back up.

'Slippery pyjamas,' I reason, with all eyes on me.

'You all look so cute in your matching pyjamas,' Rocco says. 'Like one big happy family.'

'We're getting there, aren't we?' Gail says, giving me a nudge.

'You two seem like you're really close,' Rocco points out. 'You must really like each other.'

I try to remember the exact words I said to Rocco when I was telling him about why I didn't like my step-mum – his mum, it turns out. He must be furious about that, I know I would be, but that was all just one big misunderstanding.

'I gave Billie Grandma Eileen's necklace last night,' Gail tells him. 'She always said she wanted me to give it to my first daughter and now I have one of those.'

'Oh, that's so lovely,' Mum says.

'You never told me you were doing that,' Dad joins in. 'That's great.'

'Let's see,' Jess insists. 'Where is it?'

'I thought it might be nice to wear it today,' I say, lifting it out from under my pyjama top. Well, I did when it didn't seem like Gail's angry son was staring at me like he wanted to rip it from my neck.

'Yeah, I'm okay,' Jess says, as though she was only checking it to see if she should feel jealous or hard done by.

Rocco's eyes widen. Then he glances at me briefly. Still, he doesn't say a word.

'What do you think of the house?' Dad asks Rocco. 'All Billie's vision – if you don't mind me saying, Declan.'

'Yeah, no, not at all,' Declan says through a mouthful of waffle. 'Nothing to do with me.'

Rocco must think it's weird that my ex-boyfriend is here for Christmas, but at least he's my ex. He can't really say anything, can he?

'Being an architect, I'm not usually an advocate for the tearing down of old buildings, but with this house, I might have made an exception,' he muses. 'The classic exterior, combined with the gutting to make way for a contemporary interior, doesn't quite work. If this is what you wanted, you would have been better rebuilding.'

He's only saying that because he's mad at me. Hopefully.

I can't believe he thinks he has any right to be mad at me.

Okay, so I said some stuff about his mum before I knew it was his mum, and before we managed to find our way into a positive relationship, but come on, he's married. He's the one in the wrong. I'm the one who should be fuming. And yet he sits there, at my table, in my house, playing these childish games with me? Well, if that's what Rocco wants then game on. He should know by now, creating chaos comes naturally to me, and if this is how he wants to play then this is how we'll play. Merry Christmas, everyone.

32

As Mum serves up the Christmas dinners on the kitchen island, I deliver them to the people around the table.

As the awkward morning turned into an awkward afternoon, I retreated to my bedroom to get ready for dinner. After dragging it out for as long as humanly possible, I came back downstairs to find the gang all present and anything but correct. My parents – who have whatever they have going on – Gail, Gail's son/my... what word to even use? Lover makes me want to throw up in my mouth but, I guess that, and then there's Jess and my next-door neighbour. Oh, and don't forget my ex, although he's somehow proving to be the least problematic of all of them, now he's stopped trying to seduce me on the other side of the wall to my parents. We've got ourselves one festively fucked-up family, not that most of them know the half of it. There must be so many secrets amongst us. Christmas dinner is going to be like a tinder-box. I'd be on my nerves, if I wasn't so intent on messing with Rocco right now.

'That one is for Rocco,' Mum tells me, handing me a plate full of food.

Before I take it to him, I grab the serving spoon for the cauliflower cheese and not only give him an extra massive helping, but I make a point of dripping cheese sauce over the other items on his plate.

'There you go,' I tell him. 'The cauliflower cheese is Mum's speciality, she's so proud of it, so I gave you an extra-big helping.'

'Thanks,' Rocco replies flatly.

When everyone has a plate in front of them, we all take our seats – the same seats we had earlier.

'Come on, let's pull our crackers,' Mum insists. 'We can't start our food, until we've got our hats on.'

Everyone naturally turns to the person opposite to them to pull their Christmas cracker. Rocco hovers with his for a moment.

'Trying to pull?' I ask him.

'Yes, I'm sure you can help me out, though,' he replies.

I win, which I'm delighted about. I remove the small piece of paper before getting everyone's attention, to hear the joke.

'Why don't they play poker at the zoo?' I ask. 'Because of the cheaters.'

I have to confess, that's not the joke on the paper at all, the joke I got says 'What do they sing at a snowman's birthday? Freeze a jolly good fellow...' but I really wanted to try and get a rise out of Rocco. I can't believe he still hasn't said anything. I know I haven't either but I'm the wronged party here.

'Thanks for having me,' Kenny says as he tucks into his dinner. 'I wasn't able to go back to North Yorkshire to visit my family, I've got too much work on.'

'I would've thought this crowd was a bit old for you,' I say, unable to resist a swipe, not that anyone else gets it.

Kenny laughs.

'No, just my scene, actually,' he replies.

Everyone makes small talk as we eat. In an attempt to not ruin my dinner for myself, I try to stick to talking to the women at the table. That suits the boys, who drift into talking about work and then inevitably football. My dad, annoyingly, has always defaulted to talking about football with anyone he's around long enough, so long as they have a penis, of course. Eventually, the two groups merge again.

'Times are changing,' Dad points out. 'You just don't see family values like you used to. Look at my girls, neither of them married, and they're in their thirties.'

Jess shows all the tells of the She Hulk. If there's one thing Jess hates (well, don't we all), it's people flagging the marital/child-rearing status of women, and my sister is the kind of person who always challenges things like this when they're brought up in front of her. I'm glad that Mum raised us to be strong, fiery women, it's just that Jess tends to try and combat these situations by dumping petrol on them.

'All right, Mr Family Values, you're one to talk,' she points out. 'No one's marital status, or eggs, for that matter, are anything to do with old farts like you.'

Gail winces when Jess brings up her eggs at the dinner table.

I totally see where Jess is coming from, though, I hate it when people ask me questions like this too – and it was worse when I was with Declan. When are you getting married? When do you think you'll have kids? It's no one's business.

'All right, Jess, the past is in the past,' Dad tells her.

'You're both free to do what you want, when you want,' Mum reassures us. 'No one cares. Not even your dad.'

'It would be nice to see you both married, to get some grand-kids,' Dad continues, trying to make things better, but doing nothing apart from fan the flame.

'With messed-up kids of divorce like us lot, it's no wonder

we're all doing such a terrible job, not wanting families or kids,' Jess replies.

'I'm going to the loo,' Declan says. He's always avoided confrontation.

'I don't think that's fair,' Gail chimes in – oh, Gail, hun, what are you doing? 'Your dad has worked hard to change perceptions of him, to be a decent family man, and my boys certainly aren't messed up.'

I think it's the slight tone at the end of Gail's sentence, potentially suggesting that perhaps Jess and I do have some issues, that sends Jess nuclear.

'Right, okay, well, where to begin,' she says as she pulls herself to her feet. 'You say Dad is reformed but he's definitely having some kind of affair with Mum – or trying to, at least – and as for your perfect little boy, why don't you ask him who he's being sleeping with?'

Jess, in a full-on strop, marches out of the room.

'I should probably, er...' Kenny's sentence trails off as he jumps to his feet to follow her. He gets points for being attentive, at least, but Kenny's quality as a boyfriend is the least of my worries now. Thank you, Jess, for dropping that grenade and then running for cover.

'Sorry, what's going on?' Gail asks me – why me? Then she turns to my dad. 'Rowan, what does she mean? And who have you been sleeping with?'

Gail's gaze settles on Rocco, who is looking at me, so Gail naturally follows his line of sight until she's looking at me once again.

'You?' she says.

'You?' Dad says to Rocco. 'You and her? She's my daughter. She's your sister.'

'Oh, my God, can everyone please stop saying that we're

siblings when we absolutely are not,' I insist. 'You're barely my dad, anyway. I never hear from you, never see you until you want something.'

'I can't believe you're sleeping with my son,' Gail says as she puts her head in her hands.

'Slept,' I correct her. 'Singular.'

Unless you count the morning after the night before as a separate time, but it hardly seems worth making that distinction to my nearest and dearest over the remains of Christmas dinner.

'It's not serious then?' my mum asks.

'Absolutely not,' I insist. 'It was a mistake. Right?'

I look at Rocco. He hesitates for a moment.

'I think we both very much had a different idea about what was going on,' he eventually replies.

'Have you been messing my daughter around?' Dad asks Rocco.

'It sounds more like your daughter has been leading my son astray,' Gail insists. 'He's a good boy.'

'Okay, enough,' my mum snaps. She never snaps. 'I think we all just need to cool off for a moment. There's a lot going on here that we need to sort out.'

'Don't think I've forgotten what your other child said about you and Rowan,' Gail adds. 'We'll circle back to that when we've sorted out these two. Cheating is never acceptable, what were you thinking?'

Rocco and I stare at each other, waiting to see if anyone is going to say anything, but neither of us do.

'I need some space,' I say, pushing my chair back. By the time I reach the living room in this stupid open-plan house, it occurs to me that Jess will be in my bedroom so, without really thinking about it, I grab my keys and march out the front door. I'm at my car by the time I realise I've grabbed the wrong set of keys.

I lean back against my car and slide down it until I'm sitting on the floor. It feels so cold, through my dress, there's no way I can sit here for more than a few seconds.

I flinch as I hear the front door open and close.

'Oh, it's you,' I say. 'Congratulations, you are not the last person I want to see today.'

'Is there a trophy?' Kenny replies through a smile. 'I heard everything you just said. If you want some space, do you want to come over to mine for bit?'

I cock my head at him. Is he being nice? What's his angle? But, also, what choice do I have?

'Thanks,' I reply. 'That would be great.'

Kenny offers me a hand, to pull me to my feet.

'Seeing as though it's Christmas, and you're clearly having a bad day, I'll keep my smart comments to a minimum, how about that?'

'That would be very much appreciated today,' I reply as I follow him around to his side of the fence.

'I will be lining up ammunition for tomorrow, though,' he adds.

I expect no less.

33

I've only been inside Kenny's house a handful of times, and that was back when Beth was still on the scene, just before they broke up. It hasn't changed at all apart from one thing: it feels emptier. I don't know if Beth kept things in the divorce, and took them to her new home, or if it's just the lack of... not necessarily a woman, but another person. Another's life, things, tastes. A counterpart. With Kenny having all of these things to start with, their absence is felt. I'm lucky, with Declan leaving before the work on the house got started, it's all been me, since day one, from top to bottom.

But as we head into the living room, there is one obvious difference, one part of the house that feels like a home, as opposed to a bachelor pad: the Christmas tree.

'What do you think?' he asks me. 'It looks great, right? Jess did it for me. She turned her nose up at my crappy old artificial one, and seeing as Beth took most of our good decorations, she picked up a bunch of new ones. It was surprisingly really nice, decorating it together. I never thought I'd do that with anyone again.'

The tree is Jess through and through. It's fun, stylish, and really beautiful. I feel bad, trying to steer her away from Kenny, but he just isn't a good guy. Not for her or for any woman.

'I really like your sister,' Kenny says, reading my mind. 'I know you don't think I'm good enough for her.'

'You're not,' I agree. 'I see the girls coming in and out of here. I heard the stories from Declan, about what you've been getting up to since you binned Beth off. I felt so sorry for her—'

'You didn't like her,' Kenny reminds me with a scoff. 'You thought she was stuck up.'

Well, she was stuck up. I remember her making fun of me over a word I used that she said made me seem like I was a lower class than her – I can't even remember what the word was what now, that's how petty it was.

'I never really got to know her,' I remind him. 'Before you got rid.'

'Can we sit down for a minute?' Kenny suggests, gesturing towards the pristine black leather sofa.

'Sure,' I reply. I wouldn't normally be so keen but anything to avoid going back home.

The look on Kenny's face shifts into something I haven't seen before, as he searches for the words to get going. The usual smug, smarmy grin I know on him is nowhere to be seen. I instantly soften, which annoys me. Is he playing me?

'Seeing as though it would appear you've made your mind up about me via Declan, and monitoring my house guests, apparently, I'm going to set the record straight,' he starts. He takes a deep breath and then... 'I didn't leave Beth, she left me.'

'She left you, but you kicked her out, right?'

'Not exactly,' he replies. 'To make a long story short, we'd been married for a couple of years, and we had talked about having kids previously, but only in a really general way. But when I brought up trying for a baby, because I really did want kids,

Beth finally confessed that she didn't. I think she had hoped to change my mind, and while I never would have tried to change hers, it became very clear that we wanted different things, so we decided to separate.'

'I'm sorry,' I say genuinely. 'That's rough.'

'It wouldn't be so bad, if she hadn't met someone new almost right away, and if I hadn't almost bumped into her in town a few months ago, with a baby bump the size of a football and her new bloke carrying the pram they had just bought.'

I wince.

'And if you think that's as tragic as things get, think again, because I did what any smart, mature, rational thirty-something professional adult would do, and I crouched down on the floor to hide behind a bin.'

'Sorry, Kenny, I had no idea,' I reply. 'Declan just told me you guys didn't want to be together any more, and that you had turfed her out.'

'No offence, but I was never going to be able to talk to Declan about the details, was I?' he replies. 'I was going out more, to be home alone less, and trying to have a good time, and Declan loved it, but I was miserable.'

'He idolised you,' I say. 'He thought you were living the dream, sleeping with a different girl every night – and I've seen a few here myself, this week even, but I'm sorry for judging you, if you've been going through a difficult time. I know what it's like to be suddenly single.'

Kenny relaxes in his chair a little, now that he's got the hard part out, his face starts to look more like him again.

'This place doesn't have the revolving door you think it does,' he says.

'Okay, well, it has these past couple of weeks,' I can't help but reply.

'The women you've been seeing here – you know it's been the same woman, right?'

I stare at him for a second.

'What?'

'My cousin had been staying with me, visiting friends at the uni before they go home for Christmas,' he replies. 'How old are you, that you can't tell twenty-year-olds apart and not realise you're seeing the same one?'

Oh, God, I feel mortified.

'Hey, come on, don't feel bad,' Kenny insists. 'Sometimes we see what we want to see, or what we really don't want to see, but you know now. The only girl who isn't related to me – because some of us prefer that – who has been here is Jess. I really like her, Billie. I'm not messing her around. If anyone is going to hurt anyone, it's going to be her hurting me, when she leaves after Christmas.'

'I'm so sorry,' I insist. 'More sorry by the minute. I've had you all wrong, all this time.'

'I'm sorry if you feel like Declan left you because of me,' he says sincerely. 'But if he saw me, miserable, drinking every night, and thought that seemed like a great life, then maybe I did you a favour. And at least he's going to sign the house over to you.'

'Yeah, we'll – wait, how do you know that?'

'Because I told him to,' Kenny replies. 'We had a heart-to-heart. I told him what I went through with Beth, when she left. The house was mine; I'd bought it before we got married, but I had to buy her out. I had to quite literally work overtime to do it. I told him not to be that guy, who put you through what I went through. He didn't take much convincing, to be honest, he's a crap boyfriend, but he's not a total arsehole. Just a bit of one.'

Kenny smiles. I'm speechless.

'Anyway, I told him I'd represent him, so you're going to need to find your own conveyancer,' he continues. 'But it's still my weird Christmas gift to you, in a way.'

Before I know what I'm doing, I'm throwing myself at Kenny, flinging my arms around him, squeezing him tightly.

'Thank you,' I tell him, my voice catching in my throat as tears prickle my eyes. 'I can't thank you enough.'

I think until this moment, just now, I had still been worried that Declan might not be being straight with me, or might not have been in a position to do what he said he would, but I feel like Kenny being on his side makes all the difference. It feels real. My house is going to be mine again.

How is it possible I've had Kenny so, so wrong all this time? I think he's right. We see what we want to see, or, more accurately, don't want to see, and what I didn't want to see was a man doing to a woman what my dad did to my mum, and what Declan did to me. And what Rocco is doing to his wife too. But Kenny has shown me that they're not all bad. Jess may have actually found herself a good one, for the first time.

'Kenny, would you like to spend Christmas Day with us?' I ask him.

He laughs.

'I thought I already was?'

'Yes, but I didn't want you there before, now I do,' I say with a smile.

'I'd love to,' he replies. 'Fancy hanging out here for another fifteen minutes or so before we head back? Give things chance to calm down?'

'That would be great,' I reply. 'Thanks for everything, you're my knight in shining armour.'

'Nah,' he says with a casual bat of his hand. 'I'm just the guy who is going to do the paperwork.'

I know it sounds kind of sad – more so because it's my sister's man – but Kenny has given me hope that there are still good guys out there, and maybe I can find one. Forget the ones in my house, eating my food, ruining my Christmas. There will be other guys, and plenty of time.

It's just such a shame, though, because with Declan I knew things weren't great, even when we were together, but I thought comfortable was as good as it got, and that expecting something closer to perfection just wasn't realistic. But then I met Rocco and he seemed so right for me. I think that one's going to take a bit longer to accept, but cheating repulses me to my core, and if that's the kind of man he is, then he isn't who I thought he was.

It's so stupid, how I feel more upset over losing someone who I've known for days, versus Declan who I knew for years. Looking back, I think it was the hurt of being abandoned, the way it made me look at myself differently, wondering what was wrong with me – coupled with the logistics of breaking up with someone I owned a house with – that made it feel so spectacular. Somehow, with Rocco it hurts even more, because it really felt like we had the potential to have something truly great.

And now I have to go back home and face all of it, but at least I have Kenny on my side, and Jess, and Mum – even Dad. I might have lost Gail, briefly, but I've won her over before, I'll do it again.

Okay, here we go, time to face the music. Wish me luck.

34

Back in my living room, the tension is unbearable. Dinner has been cleared from the table but, instead of Christmas pudding, the only thing on offer is an intervention. Well, that's what Jess and I keep calling it but Gail, our resident therapist, keeps correcting us.

'This isn't an intervention, this is a circle of truth,' Gail explains. 'And this is a truth stick. This family needs to heal.'

'That's not a truth stick, it's a wooden spoon,' Declan says with a snort. 'Do I need to be here?'

'He probably doesn't need to be here,' I chime in.

'He's your boyfriend,' Gail reasons. 'It might be good for him to be here.'

'Declan's not my boyfriend.'

'Declan's not her boyfriend.'

Jess and I both speak at the same time. I love that she always has my back.

'Your dad said he was your boyfriend?' Gail replies.

'Yeah, that was a mistake,' he tells her. 'Ex-boyfriend.'

'You said they owned the house together?'

'Not for long,' Declan adds. 'Can I go? This happy-clappy stuff isn't for me.'

'You can go,' I tell him. 'Honestly, things like this just go so much easier without him.'

I wait until he's left the room before I say the second part.

'Wait, he isn't your boyfriend?' Rocco asks.

'No,' I reply. 'We broke up over a year ago. Wait, did you think he was my boyfriend? Is that why you were mad at me?'

'Wait, wait,' Gail insists. 'Hold the stick of truth. No one apart from me is allowed to talk without it. Who wants it?'

I grab it, before Rocco can.

'Did you think I had a boyfriend?' I ask him, then I turn to Gail. 'Can he nod?'

'Yes, okay, he can nod,' she replies.

Rocco nods.

'And that's why you've been so mad at me today?'

He nods again.

'Well, that's highly hypocritical of you,' I point out. 'Considering you're married.'

Mum gasps.

Gail reaches out to take the stick from me.

'Rocco and I had a chat, while you were gone,' she tells me. 'I think he has something he needs to tell you.'

Rocco pulls a face at his mum.

'Is this really the way to do this?' he asks her.

'This family needs to heal,' she reminds him. 'It all needs to come out, to everyone, right now.'

Rocco sighs as he takes the stick of truth.

'I'm divorced,' he says directly to me. 'I've been divorced for a while, but I didn't tell my mum because, well...'

Rocco gestures as if to say, 'something like this would happen'.

'I'm sorry I didn't tell you, Billie, but it felt weird to tell you when we'd just met, and before I'd told anyone in my family,' he explains.

'I was only mad at you because I thought you were still married,' I point out. 'I don't care if you're divorced. We've all got our baggage, look around the room.'

He smiles at me.

'Stick me,' I say to him, reaching out to take the spoon.

'Again?' Jess jokes.

Oof, too soon.

'I'm also sorry for saying I didn't get on with your mum,' I tell him. 'We had a heart-to-heart last night and we realised we were both being a little bit hostile.'

'Give the stick to Dad,' Jess insists. 'Or Mum. We need answers.'

The only real question left on everyone's lips is what on earth is going on with my mum and my dad.

'Yeah, give it to me,' Dad demands. 'I'll go first.'

I hand over the stick before glancing back over at Rocco.

'Sorry,' he mouths to me.

'Me too,' I reply.

'Look, I know I've not been a great dad,' he starts – we didn't need a stick of truth for that. 'I thought this Christmas could be a new start for us, to try and get back to being something like a family. The insurance did offer us a hotel room. I just thought it might be nice to stay here. I just want to build bridges.'

'Bridges to our hot mum,' Jess says under her breath.

Dad hands Mum the stick of truth.

'Tell them, Katie,' he says to Mum with an encouraging smile.

She smiles back at him as she takes the stick.

'Girls, there's no easy way to say this,' she starts before taking a deep breath. 'I have a boyfriend.'

'You have a boyfriend?' Jess squeaks back at her.

'Bloody hell, Mum, I thought you were dying,' I chime in. 'A boyfriend is fine.'

'And who is this *boy*?' Jess asks, snapping into mum mode, which is cute.

'Well, he's not a boy, he's a fifty-two-year-old man,' Mum replies. 'His name is Dennis, he's a dentist.'

'Dennis the dentist,' I say.

'Drilling our mum,' Jess jokes.

'Jess!' Mum ticks her off. She gets serious again. 'I really like him. I love him, actually. I hadn't known how on earth I was going to tell you about him, but your dad encouraged me to, telling me that it would be fine, that you were both wonderful young ladies.'

'Eggs and all,' Dad jokes. That's actually pretty funny.

'We'll meet him,' Jess says. 'Kick his tyres. Not in a keeping it in the family way, not like Billie and our brother.'

'I'm taking back your Christmas present,' I tell her. I dare to laugh, though, just a bit.

'Is that everything out in the open now?' Gail asks. No one says anything.

'Oh, actually, I have one more thing,' I say, taking the spoon. 'Jess, I had Kenny all wrong, you were right, he is a good guy.'

'Ha! I told you so,' she replies.

We all fall silent again.

'So, what now?' Jess asks.

A few more seconds of silence.

'Cuppa tea?' Mum eventually says. 'Bit of Christmas pudding?'

'I'll have a cup of tea,' I reply.

'Me too,' Jess says. 'I'll call Kenny, see if he wants some pudding.'

'I could definitely go for some Christmas pudding, I am starving,' Rocco adds. 'Someone ruined my dinner with my least favourite food.'

'Sorry,' I say again.

As everyone springs to life again, getting back to something close to a Christmas Day, I think we all feel lighter, after airing our dirty laundry at the dinner table, and straightening everything out.

As for the future, well, I'm not quite sure what any of this means for anyone, but I'm hopeful. For now, though, it's Christmas. We can worry about all that in the new year.

35

20TH DECEMBER 2023

Quiet-ish Christmas 2023 has finally begun.

After a crazy Christmas last year, when all I wanted was to be left alone, all hell broke loose. This year, things are going to be different. This year, I'm going to get the nice, quiet Christmas I wanted last year. Well, sort of.

I can't help but admire my Christmas tree. Like last year, I've chosen a theme for the decorations, but the main difference this year is that I've added in a few sentimental ornaments, which Mum distributed between herself, me and Jess, so we could all have a bit of nostalgia on our trees. And, after moving into her house in January, Mum used the bonus money from her house sale to go travelling with Dennis. They picked me up a Christmas decoration almost everywhere they went, so my tree is looking like a real adventure. It's making me excited to have my own adventures someday, but not yet, I want to enjoy my house for a bit longer first.

I've spent some of the past year refreshing my décor, not because it needed it, just because I find it fun. Another reason why living here is suddenly much better is because last month,

Jess moved in next door, with Kenny, who managed to graduate from being my least favourite neighbour to my favourite, with just one act of kindness.

Quiet Christmas 2023 starts today but it ends on the 24th, because I'll be hosting Christmas dinner again – although intentionally this time, and I've invited Jess and Kenny to join us. Mum and Dennis will be joining us too, as will Dad and Gail. It's been a better year with Dad. Any events we've celebrated, we've invited him over, so we're spending more time together at least. And Gail is great. There's a lot to be said for having a therapist in the family, although thankfully the stick of truth has stayed in the drawer over the past twelve months.

'Quiet Christmas is great,' Rocco starts. 'But I'm pretty sure disco bowling is on tonight.'

I cuddle up closer to him on the sofa as I laugh at his joke.

'Get Leila and Tobias on the phone, let's do it,' I kid.

'I still can't believe they're getting married,' Rocco says as he changes the channel.

'Oh, I can believe it,' I reply. 'The day I saw her scream at him for knocking the scones on the floor, I knew they were destined to be wed.'

'I was thinking of mentioning the scones – the truth about the scones – in my best man speech,' he says. I'm sure he's kidding.

'Don't you dare,' I warn him.

'Yeah, maybe you're right,' he says. 'And maybe quiet Christmas is better than disco bowling. It's nice, just the two of us.'

'It's our first Christmas in our home,' I say. 'I don't want to share you with anyone. Christmas Day is my one exception.'

'Well, that's what my girl is going to get then,' he replies. 'Although I might need to give you your present the night before, if that's the case.'

'I can handle that,' I tell him with a smile.

We kiss, but only for a few seconds, interrupted by a knock on the door.

'Who is that?' Rocco says as he heads for the door.

I jump to my feet and run after him.

'Ooh, I hope it's carol singers,' I say excitedly. Rocco looks back at me for a moment.

'What? I want a quiet Christmas, not a silent one,' I inform him.

I cuddle up to Rocco as he opens the door but instead of carol singers, it's a couple in their forties and four kids. The eldest kid has a dog on a lead, the smallest kid has a rabbit in his arms. The dog seems to really want to eat the rabbit for some reason. The only other thing I notice is the suitcases piled up behind them.

'Hello, bro,' the man says.

'Michael, what are you doing here?' Rocco asks him.

'We thought we'd surprise Mum for Christmas, but she's been decorating, so there's no room for us,' he replies. 'She said she was spending Christmas here, so... any room at the inn for six small ones and a couple of pets?'

Rocco and I just stare at each other.

Well, here we go again...

ACKNOWLEDGMENTS

Huge thanks, as always to my wonderful editor, Nia, and to everyone at Boldwood Books for all of their continued hard work on my books. I can't believe this is book number eleven!

Thank you so much (and a very merry Christmas) to all of the wonderful people who read and review my books. It means the world to me.

Massive thanks to my family – who I loved having at my house last Christmas, so please don't read anything into this story, it's not a hint. Thanks so much to the wonderful Kim – the reason you can never buy my paperbacks in my hometown – and to Pino for all their support. Thanks to the amazing Aud for always being so loving and supportive – I'm sure everyone says this, but I do actually have the best gran in the world. Super thanks to James and Joey, who always have my back, and help me endlessly. The same goes for Darcy, who helps me more than she realises.

Finally, thank you to my husband, Joe, for the endless love (and the endless DIY) and for putting up with me while I wrote not one but two Christmas books this year. I promise to get you a good present.

MORE FROM PORTIA MACINTOSH

We hope you enjoyed reading *Just Date and See*. If you did, please leave a review.

If you'd like to gift a copy, this book is also available as an ebook, digital audio download and audiobook CD.

Sign up to Portia MacIntosh's mailing list for news, competitions and updates on future books.

http://bit.ly/PortiaMacIntoshNewsletter

Discover more laugh-out-loud romantic comedies from Portia Macintosh:

ALSO BY PORTIA MACINTOSH

One Way or Another

If We Ever Meet Again

Bad Bridesmaid

Drive Me Crazy

Truth or Date

It's Not You, It's Them

The Accidental Honeymoon

You Can't Hurry Love

Summer Secrets at the Apple Blossom Deli

Love & Lies at the Village Christmas Shop

The Time of Our Lives

Honeymoon For One

My Great Ex-Scape

Make or Break at the Lighthouse B&B

The Plus One Pact

Stuck On You

Faking It

Life's a Beach

Will They, Won't They?

No Ex Before Marriage

The Meet Cute Method

Single All the Way

Just Date and See

ABOUT THE AUTHOR

Portia MacIntosh is a bestselling romantic comedy author of over 15 novels, including *My Great Ex-Scape* and *Honeymoon For One*. Previously a music journalist, Portia writes hilarious stories, drawing on her real life experiences.

Visit Portia's website: https://portiamacintosh.com/

Follow Portia MacIntosh on social media here:

facebook.com/portia.macintosh.3

twitter.com/PortiaMacIntosh

instagram.com/portiamacintoshauthor

bookbub.com/authors/portia-macintosh

Boldwood

Boldwood Books is an award-winning fiction publishing company seeking out the best stories from around the world.

Find out more at www.boldwoodbooks.com

Join our reader community for brilliant books, competitions and offers!

Follow us
@BoldwoodBooks
@BookandTonic

Sign up to our weekly deals newsletter

https://bit.ly/BoldwoodBNewsletter